THE SECLUDED VILLAGE
Murders

SHELLY FROME

BQB

Virginia

Published in the United States by BQB Publishing
(an imprint of Boutique of Quality Books Publishing Company, Inc.)
www.bqbpublishing.com

978-1-945448-20-1 (p)
978-1-945448-21-8 (e)

Library of Congress Control Number: 2018947093

Book design by Robin Krauss, www.bookformatters.com
Cover design by Marla Thompson www.edgeofwater.com

First editor: Pearlie Tan
Second editor: Olivia Swenson

In memory of Susan and our ventures across the pond.

Chapter One

On that fateful early morning, Emily Ryder was doing her best to end the call from her mother on a positive note.

At the moment, her mother was on a short trip on her own to compare notes with other B&B owners and had just crossed into Vermont. She did so at the end of every summer in preparation for the fall influx of leaf-peepers to their village of Lydfield, a gateway to New England's famed Berkshires. This year, however, was more problematic, with rumors circling about an encroaching developer with an eye on the high meadow adjacent to her mother's property.

Ensconced in the guest cottage behind her mother's B&B where she stayed whenever she was in town, Emily continued to reassure her mother over the phone. She was hoping to quickly ease her way back to putting the final touches on another guided tour across the pond to Lydfield's sister village, Lydfield-in-the-Moor, a quaint historic village nestled close to storied Dartmoor in the United Kingdom. In point of fact, both her mother's B&B and the lure of moorland attractions had been marketable ventures for years. Until just recently, that is, when everything seemed up the air.

"Mom, it's going to be okay," said Emily, trying a little

harder to keep things on an even keel. "Matter of fact, Will, that new handyman, is off this very minute."

"Doing what?" her mother replied in that skittish way of hers.

"Making your B&B the envy of New England. Plus acting as sentinel along with Oliver, his frisky golden retriever, while you and I are both away for the next few weeks."

"Well . . . I still just don't know."

"The dog will help keep away any of those pesky realty people who are after your property. Will and Oliver, the dynamic duo. Think of it that way."

It wasn't the greatest of arguments, but it was the best Emily could come up with.

After a bit more reluctance on her mother's part, she finally agreed to try to worry a bit less as long as she was kept apprised of the latest goings-on.

"Absolutely," Emily said. "You've got it."

This was followed by her mother's sigh and the usual small talk about the plight of those in the tourist trade until they said their goodbyes.

All things being equal, it could be said it was all simply a matter of two tour businesses.

But all things weren't equal, and Emily found herself experiencing a growing sense of unease.

She padded over to the desk in the little living room that afforded a cozy view of the yard and rear entrance of the B&B. She pulled up a chair, caught sight of the gunmetal hue of the sky hovering overhead like a premonition, and couldn't help noting the change in the weather. And, once again, she couldn't help considering the realities.

There was the actual state of her mom's B&B, which was in somewhat disrepair and in need of renovation. There were the rumors emanating from the village Planning Commission with Chris Cooper, her longtime mentor and family friend, at the head. These innuendos centered on the Gordon Development Corporation, who apparently had their eye on the adjacent property. Not to mention her own struggles with the way her tour guide business was going.

In short, it was getting harder to be intrepid Emily, fit and trim, coolheaded, and able to handle whatever came her way. Of course, she knew full well how much her mother depended on her ever since Emily's dad left them in the lurch when Emily was just a little girl. Over the years, given the state of her mother's nerves, it had become a tenuous balancing act for herself and Chris Cooper to keep everything afloat.

She closed her eyes and took a minute to center herself. Then, with a barely audible "Okay . . . right," she returned to the task at hand.

As a specialist in exploring captivating places in England, she had a pressing to-do list. An incurable rambler, she loved the job she'd created for herself exploring hidden worlds in the west country of England. She'd already confirmed reservations in Bath and Devon, staying in the sister village close by the wilds of Dartmoor, then continuing on to Fowey and St. Ives on the Cornish coast.

Which brought her thoughts back to her clients, the Curtises. As it happens, they lived just over the rise of the adjacent high meadow, and she had worked one summer for Silas, the eccentric brother of the equally eccentric spinsters, helping out with his mail-order antiques. All three thought it was such a big deal to be invited to take part in the Twinning portion of the annual fete in Lydfield-in-the-moor—the Twinning alluding to the on-again, off-again exchange between the "twin" villages. Harriet was in charge of this year's flower show; Silas, the historical aspects of the Twinning; and Pru, the stepsister, incorporating bits of her storytelling.

Emily never quite understood why Harriet, the eldest, was at odds with Silas and Pru. Emily simply put it down as a dysfunctional trio. What it would be like saddled with all three only added to her list of concerns. But the way business was going lately, she had to make do. Perhaps after she got through with this episode, things would pick up again.

Undaunted, she segued to the next item on her agenda—checking the specific route in the latest UK road map since her last foray. The plan was to meet the Curtises in Bath the day after tomorrow, rent a car to take them to the fete (the holiday festival), stay a few days, and then continue on to those other enticing points. This called for Emily to fly to London the next day, spend the night, take a train, hook up with the car rental agency, and so forth. She told herself, *So far so good*. She was on schedule; she was busy.

She was fully engaged studying the map when it all began.

It started with the squawks of wild turkeys above the trail and then a slew of loud obscenities that seemed to be coming from the same direction. She caught a glimpse of

Oliver as he burst through the doggie door of the B&B and raced into the darkening Connecticut morning.

Emily tried to ignore the ruckus. She focused on some new details in her map as the noise level picked up another notch.

Getting flustered, she put the map to one side and peered out over the yard at the back steps on the off-chance Will was around. The dog would scamper back, the racket would cease, and she could go on with her work.

But no such luck. No sign of Will or his approaching pickup; no muscular, pale-yellow canine bounding back down the slope to the spot where he belonged. Just his incessant barking. Not only that, it was starting to drizzle. Oliver was young, still in his rambunctious puppy stage, and she couldn't just turn a blind eye and let him get into all kinds of mischief. He might even run off like he did once before.

Rising up from the desk, she slipped on her windbreaker, left the cottage, and was soon clambering past the sprawling roots of maple trees. With each passing second, her thoughts drifted past Oliver and began to center again on the possible machinations of the Gordon Development Corporation and its alleged dealings with the village Planning Commission.

Emily heard more shouts coupled with echoing barks and squawks as she gained on the verge through the soggy leaves and tangled underbrush. The surging bedrock, maples, and spindly birch finally gave way to the half-mile-square expanse of high meadow.

As she crested the rise, she caught the tail end of the

melee about twenty yards away. A hurled branch flew through the air. Three or four wild turkeys refusing to give up ground lingered and squawked, their jutting beaks and flapping wings at the ready. Then they suddenly retreated, ashen wingspans fully displayed, a few hops and a takeoff, swooping close to the ground and away like tattered gliders. All of this fused with Oliver playfully darting around in pursuit of more hurled sticks as the man's curses dissolved to an obscene gesture.

Then it grew still, save for Oliver's sniffing survey of the spoils left by the turkeys.

Brushing himself off in the soupy mist, a stocky figure with a thick neck, pasty face, sagging raincoat, and dark, baggy trousers yelled out to no one in particular, "Hey, what is this? Can't a guy even walk around for Pete sake?"

She could have told him the turkeys were foraging and he'd overreacted. But she didn't want to get into any drawn-out discussion about the ways of the wild. All she was after was a clue to what the guy was up to, getting hold of Oliver, and returning to her agenda.

The second he noticed her, the man changed his tone. "Oh, how you doing? This your dog, I take it?"

Through the drizzle, Emily spotted a glittering, gold GDC emblem under his lapel.

"No," said Emily. "He's Will Farrow's retriever."

"Will Farrow? Right, you mean the fix-it guy, staying at the B&B while he patches it up?"

Though he was trying hard to be friendly, his voice had a raspy, cynical edge, and Emily didn't appreciate the way he was looking her up and down. Judging from his cropped gray hair and the deep creases in his face, she assumed he was in his early fifties. She also took him to be a point man for the development company. Otherwise, why would he be scouring around on his own, seemingly taking note of everything, checking out the lay of the land?

Stepping back onto higher ground, apparently self-conscious that Emily was a good two or three inches taller, the man reached into an inside pocket and took out a few printouts. In turn, Emily unfastened the collar of her windbreaker and pulled the hood over her head. All the while, Oliver looped around, sat and nuzzled his blocky head against Emily's thigh, and looped around again.

"Ah." The point man jabbed his finger at the top of one of the pages. "I got you covered. You're the B&B owner's daughter, used to play college soccer, but now you're some kinda tour guide. Carting a few locals around spots overseas. How am I doing?"

Emily shot him a wary glance, but he went on unfazed. "So good, so maybe you could be of some use, seeing how your ol' lady is off on some kinda busman's holiday. And her place is in need of lots of maintenance, right? But in this market and as far as the fall-foliage thing goes, what can I say about it all going down the drain?"

"How do you know all this?"

"I just do, all right? So, for openers, we got mom holing up somewheres in the boonies and not something to bank on."

"So, for openers, what are you driving at?"

Pocketing the printouts, he said, "Are you kidding me? Nailing down a right-of-way, what else? For the construction site, right where we're standing. The name so far is Lydfield Woods. Get it? Lydfield, Connecticut—Lydfield Woods. Hey, as long as we're at it, I would appreciate your take on this."

"My take is, you're wasting your time. You'd better go back to the drawing board."

"Obstacles, right. Exactly what I've been saying. Which brings us back to how far this thing is gonna have to go."

The exchange broke off as Oliver dashed away into the mist. Seconds later, he returned with a gnarled branch gripped in his teeth. The point man ignored him, but Oliver went straight up to him and pawed at his trousers. The point man flung the stick far back into the woods in the opposite direction. Oliver's ears perked up as he dashed off again.

"Right," he said. "Something I should know before I make my move?"

"Meaning?"

"Come on, will ya? Cut the tap dance. I'm talking Chris Cooper, head of planning, who's gonna cast the deciding vote. I'm talking the old roofer guy and conservationist. I'm talking the number one issue. What's he trying to pull? What's he suddenly got up his sleeve?"

Emily pulled back. This was a veiled threat aimed not at the Planning Commission per se, but at her mentor. Her surrogate father since her real dad skipped out. In a word, he was after her best friend.

"I'm talking blowing the whistle, okay? Is that plain enough for you?"

Emily readjusted her hood and brushed her damp hair away from her eyes. "Go on."

Just then, Oliver returned with a new stick. Just as quickly, the man yanked it out of Oliver's mouth and pitched it out of sight. The fog hung a tad lower, cloaking everything in the near distance. Clueless, Oliver took off, this time heading south toward the far reaches of the meadow where the ground sloped down again, falling away to the Village Green.

The point man's eyes hardened as more droplets ran down his face. "Look, I appreciate how you're jerking me around and how you don't back down even though we're alone up here. So seeing you're about to go futzing off to England and we're both pressed for time, how about getting off it while I maybe do something for you?"

Oliver returned stick-less as the drizzle picked up.

Tired of this game, Emily said, "Okay, mister, let's have it."

"Okay. We're talking here about ratcheting the grand list—lower taxes, new fire trucks, snow plows, and all the infrastructure la-di-da. So talk to me. Give me the skinny on this Cooper guy before things get outta hand."

Getting testier by the minute, Emily gave him nothing.

"What do you think, I got nothing better to do? Here, you want my card? Will that do it for you?" He no sooner reached for his wallet when a cell phone jangled. He put the wallet away, pulled his cell out of his outer pocket, and turned his back.

The man's raspy voice cut off the protests at the other end. "Okay, okay, I hear you. Yeah, yeah, I'll take care of it. I set it up, didn't I?"

Muffling his voice, he walked further away. The only

other words Emily could make out were, "All right, already. I gotcha. Right away."

"Great reception up here," he said, returning. "Another plus. Think about it. A hundred and twenty townhouses that can't miss no matter what. Toss in a clubhouse, pools, recreation facilities, and whatever." Fumbling inside his raincoat, he pulled out a brochure. "Twenty-two exterior looks, and that's for openers. They got lawyers, experts, and an eye to grab up enough land to keep 'em going for the next twenty years."

"I'm still waiting for an answer. What exactly are you up to?"

His cocky grin slid away. "Well, I ain't waiting no more." With that, he turned on his heels and scurried across the waist-high grass that could accommodate anything the GDC could come up with.

"Hold it," Emily said.

"Look, I'm under the gun, gotta step on it. Besides, I've had it up to here with the wet and the turkeys and the attitude. Enough already."

"And what's your name anyway?"

The raspy voice called back as it tailed off in the gauzy whiteness. "Doc! Okay? Just make it Doc!"

Emily held still. As her old soccer coach used to point out, one of her failings was confusing motion with action. But how could she ignore his threatening words in that harsh, Lower East Side tone? *Before I make my move . . . things get out of hand . . . I'll take care of it right away . . . I set it up, didn't I?*

There was something else, come to think of it. A few days

ago, when she'd returned from her latest tour, apparently a hot plate had been left on that almost burned down Chris's greenhouse. Something bothersome about the incident, but she couldn't put her finger on it. All she knew was that something was wrong.

Emily headed back to the crest of the trail with Oliver in tow. She worked her way down, dodging the glistening roots, tightening her hood as the water dripped from the overarching branches. She reached the bottom just as Will's red pickup pulled into the driveway. The second his lanky form appeared out of the cab, Oliver leaped up and smeared Will's Levi's jacket with his muddy paws, spun around, and smashed through the hinged flap of the back door.

As laid-back as ever, even though the rain was pelting his face, Will said, "What was that all about? On, no, don't tell me. Did he take off again?"

Emily ducked under the overhang of the cottage. "Sorry, I've got something I've got to look into."

Will shrugged and ambled over to the B&B. Calling across the yard, he asked, "Sure you don't want some hot coffee and an omelet? I can do it with chili or asparagus."

At any other time, she would have liked nothing better than to take a break and find out how his work was going. She'd only known him for a short while, dropped in for coffee once or twice, and he couldn't be that much older, maybe in his mid-thirties, and you never know. But at this moment, that was out of the question.

"Tea? Supper?"

"Maybe. But right now I've got to—"

"Around five or so?"

"I guess . . . sure, fine."

"Then you can tell me exactly what Oliver's been up to."

"I will. Later, okay?"

Stepping inside the cottage, Emily made straight for the kitchenette. All other issues were secondary now given the way her thoughts were running. Rambling and moving on was her primary modus operandi. But her encounter with this Doc guy meant there was no way she could shrug this off.

She snatched up the handset and punched in the numbers.

The familiar gravelly voice that went with the elongated weathered face picked up almost immediately. "Yes?"

"Chris, I met a guy just now on the high meadow who's got to be from New York. He seems to be—"

"Emily, can this wait? I've got a by-me to take care of."

"By-me" was their code for "by my own hand, I am responsible." The alternatives were "to-me," or "everything happens to me," and "through-me," meaning "let it go, let it pass." When Emily's dad ran out on her and her mother, Chris pushed the "through-me" tack. *All things being equal, through-me looks like your best bet, kiddo.*

"Look, Emmy," Chris went on, "it's a by-me 'cause I just got a phone message that I botched a job on North Lake Road. As if I didn't know my business, didn't know how to weather-tight a slate roof. So I'm off to see what's going on."

"Now? In the rain?"

"When else? Claims there's a bad leak, all my fault. Anyone who knows me knows that is bogus."

"Chris, listen to me."

"Whatever it is, whatever you want to discuss, I'm sure it'll keep," Chris said, obviously in a rush. "Let me see to this. We'll kick back later and you can tell me all about it."

"Will you please wait a minute? This is not a good idea."

But it was no use. Chris offered his quick apologies and hung up. Hitting the redial brought her nothing but his answering machine.

She replaced the handset and thought it over. Was she jumping to conclusions? Was she, once again, about to confuse motion with action? Shouldn't she at least think it through?

But she couldn't just stand there.

Unable to contain herself a moment longer, she left the cottage and hurried down the drive, past Will's pickup and the clapboard siding of the B&B and the front lawn. She slipped behind the wheel of her old Camry, had a few more second thoughts, hit the ignition, and headed down the hill.

As she passed the expanse of wetlands and uplands, it didn't register that the tract the GDC coveted was bracketed by her mother's property and the Curtises' ramshackle colonial at the foot of the hill. Nothing registered except a need to talk Chris out of climbing up onto that slate roof.

He was over seventy but refused to admit he was no longer agile and had had a few recent close calls. Steadfast to a fault, thinking only of his artisanship. Unless she missed her guess, he would be going up to the Tudor house on North Lake Road if she didn't intercept and get him to change his mind. The vacant McMansion was owned by the UK's own Miranda Shaw, a pampered guest who had stayed at the B&B while her McMansion was under construction. Who may or may not have made the call that set Chris off. After all, Miranda was currently in far-off Bovey Tracey, on the outskirts of the moors.

Driving on, everything receded, including the stately elms and the file of Federal style homes on both sides of North Street with their low-pitched roofs, flat façades, and black, louvered shutters. So did the white congregational church on the Green with its Christopher Wren steeple dissolving instantly as she turned right onto West Street and whisked by the old brick shops, Village Restaurant, and the town hall and state trooper's office.

Picking up speed, she passed the rows of Victorian houses with their pilastered front porches and attached shutters in homage to last century's Colonial Revival. She'd grown up here, always lived here except for college and her transatlantic jaunts. But at this moment, her village might as well be a scattering of old photos.

Before she knew it, the rain was beating down harder, her wiper blades barely able to keep up. Among the nagging questions flitting through her mind was how could Miranda Shaw have suddenly gotten wind of her leaking roof? Or did somebody just put her up to it, to get Chris rushing pell-mell in the rain so he would . . .

Emily eased her foot off the pedal, barely able to see through the downpour. She switched the wipers on high and kept her eyes on the road, intent on avoiding an accident.

Minutes later, she pulled into Miranda Shaw's place at a slow but steady crawl. As she reached the circular drive, straining her eyes through the thwacking blades, she peered up two stories above the stone archway.

There she caught sight of the familiar gangly figure climbing higher toward the peak of an eight-sided turret. At a point where the grayish-blue slate, copper flashing, and a mullioned window merged, the figure suddenly became a shuddering blur.

Emily honked her horn, blasting as loud as she could. But it was too late. The figure flopped over and slid down the turret, glanced off the aluminum ladder, and toppled like a broken doll until the cobblestones broke its fall.

Chapter Two

"Just think about it," said Emily.

"I have," said Trooper Dave Roberts.

"Not hardly at all."

"I listened and now, if you don't mind, I have work to do."

"Terrific, Dave. That's just terrific."

It was close to noon on that same rainy Monday. Emily was down in the basement of the old fire station in a gray-paneled office that suited Dave Roberts perfectly. The room matched his uniform, standard-issue features, crew cut, and build. Despite Dave's attempt to brush her off, Emily remained rooted in front of his desk.

Dave started rifling through a file cabinet, pulled out some papers, plunked himself down on his swivel chair, and began to read. After a few moments of strained silence, he looked up.

"Come on, Em. It was an accident. How many times has he rolled off a roof and broken something? This time it happens to be worse."

Emily continued to wait him out.

"Okay," Dave went on, "I know. I heard. Looks like it's

touch and go, iffy vital signs, and they're not giving out details. But that doesn't change a thing."

"Except . . ."

"Except what?"

"If I'd gotten there sooner or been more insistent over the phone—"

"And if the dog hadn't gotten loose or the sun was shining or Cooper had used some common sense . . ."

Holding her temper, Emily went at it again. "Okay, I can't prove it. But I'm telling you somebody was counting on him shimmying up that turret. Counting on him to—"

"What? Lose his footing? Be totally out of it so his Planning Commission alternate, slick Brian Forbes, bank vice president, would rubber-stamp the GDC's application for site development? All by the hand of some Doc character you ran into up on the proposed site? Is that what you really think?"

"Maybe."

Tossing the papers aside, Dave stood up again. "Face it, will you? You saw something that shook you up. You're antsy. And you're stuck with your clients, the wacko Curtises, and this stupid twin thing you were working on just before this happened."

"Twinning. It's called a Twinning—twin villages, a twin exchange."

"Right. Like when we still had a soccer field, and the Brits came over every couple of years and we'd do our thing with sports and go over there for their fete or what-you-call-it. And our village council wanted to keep it going until finally there was no real point. But now, you're trying to maintain some last ditch thing with the Curtises, of all people. Hanging by a thread. Like Cooper scrambling on a soaking-wet slate roof trying to hang on to his reputation. Same reason—trying to hang on. And for what?"

"Open space, for your information."

"Open space? Where are we now? How many circles do you want to go around? First it's what you call a suspicious accident, and then it's some environmental issue. In case you haven't noticed, I am actually trying to accomplish something."

"Right. Wonderful. Thanks for your time, Dave."

Dave Roberts plopped down on his swivel chair and went back to his paperwork.

Emily walked away and stopped at the doorway. "Tell me, what would it take?"

"For what?"

"To get your head out of that folder and do your job?"

Dave sprang back up, brandishing the sheaf of papers like a warrant.

"You see this? It's full of tangibles. One: The glass front door of Lydfield regional fourteen high school was smashed. Two: The alarm system was tampered with. Three: Library books were ripped and flung all over the place. Plus honors plaques broken and school bus tires slashed. Conclusion: It's an inside job. Bottom line? One of those kids who flunked out will supply us with a lead or incriminate himself. No lame conspiracy theories about an old guy falling off Miranda Shaw's roof while she's off in jolly old England."

"Is that what you think of Chris? Some old guy who fell off a roof?"

Dave cast his gaze up at the fluorescent lights as though searching for an exit line. Then, looking directly at her, he said, "All right, Emily. Let's play Clue. What I would need is for something to cast a shadow."

"Go on."

"Say Miranda Shaw is in touch with some busybody neighbor and asks her to watch out for prowlers. The busybody spots some stranger trespassing or an alarm's been tripped or tampered with on the premises. Perhaps Cooper's housekeeper signs a statement that Cooper's been harassed by this Doc guy you ran into."

"If he had a housekeeper. If he wasn't a bachelor who lives alone."

"You see? That's what comes of concocting stuff way out in left field. But take you, for instance, alone in the cottage."

"What is that supposed to mean?"

"That Will Farrow, the handyman nobody knows anything about, is all by his lonesome in the main house. What guy could resist that perky, trim bod? Not many females with those qualifications around these parts. So, if something happens to you, we've got probable cause."

"Get off it, Dave."

"And you get off it. You wanted to play, we played. Game's over."

"No way. You haven't even checked it out."

"Come again?"

"Drive up to Miranda's place and look it over. Won't take you more than twenty minutes."

Dropping the papers on his desk, Dave spread his hands in mock surrender. "Is that it? Will that do it for you?"

"It would be something."

"Fine, I'll take a look-see. But the price is negotiable."

Emily slipped out before he had a chance to name his price. But he did manage to tack on, "You know, Em, I still think we'd make a good team."

Famished, Emily crossed the Green, settled into a front booth at the Village Restaurant and waited impatiently for a salmon-cake platter and a cup of hot tea. Now almost two in the afternoon, Emily was still mulling over the cursory report that Dave Roberts had run by her back at his office. His "look-see" had turned up nothing except the obvious. There was an aluminum extension ladder skewered to the side of the stone archway and Chris Cooper's bag of tools was sitting up high next to one of the chimneys.

Making matters worse, Dave had come up with his price for humoring her and wasting police time. He had found out that the proposed development was geared for retirees with disposable income. A strip mall with a multiplex was in the works, slated for the old soccer field grounds—anything that would draw well-off buyers. Coinciding with what he called Emily's obvious need for a career change, he told her that all she had to do was get hold of a limousine, hire herself out, and take the bored condo owners into New York for shows, up to the Berkshires for the summer music festivals, and be on hand to chauffeur them back and forth to the airport. After Emily returned from her trip, Dave would have it all outlined for her, over dinner.

He left her with the prediction that as soon as this "twin thing" tanked, she wouldn't have to think it over. She'd been at it now for over seven years and the handwriting was on the wall. She'd have to come around.

His remarks only added to her frustration. There was nothing she could do for Chris at the moment. He was in the intensive care unit of the Sharon hospital miles away. Visitors were not allowed and he still hadn't regained consciousness. Just obtaining that bit of information had taken a lot of finagling. If Emily hadn't gotten hold of a duty nurse she'd dealt with the last time he broke his leg, she would've been completely in the dark. At a loss, she had a bouquet of cut flowers delivered anyway.

Now, still waiting for her order, she was filled with a twisty feeling in the pit of her stomach coupled with the same abiding guilt over not interceding in time.

To deflect for a moment, she turned her thoughts to her business. Dave was right. Prospects were not looking good. Continued job losses, people dipping into their 401Ks and postponing retirement, and the fear of terrorism aloft or in terminals and what-have-you overseas had resulted in a number of recent cancellations.

She'd heard the same excuses: "Sorry, Emily, love to but perhaps we can do it in the spring . . ." and "Can we take a rain check?"

Continuing to deflect, she reassessed her website and a typical testimonial she knew by heart:

"If you want to get off the beaten path and leave the tour buses behind, you can't do better than a personalized jaunt with Emily Ryder. Always enterprising, at the ready to make adjustments, there is nothing like her incomparable rambles. Take it from us, log onto 'Hidden Britain.'"

—Fred and Mary Showalter
New Milford, Connecticut

She thought of the photos on the site. Perhaps they could use some revising. Like the one of her deep in the moor, leaning up against the jutting ancient rock. Echoes of all those times in the wilds, scurrying around the stone circles and the shifty weather patterns. The critical difference between the peat beds with heavy, firm grass around the edges and the featherbed of sphagnum moss that sucked you down and covered you over. Perhaps she should cut even the remotest allusion to anything of that sort.

It was only a short while ago that she was tramping around on a misty, rainy morning not unlike today, pointing out the dangers to the Showalters. It was that same thin line between jeopardy and adventure she was so drawn to. Underscoring the sense of light and dark, ups and downs, then it was back to the nearby confines of Lydfield-in-the-Moor, dinner at the old Elizabethan Castle Pub, and the rest of the cozy amenities.

All of which, in conjunction with today's events—misty,

raining, then dreadfully dark—only exacerbated that twisty feeling and sent her thoughts reeling back to Chris's plight.

Pulling herself together as the food was set in front of her, she remembered that she had a meeting at the rickety Curtis colonial at four to go over last-minute details. She'd continue to check on Chris's condition and, in the interim, return to her maps and last-minute preparations.

She had taken a sip of her chamomile tea when Harriet Curtis burst through the door.

"Ah, there you are!"

Framed against the green-and-white-striped wallpaper of the empty restaurant, Harriet was a sight, even for those who knew her, with her ill-fitting charcoal blouse and skirt, stoop-shouldered figure, and lank white hair.

"Listen," Harriet said sharply, juggling a pile of slick catalogues and envelopes under her arm while grappling with an open shoulder bag. "There's been a change of plans."

"No, Harriet. Sorry, not at this late date." Thrown for a loop but holding on to a sense of professionalism, Emily added, "I'm sure you recall my cancellation policy."

"Don't interrupt me. My mind is made up and I don't have time to mince words."

It was Harriet at her worst. The domineering head of the library board and Historical Society, and chair of the local League of Women Voters and Lydfield Beautification and Garden Society, Harriet was a perfect contrast to her distracted brother, Silas, and her pixilated stepsister, Pru. Though Emily was in no position to lose a client and would have liked nothing more than to call off taxiing all three Curtises around the west of England, there was no way she was going to let Harriet push her around. Especially not today.

"Now listen carefully," said Harriet, still attempting to keep the assortment of slippery catalogues from squirting out of her grasp. "I'm taking a late flight tonight and—"

"Wait a minute. The inn in Bath isn't booked until the day after tomorrow."

"Nevertheless. I shall stay at the Windermere near Victoria Station, take the train to Bath the next day as we planned, and go over my concerns with the organizers of the fair."

"Fete."

"Fete, fair, Twinning—what's the difference?"

"The Twinning is just a segment," Emily said, trying to keep the newfound edginess in her voice in check. "Let's stay calm and keep everything in proportion."

"Oh, will you please stop interrupting me, Emily?" Rattled, Harriet clutched harder at her slipping catalogues. "Now where was I? Ah, yes. As I was saying, I shall see to matters with the organizers by phone and then await your arrival the day after tomorrow. We shall rendezvous in Bath, where you will transport me via rental car to the moor and the sister village as planned."

"Why do you suddenly have to leave a day early? And what about Silas and Pru?"

"What about them? Are they judging the flower show? Do they have a major part to play at the festival? Anyway, I don't wish to discuss it."

"Harriet, make sense. Are you trying to run off and ditch your siblings?"

"I need time. I need space. I can't be boxed in like this —under the gun, as it were. I'm sure you can think of something to keep them at arm's length. Keep everything at arm's length."

Deflecting, Harriet started jabbering about the need to do some extra research about English floral varieties, including Michaelmas daisies, montbretia, and certain amaryllis hybrids. Then, pitching her flinty voice a bit higher, she said, "I have spent the last few hours making these arrangements and have my confirmation numbers right here, if you like." To drive her point home, Harriet reached into her open straw bag but lost control of the catalogues and whatnot, scattering them all over the plank floor.

Reluctantly coming to Harriet's aid, Emily slipped out of the booth and gathered up most of the pile. She placed the envelopes on top while Harriet contended with her bag and crumpled e-mails.

Snatching the stack out of Emily's hands, Harriet said, "I would greatly appreciate it if you would deal with Silas and Pru."

"Harriet, this is ridiculous. Arrangements have been made. I've scheduled everything for all three of you. We have a contract. I am a professional, in case you've forgotten. I don't work this way."

"Can't be helped. Come by at four as planned. We'll finalize whatever needs be and I'll be on my way. Right now, I have some banking business to attend to."

Before Emily could say another word, Harriet scuttled out the door.

Emily finished her lunch, left a tip, and asked the waitress if she could use the phone by the kitchen. She reached Will on the third ring and, as a matter of courtesy, asked if she could postpone the tea he'd offered until around five-thirty. He said that would be no problem.

She made another call to the Sharon hospital. No word about Chris except that he was still in critical condition.

Emily left the restaurant and stood motionless under the overcast sky. She glanced across the street to the corner of West and North where the bank sat conspicuously across the Green and catty-corner to the congregational church. Presently, she began to sense a hazy thread tying together the events of this morning with Harriet's unexpected day-early escape route. A thread linked somehow to the long business envelope she'd scooped up in Harriet's wake, addressed to Harriet Curtis, marked *Confidential*. The return address was embossed with a gold GDC logo. The envelope might very well contain a check that Harriet assumed was still in her possession.

Chapter Three

Emily watched and waited under a spreading elm at the edge of the Green as the late summer sunlight filtered through the cloud cover. All along she'd wondered where the money for this excursion was coming from, especially considering the Curtises' sparse lifestyle, the shape their home was in, and the fact they didn't even own a car. From all indications, the answer was still hidden in the envelope tucked in Emily's jacket.

Soon enough, Harriet hurried out of the bank, passed through the white colonnades and stopped short. From her vantage point, Emily could see that Harriet continued to struggle with her slip-sliding mail. As she fumbled around, Chuck, the balding security guard, came to the rescue with a clear, plastic shopping bag. No surprise on that score. Predictably, Chuck was eager to please, delighted to have something to do besides open doors. But expectedly, Brian Forbes, second in line at the Planning Commission, head of the Business Association, and bank vice president, quickly exited the bank and shooed Chuck inside.

Conscious of his image as if always on camera, Brian offered Harriet a chivalrous hand. His outfit consisted of a tailored, light-blue blazer, a matching tie, and crisp, white slacks.

What Emily had been looking for was some sign of panic on Harriet's part over her missing check. But Harriet brushed aside Brian's proffered hand and made her way down the marble steps. Then she spun around and shouted, "You're the cause, Brian, if you think about it! It started with you, and now look at me!" With those parting words, Harriet scuttled away, leaving Brian standing there looking bewildered.

Emily crossed the street and caught Brian's attention as he reached for the burnished doorknob of the bank. "Brian, have you got a second?"

"I'm in a little bit of a rush," said Brian, flashing his studied smile. "You know, it's one of those typical Mondays."

Before he could slip back into the foyer, Emily bounded up the steps and said, "It's about Harriet. Couldn't help overhearing what she said, and I need you to clear something up."

Brian stepped away from the door and moved well out of earshot of bank customers and employees as Emily joined him.

A glint of sunshine radiated across the colonnades. Emily reached for the envelope.

"Harriet dropped this in the restaurant after announcing she was taking a last-minute flight to London. Which, as you know, must cost a bundle, not to mention checking into a decent hotel."

"So?"

"So, given Harriet's circumstances, doesn't that strike you as odd? Unless there's a nice fat check in here," she added, pointing out the GDC logo. Emily knew she was pushing it, responding to Harriet's outburst about it all being Brian's fault, but at the moment she was unable to contain herself about this direct link with the GDC.

"Losing it, depending on this juicy sweetener to see her through, plus whatever set her off just now, including her plans to dump her brother and step-sister, is compromising my tour. Not to mention raising all kinds of questions."

Brian gingerly took the envelope out of Emily's hand. Just as hesitantly, he said, "Thanks, she'll be greatly relieved. I'll give her a quick call."

"Brian, I think you're dodging the issue."

"Ah, you mean her sudden departure. I'm sure it's all a misunderstanding."

As he attempted to turn away again, Emily said, "But that's not all. This is not a typical Monday, as you just said. I'm sure you've heard about Chris Cooper's fall during the downpour this morning. And not just an accident. He's barely hanging on! As if you, of all people, weren't on top of things that concern you directly."

Brian modified his fixed grin before coming out with, "Now, Emily, since when are you interested in politics?"

"We're not just talking about politics."

Brian adjusted his tie nervously and came up with a lame retort. "Of course. And I understand that you and your mom are worried about the effect of the new GDC project on property values and the B&B. Well, my advice is, best to ask Martha. Not only is she my better half, she, as you well know, is the principal realtor in town."

Before Brian could offer any more *non sequiturs*, an elderly couple approached the marble steps. And before

Chuck had a chance to step back out, Brian gave the couple his best Iron Bank welcome, held one of the looming doors open for them, glanced back at Emily, and said, "Too bad you're off again. Love to have had you at the hearing. You could've learned all about the wheels of progress."

As the couple entered the bank, Emily pressed harder.

"Wait a minute. Harriet's payment from the GDC aside, are you really telling me you know nothing about Chris? Or the fact he was up on Miranda Shaw's roof when it happened?"

At the mention of Miranda Shaw's name, Brian's fixed smile wavered.

Again, Emily knew she was pushing it by assuming Brian knew full well about what happened to Chris this morning and was obviously brushing her off.

"You know, Miranda Shaw's overpriced, fake English Tudor. The one Martha has failed to unload."

There was a long silence as Brian continued to look out at nothing in particular.

"I don't get it, Brian. Why can't we communicate? You, your wife, Miranda Shaw, and the scene of Chris's dreadful fall. There is an obvious connection."

Just then, Martha Forbes came sauntering into view and abruptly halted. Brian altered his gaze in her direction. They were no more than twenty yards apart but neither of them spoke. For a time, they simply regarded each other. Brian fluttered a few fingers in a tentative wave, planted the smile back on his face, and raised his voice.

"Well, Emily, you're in luck. Here's Martha now. And if I don't see you beforehand, have a good trip."

"Right, Brian. Just keep ignoring me."

"Yes, there she is." Brian's smile switched off completely as he clutched the envelope. "She's the realtor, I'm the banker, and we each have our separate roles to play."

Emily let it go, doing her best to file all of this in the back of her mind. She ambled down the steps and started back toward the Green and her Camry, realizing she and Martha would cross paths and have to exchange pleasantries. Unless Emily wanted to delve further, which would only overload the circuit even more.

"Hi, Martha," Emily said, pausing on the walkway as an act of courtesy.

"Hello," said Martha, pausing as well but glancing up at the bank entrance as though making up her mind whether or not to enter. Like her husband, Martha Forbes never failed to make Emily feel like an underling. Sporting a trim, tailored suit with a white, frilly blouse and turquoise silk neckerchief along with her impervious smile, Martha affected a note of concern. "Mind if I ask what caused my husband to look so sheepish?"

"We were talking about Miranda Shaw's place, among other things."

"Ah." Switching gears, Martha came out with, "I must say, I often wonder how you do it. Carefree, short hair and khakis. Footloose. What is your secret?"

Emily wanted to cut through the chitchat, but Martha switched gears again and went into her business mode.

"At any rate, be sure to inform your mother that I'm positive I can get a decent price for her place if she will listen to reason and act quickly. Oh, and while we're on the subject, about that handyman of yours. I understand he had a charter boat business in the Keys. How on earth did he wind up renovating houses in the northeast? Is he any good?"

Martha's sales pitch only made matters even worse, if that was possible. Emily did her best to let it pass. Needless to say, selling the B&B, the only home she'd ever known, was the last thing she wanted to contemplate.

As the elderly couple reappeared and made their way down the steps, there was no telling if Martha was actually talking to Emily or stalling while collecting her thoughts vis-à-vis her husband. With a sigh, Martha pivoted smoothly on her low heels. "You'll be leaving tomorrow and Devon is on your itinerary, I hear."

"That was the plan."

"Well, have a good trip and don't forget to contact your mother posthaste." With that, Martha continued briskly on her way.

As the pearl-gray hue of the sky held steady, Emily watched Chuck usher Martha into the bank.

Getting more edgy by the second, Emily sensed that everything in her world was wrong. Chris was in critical condition, Harriet had likely been bribed and was taking off, and Brian and Martha wanted Emily and her mother to sell out and get out of the way as well. Emily thought back to Doc's mysterious phone call in the downpour this morning, that, in effect, had possibly erased Chris Cooper from the scene.

She walked briskly past the glistening elms that dotted the Green, opened the trunk of her Camry, exchanged her walking shoes for her old cross trainers, and slipped on her running jacket.

Jogging past the post office and library on South Street, Emily noticed a crew tackling a huge copper beech on the other side of the street. High above, one of the men in the crane bucket worked away with his chainsaw, ripping into the uppermost reaches of the stately tree. At the same time, four men and a woman below egged them on.

As Emily cut to her right down Gallows Lane, there was a hush, a resounding thud and a hearty cheer echoing behind her. She picked up her pace. Unbidden, something Chris Cooper had once said to her crossed her mind. Something from Thoreau about mourning what had needlessly been cut down.

Passing by the water lilies alongside Longmeadow pond, she knew there was no way she could run past her deepest worry and do a through-me as Chris would usually advise.

The tinge of guilt over not intervening in time shook her once again.

Chapter Four

Almost finished with her run, Emily had no sooner passed the Central School when a sharp whistle caught her attention. Then a shout.

"Hey, Ryder, what's the story?"

Then Emily remembered. In a way it was a coincidence. In another way it was a solution to a double bind. She couldn't be in two places at once—here with her growing suspicions and anxiety over Chris; about to go abroad with its own dicey implications starting with Harriet. She doubled back to the verge of the school's front lawn. Bent over with her hands on her knees, catching her breath, she paid no mind to the Nikon camera clicking away.

"Hey, what can I say?" said Babs Maroon, employing her usual mocking tone. "You're over the hill, pal. Over the hill."

The mop of tousled red hair that framed the pinched face of Emily's old school chum glinted under the fickle cloud cover. As usual, Babs sported a loose-fitting, periwinkle cotton top tucked inside a pair of bib overalls. Babs had recently become a features reporter for the *County Times*, which could very well prove useful.

Straightening up and stretching, Emily said, "Babs, glad I ran into you. I could use a little information."

"Righty-o," Babs countered as though they were still grade school cheerleaders. "For your information, you happen to be late."

"Oh?"

"Hey, don't give me that look. I allotted myself thirty minutes here, tops, in our beloved backwater. Then it's on to Falls Village, Cornwall Bridge, and a few other Sleepy Hollows that time forgot."

"Sorry?" Then Emily remembered. "Oh right. So much has happened since this morning. We had an appointment, a photo shoot and all."

"Gotcha. As payment for wasting my time, I've narrowed it down to three finalists for the funny name contest for the paper. Pick one and spare my fevered brain. 'Rhoda Horsey,' 'Ella Funt,' or 'Dudley Bumpus.' And the winner is . . ."

"Look, Babs, this is the last thing I need right now."

"I happen to be serious. Trying to keep afloat even if the price is these mindlessness stories to humor the editor and keep up circulation. Oh, never mind, I'll just give it to Ms. Rhoda. She's actually got her fingers crossed, hoping to win the stupid thing to get back at folks for teasing her all these years."

Amazed with what Babs had to put up with to keep gainfully employed, Emily said, "Okay then. My turn."

"Not so fast, not so fast," said Babs, shuffling backward and snapping shots of Emily in motion.

"Babs, hold still, will you? I need to ask you something."

"Oh, yeah?"

"Yes."

Keeping up with Babs until they were at the school crossing, Emily stopped short. "Harriet Curtis."

"At last count, you've given me nothing I can use here," said Babs. "And what about Harriet Curtis?"

"Why would she scream at Brian Forbes outside the bank? Accuse him of being the cause of something, that 'it' all started with him? She said she was under the gun. What pressure is she under? And why would she skip town a day before our scheduled departure?"

"Whoa, what is it with you? Haven't you heard what's up with the Curtis house? Go check the updated list."

"What list?"

"Ryder, don't you ever read the paper? The tax collector's list. They're threatening to foreclose."

Resuming taking shots of the bus stop and the old brick school, Babs went on. "As it happens, not only is good ol' Harriet in arrears due to uncollected back taxes, but as the principal heir to the estate, she's responsible for a second mortgage her late father took out ten years ago. In short, my sweet, the wolves are at the door."

"Okay then, how does Brian Forbes figure in? Why would Harriet accuse him of causing everything and how is that linked to the GDC proposal?"

"Can you back off a little?"

"Just answer me, okay?"

While eyeing the camera's display window and erasing some of the shots, Babs made some offhand remarks about Brian that were strictly personal and of no help. Then she came out with some reference to GDC tactics.

"Got to hand it to him, that Martin Gordon. Crafty guy. Always brags he never once foisted himself on a community."

"What are you saying?"

"You see," said Babs, "even if the whole town rose up against him, his trick was to hire a team of lawyers who threatened to sue for obstruction. Commission members became so anxious over legal fees at the expense of the taxpayers, they caved in."

Emily held stock still, beginning to see how shady this whole enterprise was, and getting some inkling as to what she was up against.

Rounding off her spiel, Babs said, "Then clever Gordon would hand it over to Hacket, his silent partner, who would raise the price of the condos exponentially. Hence, the GDC could continue to claim they never went where they weren't wanted."

Babs absentmindedly checked the display window on her camera again. "But let's get down to more pressing matters. How's your sex life? Dave Roberts still trying to jump on your bones? Or are you opting for Will Farrow, the drifter caretaker, and a trial run at older men?"

Emily ignored her. Despite sensing that all the twisted threads were getting beyond her, she couldn't let this one go. Couldn't erase the recurring image of Chris's violent spasms and dreadful fall.

"Babs, can you just for once stop messing around? I am trying to get a bead on what's going on around here. Tell me the latest on Miranda Shaw."

"Why?"

"Just humor me, okay? Please?"

Affecting an erect pose as if reciting the answers to a quiz, Babs said, "Miranda Shaw, busty English wench, poaches enticing males in our midst up until late summer. Does God-knows-what whilst at home in the UK. As for the unmovable fake Tudor, I haven't a clue. In short, I wouldn't be surprised if she's got her claws into someone local, who will go nameless for now. But she's back in the UK at the moment, while trying to move her McMansion here, and playing both ends against the middle."

Suddenly, Babs looked up from her camera and stared at Emily. "Hold it. Why do I have the sinking feeling I've been duped? That you've actually totally forgotten all about tomorrow?"

When it finally came to her, Emily said, "Right. We had an arrangement."

"Damn straight. Why, pray tell, did I just take all these stills of your healthy, glowing countenance? Why did you prod me the other day, saying a promo and sidebar would be so great? First day of school, appealing to the little brats who, in turn, would prod their parents to hook up with one of your oh-so-special guided tours. What is this, sudden amnesia?"

"Look, Babs, I'm booked to take off first thing tomorrow. After what I've been through—I mean with Chris and all this stuff that's percolating underneath . . ." Emily stopped herself, realizing that none of what she'd been alluding to made any sense.

"Something happen to Chris?"

"Yes. He fell off that fake Tudor roof."

"Wow." Babs got off her signature flip repartee for a

moment, quickly recovered, and carried on. "Anyway, no taking off first thing. First thing tomorrow, first day of school, you're going to tell the kiddies what wonders Auntie Em is going to bring back for show-and-tell about her wild adventures in the spooky moors. You are not going to leave me holding the bag."

"I'm telling you, I don't see how I can the way things are going."

"The way things are going, pal, is what we call life." Babs segued to a few clichés about fulfilling one's obligations. Dropping that tack, she said, "Okay, let's have it. What is the upshot here?"

Emily realized that, given the drastic change of circumstances, she hadn't taken this under consideration. Hadn't come up with some way to juggle the meeting with the kids on the first day of school, which had completely slipped her mind, while enlisting Babs's help to keep tabs on the machinations back home while she was off in England. At the moment, all Emily could say was, "I'll get back to you."

Walking off, Emily barely heard Babs yelling behind her. "Hey, what is this? Fair is fair. Ever hear of it?"

Emily hurried back to the Green as Babs's shouts trailed off. Enlisting Babs's help was not the first thing on her list. The first thing was dealing with Harriet as she attempted to leave Silas and Pru in the lurch. Stop her from taking off and make her have it out with her siblings—or something to that effect.

Percolating beneath her thoughts were Doc's insinuations coupled with the GDC's ploys and resources.

Which, by some hook or crook, led somehow to Chris's tenuous hold on life and was linked to the phone call and Miranda Shaw's leaky roof. She thought about Brian's and Martha's response to the very mention of Miranda's name, back again to Harriet's sudden panic, and the seemingly taboo subject of Chris's fall. Emily was speculating like crazy. Whatever way she looked at it, there was no way she could get her mind around this jangle of loose ends while groping for some way to deal with her obligations.

Even so, there was so much at stake here, including promising her mother that she would keep track and make sure everything was okay back home. Even so, there was no way Emily could dismiss any of it.

Chapter Five

Emily pulled over across from the ramshackle Curtis colonial. She let the motor idle for a while as a few cars zipped up the vertical curve on their way to the Massachusetts border, the southern Berkshires, and beyond.

Seen from this angle, the Curtis place held its own as the oldest house in Lydfield. In the hazy afternoon light, it stood with its flat Federalist façade, white clapboard beneath a steeply-pitched roof, black shutters flanking paned windows, and a semi-circular fanlight above the central entry. Just as traditional was the left front door, added on to eliminate the prospect of walking straight into the stairway.

Looking more closely, what marked the Curtis house— apart from the sagging roof and peeling paint—was the absence of a front stoop that had long since rotted away. Even more curious were the steps to the side entrance that had also rotted away. In their place were loose wooden planks supported by concrete blocks. It was a wonder to Emily how Harriet, Silas, and Pru managed to venture in and out, especially in winter, without spraining an ankle or worse. Especially Harriet, in her late sixties, ungainly and accident prone. All in all, it was patently obvious that the Curtises were strapped for cash.

But what really caught Emily's attention was the sight of red flags, like the boundary lines of a foot race, leading away from the Curtis side yard and up the slope to the tree line and the high meadow. As she eased her car back along the road, it dawned on her that it would be highly dangerous for the GDC to place the entrance to a gateway community of 120 luxury townhouses, a clubhouse, and whatnot on such a steep curve. The surging bedrock would make it almost impossible and prohibitively expensive to construct.

Emily drove off, passed the crest of the hill, made a U-turn and stopped in front of her mother's B&B. If her mother did sell out, with a bit of excavation, the GDC could use their driveway to connect to the trail up to the meadowland. But the GDC wouldn't have filed a site application banking on that remote contingency, which Doc had already intimated was a highly iffy option and not the optimum linchpin.

On the other hand, driving back down the vertical curve and past the looming rise of the meadowland, the solution became glaring. There, less than a hundred yards back, the tiny red flags leading up and away from the Curtis side yard created a safe entrance from the point where the road flattened out, past the long side of the Curtis estate, to an easy access up and onto the coveted site.

Emily switched off the motor. One way or another she was going to confront Harriet about the flags and the check she had ostensibly received from the GDC. This represented not only the end of Emily's mother's way of life due to the imminent excavation and destruction of the high meadow, but the very quaint, historic character of the village. A peaceful and cozy ambiance that affected everyone.

But as luck would have it, Emily's timing was off. She had no sooner gotten out of her car when a blue cab with yellow markings swerved in front of her and parked. The cabbie, a scrawny man in a tacky brown shirt and green tie, popped open the lid of his trunk and headed down the front lawn toward the loose-plank steps. Harriet appeared at the side door lugging a suitcase. While the cabbie was struggling to grab the suitcase and keep Harriet from stumbling, into the mix, hot on Harriet's heels, came Doc, dressed in his shirtsleeves.

"Hold it! I tell you, we gotta talk. Where you think you're going?" Doc yelled.

"I have nothing further to say to you," Harriet called out in that flinty voice of hers. "I have nothing further to say to anyone."

"Oh, yeah? Well, lady, you got another think coming."

The befuddled cabbie threw the suitcase in the trunk, slammed the lid, slid behind the wheel, and gunned the motor. Harriet jerked open the passenger door handle and shouted back, "It will simply have to wait!"

"Like hell," said Doc, waving his hands like a traffic cop. "You can't pull this now."

Emily wanted to do something, step in somehow, but in all the confusion she hadn't a chance.

Spotting Emily, Harriet peered out the passenger window and called to her over the noise of the motor. "Handle Silas and Pru for me, won't you? As I asked. Come up with something, anything. Our situation, our association, is completely untenable. And don't forget the logistics—our rendezvous time and itinerary."

Before Emily could reply, the cab took off with a lurch, heading east to beat the traffic on its way to Granby and the Bradley Airport north of Hartford.

"How do you like that?" said Doc glancing at Emily. "Looks like now I got to deal with you."

"Keep away from me, okay?"

"Fat chance."

They were standing approximately the same distance apart as they had during their exchange in the drizzle up on the high meadow that morning. Except that now they were in full sight of passing cars and there was no way Emily could put up with him.

"Okay, all right," said Doc, softening his tone. "When you wouldn't even take my card, I could see I was maybe coming on a little strong."

Emily pondered her next move as Doc carried on.

"So, we got off on the wrong foot. You might have heard something I said over the cell phone about taking care of it right away, and then it was raining, really coming down. And then—I mean, these things happen. And now with this Harriet fleeing the coop, it's all too damn much. Am I right or am I right?"

Frustrated over Harriet's sudden getaway, Emily decided her only option was to pick up the pieces. She turned back toward the house.

Following close behind, Doc said, "Wait up, huh? You want to talk soccer? I know soccer. You were a striker, right?

What happens when you get tripped up? You get on the ball, chip it over to a wing, get it back, and bang it home. So use your head, make like I'm the wing."

Ignoring Doc completely, Emily made for the loose-planked steps.

Doc grabbed her elbow. She yanked herself free.

"Don't be like that. Look, you tell me what logistics this Harriet was talking about and I'll figure some way we both make out. Just tell me exactly when and where you're gonna meet. We both need everything nailed down, right? What can you lose?"

Emily had only one thing to say as she stepped up to the side entrance. "You're on my list, Doc."

"Oh, that's cute. That's real cute."

She passed under the weathered plaque inscribed with "Elijah Curtis 1781" in wrought iron. As she entered, whatever else Doc may have had to say evaporated into the woodwork as he left the premises, his curses tailing off.

Making her way into the dingy interior, she sloughed off the musty odor, the shabby upholstered wing chairs, and frayed silk draperies, fixing her gaze on a drop-leaf table where a number of papers had spilled out of a double-sided satchel. She made a sharp turn into the keeping room, past the sooty fireplace with the dangling cast-iron pots and ladles, and called for Silas.

There was no reply. She called for Pru with the same result.

No matter what, she had no intention of taking off tomorrow and winding up alone with Harriet, who was up to God knew what. She hoped that she'd never wind up alone with any member of this flaky trio under any circumstances, but with Silas and Pru as a buffer, she might somehow be able to manage the tour and, at the same time, get a bead on the troubling games being played from across the pond. Which meant making sure Silas and Pru were squared away. Perhaps with all three in tow, Harriet would be rendered harmless, slip up somehow, and come to terms. Perhaps, by some stretch of the imagination, the tour would eventually run its course as planned.

Presently, Emily heard shuffling from below and started down the rickety cellar staircase. As she was about to call out again, Silas rushed up. Sidestepping both Silas and the oak case he wielded that probably housed one of those antique dueling pistols of his, Emily let him pass.

A few steps above her, Silas muttered, "After all I did for her . . . all I've done . . . and this is what I get." He turned, peered over his silver-rimmed bifocals and, as if Emily had been there all the while, said in greeting, "Remember this?" He lifted the oak case.

Glancing up in the dim cellar light, Emily remembered the way Silas's mind worked. For Silas, time was telescoped, and yesterday and today were still fused. It was as if he was here and, at the same time, someplace else. Perhaps back in history, perhaps hanging on to something that had happened recently or long ago.

Humoring him until she could get him to focus, she made a stab.

"Bet you've got a matched pair of flintlocks with a walnut stock in there," she said.

"Plus?"

Emily couldn't possibly remember.

"Battle trophies on the trigger guards," said Silas, prompting her. "And pineapple finials. Wad cutter, ball mold, powder flask, and oil bottle in the original case. Look what I've had to resort to."

"You don't mean selling them?"

"What else can I . . .? To supplement Pru and I . . . our travel expenses, now that Harriet has skipped out. The fete is counting on us, you know. Especially because of all I can reveal about the historical link between our two villages."

Silas stopped talking and held still, as if posing for a family portrait. Except for his full head of gray, wooly hair, hound-dog face, and skinny frame, he looked every bit like Harriet's brother, his rumpled tweed jacket contrasting with Harriet's usual starched getup when flustered out on the town.

"All the same, Silas," Emily said, "I couldn't help notice the papers strewn over the table in the parlor. I hope you've gone over my instructions carefully about packing, the rate of exchange, duplicate passports, and bringing drug prescriptions, just in case."

"Yes . . . maybe. Not sure. They're counting on me at the Twinning, you know," said Silas, repeating himself. "The residents of Lydfield-in-the-Moor know little of the founding of the Greenwoods and the Western Lands. When the Brits came over, that's what they called our village. So much else to tell them, which means I am absolutely obliged to . . ."

"Sell that matched pair."

"Yes, yes, pawning this, selling that. But I shall recoup, I tell you. I can't believe Harriet going off like this, as if Pru and I were extra baggage. But I definitely will recoup."

"What about my travel instructions, Silas?"

Silas climbed up the remaining steps into the keeping room and turned. "On my desk. Bring them up and lock up tight, will you? And don't mention a thing to Pru. Let her think I had extra money squirreled away for a rainy day. She'll like that. Makes for a better story."

Emily wanted to ask where Pru could be found, but Silas kept moving off.

"Good, good," Silas muttered. "Emily Ryder over here to make sure we were included and all set with her instructions. Very good."

For the sake of expediency, she went along with Silas's wishes, though she wished playing nanny didn't so often come with the job.

As the dimming afternoon light sifted through the cellar windows, Emily skirted the converted coal furnace, stepped up onto the raised flooring, and entered Silas's makeshift vault. There it was, in as much disarray as the first time she encountered it. Cobwebs clustered in the corners of the drop ceiling; the temperature control and humming vented humidifier probably hadn't been replaced in years. UV filters and silica gel anti-humidity packets were everywhere— inside the storage cabinets and glass cases and even on the shelves beneath the framed and faded colonial maps—while the wiring running across the edge of the vinyl flooring was frayed as ever.

Her sense of unease grew worse by the second down in the dingy space.

As she vaguely recalled, an old mahogany desk occupied the center of the room and held an old Mac computer, printer, fax machine, and phone, where Silas conducted most of his mail order business. She retrieved the travel instructions and shut the computer down.

For good measure, she padlocked the display case housing the double barrel traveling pistols, ramrods, brass powder flasks and ammunition, the Colt, long-barreled cap and ball revolvers, and the like. It was a wonder there was still a worldwide market for authentic firearms from the Revolutionary War.

She noted that there was only one of a pair of hammerless, nickel-plated, .32 Smith and Wesson "Lemon Squeezers" and a box of assorted cartridges. *He must have sold that too,* she thought. But she didn't discount the oddness that went with everything else today. She continued tidying up to comply with Silas's wishes and, perhaps subconsciously, to put things in some kind of order.

Absentmindedly, she moved faster and straightened up the silhouettes of heads and shoulders, jungle creatures, and other clip-ons for target practice. She secured a second display case of old books and pamphlets with a skeleton key that hung by a set of dangling pick locks.

Just then, as the humidifier shut off, a familiar buzzing sound caught her attention. She located the model electric train perched on a plywood-and-sawhorse table in the far corner, replete with simulated green hills and valley. The replica of a steam engine caught her eye as well, along with the boxcars, freight cars, Pullman passenger cars, and a red caboose.

Just as she had in restless times during her employment with Silas, she gripped the multi-volt transformer that would send the train tooting up the first steep grade, cascading down and over a bridge and round a curve, up a steeper rise and down again through the tunnel and long straightaway till it slowed in its return to Lionel City in honor of its brand name.

On a whim, she fiddled with the dial and watched the toy train zip up the first grade and head straight down for the bridge. But something sparked along the tracks and switches and the overhead lights flickered. She shut the whole thing off.

She checked the fuse box, reset a breaker, and replaced the blown fuse. Skirting around an open toolbox and a crumpled raincoat, she unplugged the transformer and switched the lights back on.

Sitting down on a crate marked "Parts for Carlisle and Finch model trains," she decided to draw the line. Once again, she realized she was fussing around to distract herself from all that was weighing on her mind. But she was not about to put away the tool box lying by her feet or the damp raincoat.

"Come on, Emily," she muttered. "Back to reality."

She checked her watch. She had a morning flight and hadn't even started packing, let alone had a chance to fully prepare.

Nevertheless, thoughts of Chris's plight filtered back more strongly than ever, along with something else he recently said. *You know something, through-me doesn't seem to quite work anymore. Getting so I can't hardly let anything pass in dealing with town folks without wondering. Really beginning to wonder, Emmy.*

With the twisty thoughts beginning to take over again, she looked around, catching sight of Pru's Victorian doll collection behind another set of glass cabinets. In the forefront were Calico Girl, Little Girl in Cream, Sailor Girl, and Girl in Mauve. Ladies in burgundy and other satiny colors stood in various positions, elegantly fitted-out with umbrellas, pantaloons, crinolines, silk flowers, and all the rest of it.

She couldn't help but be reminded of Storytelling Pru's visits to Emily's second grade class with her spooky tales, and the time Pru had brought "something special for the girls." The others ooh-ed and ah-ed over the porcelain faces and gushed over the curls and long eyelashes as Pru told the class what befell these poor maidens in the wilds of the moors overseas in the witchy part of England. This had prompted Emily (who had no patience for dolls and tall tales and would much rather be out playing ball) to sneak off and race away from the school grounds, only to run into Chris and that quizzical Lincoln-esque look of his.

"Now, now, what's this?" he had asked.

Emily only shrugged.

"Not running away?"

Emily shrugged again.

"Emily, do we really want to make a habit of this?"

"Like my dad, you mean?"

"Not saying, not my place. Wouldn't be right to put words into your mouth. You just think about it, that's all."

"I just have."

"Oh?"

"If I had to choose, I wouldn't want to become a runaway. Much rather take after you."

"Well then, you go right back there and stick it out. You never know. Could be more to this than meets the eye."

With that, she had eased her way back to face the silly goings-on, like it or not.

As she was about to do now. She needed to go back upstairs and check on Pru, which was as off-putting as having to deal with Silas. Both of them in some other world, flitting in and out, making communication doubly difficult. All she really wanted to do was see about Chris and get a definite prognosis, then cool down the jumble of vexing thoughts and try to take it from there.

Chapter Six

Emily scanned the rear of the house from the lilac bushes to the rhododendron, and laurel to the rose arbor. Looking past the arbor, she finally spotted Pru pulling up weeds behind the ragged zinnias and cosmos, looking like her Little Girl in Cream doll with her ankle-length skirt and ruffled blouse.

Emily braced herself. Not because Pru was any kind of threat but out of concern for Pru's grip on reality. She did so much daydreaming that the way things were turning out, she might be more of a hindrance than a help. She wished she could ask her directly what exactly was going on between the three of them, about the altercation that had set them apart. But Pru being Pru would doubtless only go off on a tangent, create some comparable faerie tale, and leave the matter even more convoluted. The only tack Emily could come up with was to humor her while attempting to get her on board. But she had to do it quickly. Then she could see about Chris.

As Emily headed towards her, Pru widened her eyes like saucers and said, "Ooh, Emily, this is so-o-o good. Come help."

Letting Pru chatter away in her singsong voice, Emily

joined in the battle against the rain-soaked encroaching weeds, unsure of how Pru was taking Harriet's sudden departure or if she was even aware of it. Originally, Emily was supposed to meet with all three of them to go over the last-minute details. But with that plan out the window and Harriet's resolute order to dump her siblings, Emily had to make sure of Pru's place in the scheme of things.

"I still can't get over the way Harriet allowed things to get out of hand like this," said Pru, stagey as ever. "It's her job, always has been. Just look at the cosmos. It needs to be staked. It's as tall as me. And look at the horrid bittersweet climbing up the rose arbor, all tangled up and choking things. It's a wonder I don't get caught up and lost in it all. But who would care, 'cause I'm so tiny. Who would even know I was missing and left behind?"

After a moment, Pru beamed and added, "Now tell me, wouldn't that make a good story?"

Emily shifted to rooting out a few clumps of creepers overtaking the beds of myrtle. "I don't know, Pru. Whatever you say."

"A story for kids, of course. If you look at the rambling roses and the darn bittersweet, then inside the arbor tunnel of climbing shrub roses, with a little embellishment here and there, I'd say you've got something. A battle between beauty and devilish creeping things."

"It's okay, Pru, I get it."

Emily continued to hang back. Pru had done so many *Let's Pretend* children's shows in libraries and whatnot, Emily learned early on to slough off most anything she said. Under the circumstances, Emily needed to know not only if Pru was okay but if she was capable of getting at all serious about Harriet's machinations and perhaps even help keep a close eye on her stepsister.

They worked in silence for a while, tossing the clumps of weeds into a wheelbarrow. The wide swathe lined with little red flags leading up to the high meadow was close by. But Pru seemed to take no notice. It was as if the flags had always been there, sloping up to the tree line to the proposed construction site. But Emily had just discovered them today.

"There now, isn't this starting to look better?" said Pru. "Once they're staked, they'll stand up like happy hand-maidens."

It was getting harder and harder to put up with this nonsense, but Emily nodded anyway.

Emily carted the wheelbarrow to the pile of scraggly brush behind the arbor and dumped it. As the cloud cover took over darkening the sky once again, Pru quit raking as she started explaining to Emily about the stories she planned to tell at the Twinning portion of the fete. She was booked to keep the children amused by telling tales linked to old timey New England they could relate to.

"So I thought I'd do my version of *The Headless Horseman* with a slight British accent. For starters, I mean. To warm the kids up and make friends."

"I guess," said Emily, returning with the wheelbarrow, still trying to assess Pru's state of mind.

Sidling up to Emily, her slight frame perfectly erect, Pru said, "Want to know the real reason I'm going? Besides the honor of being chosen to represent Lydfield?"

Emily didn't have the heart to tell her the only reason she and Silas were included was to make it "worth the candle." It was all Emily could do to convince the fete committee of the Curtises' historical prominence, Harriet's floral expertise and whatnot, and what Pru and Silas could possibly offer.

"Okay, Pru," Emily said. "But let's keep in mind I only dropped by to see how you were taking all this. How you felt about it and all."

"I've been corresponding, as you know," said Pru, disregarding Emily's concern and carrying on. "And I've been informed that beyond the sister village, there's a soothsayer who knows all the old tales. Lives in a thatched hut. Knows stories about Devon pixies leading people astray on the moorland bogs. And the Dewerstone where the Devil guided a lost traveler over the edge in the fog. And fickle maidens made to run ragged around prehistoric stone circles before they were exonerated. If I can bring these stories back and make them my own, I could restart my whole career. Be booked in libraries and such all over New England."

As the cloud cover continued to hold steady, Emily found herself wondering why some of what Pru was saying had begun to slip into that hazy, jangled thread in the back of her mind. Slipped in for apparently no reason.

A few glimmers of sunlight appeared and faded. A cardinal pecked at an empty bird feeder and flew off, causing Pru to say, "See, Harriet even let the feeder go to pot. Soon the songbirds will give up on us altogether. And what about the bittersweet? It's choking the whole arbor. I tell you, it's strangling it."

"When we get back from our trip, we'll tackle it, okay?"

"You mean it?"

"You bet."

"Oh, I really hope you mean it." Pursing her lips, Pru said, "We can't let Harriet ruin things, can we? That would be a crime."

"Exactly. For now, let's say she's just gone on ahead, and as far as everything else goes—"

"Everything else? What do you mean?"

Emily was not about to get drawn into some endless explanation. Instead, she came right back with, "We have to handle it one step at a time. Play it as it lays, as the gamblers say."

"Meaning? Is there something you're holding back?"

Reluctantly, Emily skirted around the issue, saying that Chris had had a bad fall and a lead man for the developers had been nosing around. She could have asked Pru about the red flags and all manner of things, but with the way Pru's mind was still flitting around coupled with Emily's own anxiety, she wished she hadn't said "everything else." Wished she hadn't spoken at all.

"So," said Pru clasping her hands together, "we're going to have to watch our step. But you'll be at our beck and call. That's why we chose you. Steadfast and true."

Actually, there was no one else they could have chosen, no one else who had even a vague connection with the Twinning and could set up a semi-exchange.

"Great," Emily said. "You just hold onto that upbeat attitude." Before Pru had a chance to toss in another "What do you mean?" Emily told her that she was on a tight schedule and had to go. She slipped away, got back in her car, and drove off.

Continuing up the vertical curve, she tooled past the B&B and kept going until she reached an elevation high enough to get a decent signal due to the problematic cell tower. She pulled over, snatched her cellphone out of the glove department and hit the speed dial for the ICU. Perhaps this time the duty nurse could give Emily some idea of how long it might take for a victim of a horrific fall to come out of a coma. Perhaps there was an off-chance the Planning Commission would delay the application for site approval, buying Emily some time to sort things out until Chris regained consciousness.

But it simply wasn't to be. The nurse was sorry to inform her that only a short while ago, Chris Cooper had passed away.

Chapter Seven

Crying softly, Emily drove aimlessly around the foothills as memories filtered in and dovetailed. She thought of all the times Chris had come over to talk to her mother after Emily's dad had walked out on them for the last time. Long talks in the kitchen about staying solvent and other matters Emily was too young to understand. Chance meetings atop nearby Mohawk Mountain after the tourists had gone, comparing notes and discussing the changing seasons, threatened habitats of creatures and ecosystems, the preservation of upland tree canopies. Dropping in on Emily from time to time to see how she was doing with her schoolwork and her exploits on the soccer field. Then, more recently, eager to hear all about her escapades in the UK, especially her treks across the rock-strewn moors.

With the memories came an inconsolable ache. It had no name but would surely stay with her.

After a while, she remembered her early supper date with Will. She pulled over onto a dirt road. All her energy drained, she took out her cellphone and hit the speed-dial number for the B&B. He answered immediately and she asked for a grace period of another half hour or so. In that laid-back southern drawl of his, he said he was only going to whip up some quesadillas and she could take her time. The weak signal broke off, and she went on a while longer with her looping, aimless drive.

Emily sat at the butcher-block table, her back to the screen door of the B&B. She barely noticed that for the first time ever, the kitchen was inviting and scrubbed clean. The paneling was white instead of loyalist green, the cupboards a glistening chrysanthemum, the faded linoleum replaced by yellow and white tiles. Twilight was dwindling, but the new light fixtures were aglow. Oliver's heavy paw was on Emily's knee, his blocky head nuzzling against her side, his pale-yellow coat blending in with the new decor. But none of this really registered.

Canola oil sizzled in the cast-iron skillet as Will turned the front burner down and said, "Have I passed the test?"

So depressed she could barely answer, Emily said, "It's fine."

All the while, Emily hadn't given Will any inkling of what was really in the back of her mind. After all, they'd never had a conversation that amounted to anything, even though there was always something percolating underneath. Truth to tell, some part of her needed a male presence, a steadying influence, a lingering touch of Chris.

To try to deflect from her sad news she'd revealed in hesitant drips and drabs, Will continued to tell her more about himself—running a charter fishing boat in the Keys and an air boat in the Everglades and Big Cypress Swamp.

Something else about bartending on a riverboat called the *Catfish Queen*. His present stint with "fixer-uppers" was a trade he'd learned from his "ol' man" who specialized in repairing damaged beachfront properties from Cape Hatteras to Cape Cod.

But none of this made any impression either. All she could think of was the fact that Chris had no family, no one to look out for him. No one else who truly cared how he had died.

Pru, being Pru, had called her steadfast. In some way, Pru was right. Emily would not be turning her back by running off to England. She would be going after Harriet and looking in on Miranda Shaw about the call to her Tudor McMansion in the pouring rain. She'd stick with all the tangled threads for Chris's sake.

The inconsolable ache began to mesh with the abiding edginess. As Trooper Dave had intimated, her anxiety was no excuse. She knew nothing about police procedure and had no training or business becoming involved in a case that didn't exist, let alone unlimited law enforcement resources to call upon.

The only thing she could possibly hang this on was circumstantial and personal.

Too bad. It was unfinished business and she had to see to it that she could eventually call on someone to step in.

At the same time, she was aware she had to pack if she was going to carry out the terms of her tour contract. Though she had received a retainer, it was obvious that Harriet was no longer going to underwrite this venture for all three. Receiving the rest of her payment was contingent on Silas coming up with supplemental funds for himself and Pru.

Once again, Will tried to engage Emily in conversation. "I heard from your mom. She has some idea about re-decorating in different colonial motifs, like the B&B she's been staying at in Lenox. She also asked if I heard anything more about the possible threat of a big condo development next door. Up on the high meadow, I guess she means."

Pulling herself out of her stupor, Emily said, "Tell her I'm looking into it like I told her earlier. And please sidestep any reference to Chris Cooper's passing. My mom is skittish enough. It would just do her in."

"She deserves a little time off, you mean. Before dealing with the fall foliage season."

"If you like."

Will folded ingredients into two tortillas, including bits of fresh shrimp, and tossed together a salad.

Oliver began begging, resting his chin on the table top as a ploy as Will placed a bowl of nachos before her.

Will ushered Oliver into the living room where Oliver plopped down with a sigh, facing Emily with his head resting on his paws as another ploy. Any other time, Emily would have paid Oliver some attention. But Emily was no longer part of any other time.

Standing in the alcove, his lanky body blocking Oliver's forlorn gaze, Will turned to Emily and said, "He's still kind of a baby, as I guess you well know. Don't pay him any mind."

Emily began to notice that Will moved with an easy

rhythm. Even his faded jeans and Levi's shirt looked as though they just happened onto his frame, not something he deliberated over. From every indication, he took things in stride. A factor that might come in handy. Someone calm, who didn't jump to conclusions. Someone who wasn't directly involved. Exactly what she'd unconsciously been looking for.

They ate mostly in silence, Will biding his time, still uneasy about how to handle the situation, Emily commenting now and then about how good the quesadillas were.

Still deflecting, Will asked about Oliver's big adventure that morning. Trying a little harder, Emily told him about the wild turkeys and encountering this streetwise guy by the name of Doc on the high meadow. She mentioned Doc's cellphone call and promising to "take care of the situation right away," her own hurried call to Chris, and the awful thing she'd witnessed, his dreadful fall from the roof of the Tudor McMansion that she would never get over.

"Trooper Dave would only give a 'look-see,'" she added, "which was not much better than nothing. But he did mention something about casting a shadow."

"Meaning?"

"To do any more, he needs something that would cause some concern. What he calls 'casting a shadow' is a prerequisite for police intervention. He also called it 'probable cause.'"

Will took a deep pull of his Corona before speaking.

"Now hold on. Don't get me wrong, I appreciate you had

a horrible experience. And I understand how you might feel about Chris passing away like that so suddenly. I mean, I knew him. Really nice guy who set me up here, after all."

He took another pull from the bottle of beer before adding, "I do think it's worth checking out this Doc character. But you see, that's where it gets tricky. 'Cause people say things they don't mean. They also do things and don't have a clue why."

"Not like carpentry and repairs."

"Now there you go," said Will, putting the empty plates in the sink. "I rip out the floorboards upstairs 'cause they're rotten and squeak. The tiles in the bathrooms are cracked, the caulking around the tub is peeling, the grouting is crumbling. I can see what's wrong. I can fix it."

"You mean if you can't see it, there's nothing there."

"I guess."

Will worked slowly and deliberately with the cleanup chores. Oliver sprang to his feet and began pawing Will's jeans.

"Sorry," said Emily, getting up and reaching for the screen door. "My problem, not yours. I apologize for not helping with the dishes but I've got to pack. Didn't schedule my time right. But I appreciate the early supper."

Will tried to backtrack, tried to tell her she was taking this all wrong while wrangling with Oliver's rambunctiousness. In the confusion, Emily eased out the screen door, crossed the backyard in the darkness, and made her way into to the stillness of the cottage.

She didn't know him well enough to get into an argument. Nevertheless, whether anyone could see the rot and peeling, she knew something had to be done.

As Emily finished packing, she received a phone call from Silas. He wanted her to know he'd worked out some arrangement involving international priority shipping, customs, money wired to his account posthaste, and ABA and FI identifiers numbers. He added a slew of other fuzzy details as he became even more incoherent. The upshot, as far as Emily was concerned, was that he and Pru would be on the scheduled flight and meet Emily in Bath on Wednesday afternoon as originally planned.

When she asked him about Harriet, Silas muttered, "Yes, yes, what can she be thinking of? So much to take care of on this end. Must go confer with Pru. Good tips and instructions, I see here. So orderly, much appreciated." Silas muttered a few more *non sequiturs* and hung up.

Emily drifted into the narrow living room and sat on the couch. The three-room New England Cape Cod house never bothered her before. It served its purpose, earmarked for her comings and goings. But now, at the close of this Monday to end all Mondays, even the cottage seemed strangely foreboding.

She looked at the trip map she'd been perusing earlier and realized she should check her e-mail. But she couldn't keep her mind on any of it.

As the early evening wore on, her restless thoughts were

interrupted by a muffled knock on her door. Then another. Then nothing.

She rose slowly, unlatched the chain and switched on the outside light. Retreating back toward the B&B were Will and Oliver. Will turned as Oliver obeyed the hand signals to sit and stay.

"We didn't want you to go off like this," said Will, approaching the front step.

"That's okay. You're not involved."

"No, but I got to thinking. Process of elimination. Like I said, we can't let you go off wondering."

"Oh?"

"So, let's say you get hold of this English lady, this Miranda Shaw. About her McMansion, I mean, where you went and saw that terrible accident."

"Give her a call, you mean?"

"Right. Well, seeing that the trooper did such a slipshod job checking things out, you could tell her—in case she hasn't heard—what happened to Chris. And get permission for me to look into it."

"Mentioning how thorough you are," Emily added.

"And how, naturally, she doesn't want to get sued by what happened on her property to a fella she hired."

"And since she's so far away, it would ease her mind."

"That's the gist of it. All you have to do is get permission. Let me know first thing and I'll take it from there. You got enough to handle with your loss and your flight plans without wondering about this to boot."

Emily nodded. "Okay. Thanks. That's really helpful." She wished she could've come up with something better, told him how much this meant to her, but "thanks" was all she could muster before he bid her goodnight.

Reentering the cottage, Emily realized that getting Will to go along without actually spelling out all the troubling circumstances surrounding Chris's fall might only add to the complications. There was no telling what Miranda Shaw might say or what Will might dig up. But, in the state she was in, this was all she could manage.

She shuffled into her bedroom with no clue how she was going to contend with her sorrow, her guided tour, and the potential mushrooming of a murky game, armed solely with an ache that just wouldn't quit.

In the dream, Emily typed the heading, "For Chris: Preservation of open space" and the computer screen dissolved into the high meadow. Giant chainsaws ripped into a stand of maples and white birch and lopped off their branches. Dynamite blasted away at their stumps. Emily called out, but no one heard. Jumbo threshing machines ground the limbs into sawdust as flatbed trucks carted the strapped trunks away like so many wooden corpses. An excavator shot steel spikes into the ground, shattering the bedrock. Mourning doves scurried away from their nesting sites and white-tailed deer scampered in all directions.

Emily clicked away at the delete key but there was no response.

Hovering overhead, a hawk, with its rusty chest and long tail, flew lazily over the rising smoke, eyes closed.

The second it blinked, it frantically flapped its wings, rose higher, and circled to no avail.

More machines leveled everything flat and covered it with asphalt, which turned into a driveway leading up to Miranda Shaw's fake Tudor.

Emily tried moving her lips, forming the words "Go back, go back," but couldn't stop Chris's gangly form from scrambling up the ladder. She left the computer and raced to the Green. She stood in front of the bank's colonnades and shook Brian Forbes and his wife, Martha. They both turned and walked away.

Across the sea, Miranda's buxom figure and sleepy eyes came into view. She dialed a number on her mobile as Chris climbed higher. The Curtis House emerged onto the scene, all boarded-up, check stubs scattered across the scraggly front lawn.

Next, an ornate bridge appeared. It stretched from the Lydfield Green, past Doc's stocky figure and the Hudson River, across the ocean to Lydfield-in-the-Moor.

Still mute, running up and down, Emily tried to call for help but it was no use. She froze as Chris reappeared, falling from a great height. Trying to shake herself free, to get to him in time, Emily tossed and turned every which way. The tossing and turning woke her up.

She snapped on the lamp by the nightstand and stared at the luminous dial on the travel alarm clock. It was almost midnight. Ordinarily, dreams faded within seconds. Those that lingered were inconsequential. Lost in Hempstead or making a wrong turn on the Cornwall coast and getting stuck in an abandoned tin mine.

But there was no way to shake this one off.

Her alarm was set for five o'clock; 10:00 a.m. in Bovey Tracey, the town bordering the moors. Miranda Shaw would be languidly readying herself for her day's activities. When Miranda had stayed at the B&B while overseeing the construction of her Tudor white elephant, she made sure everyone knew her schedule, which included plenty of beauty rest and ample time allotted for pampering. She kept herself youthful with regular hydralessence facials and deep-tissue massages.

Even so, Emily had decided that when five rolled around, she would give Miranda no slack. She would accomplish something, get an okay for Will to check out the slate roof. That done, she could hopefully doze off one more time, shower, and wolf down some breakfast. Then she would force herself to humor Babs and the little kids at the Central School, make sure Babs was on board to keep her eyes and ears open, catch the shuttle to Kennedy Airport, and take it from there.

By functioning and getting hold of Harriet, something might come of it. At any rate, it was better than piling up dicey elements ad infinitum. But when five rolled around, the exchange with Miranda was anything but to the point.

"No, Miranda, listen to me." Standing barefoot in her pajamas, leaning on the kitchenette counter, Emily tried her best to explain. "I'm still in Connecticut."

"Good heavens," said Miranda, "it must be the middle of the night. Isn't this a horrid time to be ringing me?"

"Yes, but I need to ask you something."

"Oh, dear. But how tiresome for you."

Hammering and drilling sounds interceded. Miranda excused herself and returned several times. One of Miranda's evasions was her breakfast tea needed "hotting up." During another lull, Miranda said, "Much ado, I'm afraid. As ever, modernizing, getting the place all tarted up. Newish fitted kitchen, central heating, swagged brocade curtains, and double glazing. Of course, I simply can't abide the noise. I tell you, I am about to pop over to the salon for a long and much-deserved respite."

As usual, Emily could not get over the fact that no matter what was going on, Miranda thought that the world simply revolved around her whims.

Miranda excused herself again to ask the workmen to work a bit more quietly. It began to dawn on Emily that she never actually had any idea who she was dealing with. She never knew what arrangements Miranda had with Mr. Shaw, the London barrister, while she flitted around on both sides of the Atlantic. She hadn't a clue what was percolating beneath Miranda's purring, pampered tones, least of all what she may or may not have been up to regarding Chris's headlong rush to her property.

Regardless, Emily pushed on. "Listen to me, Miranda. Chris fell from your slate roof. He never recovered. He passed away just . . . yesterday."

When Miranda didn't reply, didn't mention the urgent call she may have made, or ask about the exact circumstances, or even ask when it all happened, Emily said, "Well, I thought you'd care. I thought at the very least you'd want to make sure there was no negligence on your part."

Still no response, only the sounds of the workmen.

Finally, Miranda repeated one of her all-purpose expressions. "Appalling, surely. Emily, I'm rather rushed, and you must be keen to get back to bed."

Raising her voice, Emily said, "It's about your leaking slate shingles in the pouring rain."

The hammering noises picked up in intensity.

Deflecting once more, Miranda said, "I see. Now tell me, when will you be coming round to chat?"

Given Miranda's way of deflecting, Emily had no idea what she had in mind.

Emily told her the tour schedule and when she might be free. Sensing Miranda was about to hang up on her, Emily said, "So you won't object to Will Farrow checking out your roof?"

"Who?"

"Our handyman. Chris thought very highly of him. May I tell him to take a look? At no cost to you."

After a barely audible murmur, Miranda said, "I suppose. But that, my dear, is as far as it goes."

"The way things are going, I wouldn't count on it."

Yet another delay until Miranda said, "My, my, I must say you sound so distraught. Do get some proper rest. Works wonders when one is unduly under stress. I have it on the highest authority."

Instead of insisting that she be notified immediately about Will's findings, she went on another tangent, sighing over how trying it was for one to forever change one's digs and mobile number.

Before Emily had a chance to ask how, in that case,

she could be reached with the results of Will's inspection, Miranda said, "Sorry, I simply must dash. But do pull yourself together. And, in your travels, do make time to pop over for tea."

Chapter Nine

With her suitcase packed, there was only her early-morning encounter with the first graders and Babs to deal with, and Emily would be off.

But then she became distracted by the need to stock up on fresh fruit and energy bars in Bath and set up a communal survival kit of snacks for the long drive. This fleeting thought may have been some kind of defense mechanism kicking in to keep her inconsolable ache at bay.

There was also a host of unknowns to think about, including whether Will would show up to see her off, what she might discover when she caught up with Harriet, and what would happen the moment Harriet met with Silas and Pru to create an unholy threesome. At this juncture, there was no way of knowing what form her emotions might take. Ordinarily, she tried to stay coolheaded as advertised and keep her feelings in check. In truth, this conundrum called for a juggling act beyond anything she'd known.

She found herself standing perfectly still, looking out though the cottage shutters at the beckoning horizon in much the same way she'd looked out yesterday morning. It reminded her of the time she and Chris were high up on a ledge in Mohawk Mountain. They could see the storm that was coming, the billowing clouds overhead, and the sleet that had just passed. She recalled Chris telling her that this was the key to dealing with the randomness of life. To regard everything from such a vantage point—centered and on top of things.

Breaking out of it, she locked the front door, flung her overnight bag over her shoulder, picked up her suitcase, and headed across the backyard. After a few strides, Oliver's pale-golden blur came tearing around the side of the B&B and blocked her way. In turn, Will ambled toward her, the morning sunlight glinting behind him.

Shielding her eyes, she said, "I was just about to throw my stuff in the trunk and ring the bell."

"Did you get the okay?"

"More or less. With Miranda you never really know."

"Guess I'll have to make do with more or less."

"Can you go over there soon? While it's all still fresh and nothing's been tampered with? Check out what might have happened on the roof by the turret window and caused him to shudder like that?"

"Yes, ma'am."

"Great."

While she fumbled for the keys to her car, Will grabbed her luggage and walked past his pickup to the front of the B&B, flipped her trunk open, and deposited her stuff. After lingering for a second or two, Oliver took off after Will.

Emily could have followed suit and said her goodbyes out on the street. Instead, she drifted over to his pickup and waited.

Will reappeared, prompted Oliver to jump onto the

truck bed, and latched the tailgate. He eased over, leaned against the side of the cab next to Emily, and crossed his lanky legs at the ankles. A shock of his sandy hair fell over his forehead, but he didn't bother to brush it back.

"So when you get to Miranda's Tudor McMansion," Emily said, leading the conversation where she wanted it to go. "Can you check for evidence or signs of . . ."

"You mean what I might turn up?"

"Yes. Trooper Dave calls them 'tangibles.'"

"Well, I'll tell you this much. If it looks iffy, I will run it by at least one other guy."

"Oh? Who did you have in mind?"

"Depends on what I find."

She could tell he was weighing his words to keep things on an even keel. Not one to jump the gun. She'd have to pull back a notch.

"It's like the wave patterns down in the Keys," Will went on. "Wind and clouds, getting a bead on where the marlin are running but—"

"You'd still like a second opinion."

"Yes, ma'am, I would."

"From a professional."

"You could call it that."

Growing impatient, Oliver started slapping his bushy tail against the sides of the truck bed.

"You see that?" Will said, leaning over, rubbing Oliver's backside. "He wants to dive right in. Has no notion about steering clear of such things as reefs and shoals."

Letting him have the last word, Emily went over, rubbed Oliver's backside as well and started walking toward her car. Will followed, patted her shoulder, and said, "I'll let you know soon as I can. We'll keep in touch. Deal?"

"Deal."

Emily gave him a quick rundown of her itinerary and promised to call from Bradley Airport before she hopped on the shuttle to New York. Will gave her a thumbs-up and touched her hand. Perhaps it was nothing and she was making too much out of it. But to Emily, the exchange, the touch, and the high sign meant something more. She was not entirely on her own.

Emily parked, rushed past the bus stop, and saw that the other elementary school kids had already filed in. What awaited her was a hyper Babs Maroon and a very young teacher trying to keep a group of antsy first graders in line. The teacher had the flustered look of someone who had just received her certificate and wasn't at all sure she could handle this assignment on her own.

"Not to worry," said Babs, as Emily took her place facing the wiggling children. "Here she is, boys and girls. Better late than never. Which is not a message you kids should take home with you."

Emily forced a smile, recalling that this outing was geared as a cute marketing ploy to attract interest in Emily's private tours. Babs would tie-in Emily's jaunt with the kids' new year and the adventures they would be looking forward to as a "brand new chapters" feature. But as things stood, Emily was playing both ends against the middle. She couldn't care less about marketing but would partially go along so that Babs would still have a feature to post while, at the same time, enlist Babs as another ally.

As Emily helped reposition the kids for Babs's photo shoot, some of them wanted to know if Emily was a Girl Scout leader. Others wanted to know why she wasn't wearing any makeup like their moms. Whipping out her camera, Babs said, "Let's just say Miss Ryder owns every shade of beige in captivity and is a no-muss, no-fuss kinda gal."

Babbling on, continuing to dig it in over Emily's apparent disinterest, Babs added, "Unless she's running in the annual Lydfield charity race. Then she shows up way ahead of time in some bright, spiffy outfit wearing little dabs of makeup. Not exactly girlie, but looking good."

The hurried photo shoot called for a group eager to begin classes. As the kids complied with bright, smiley faces, Babs announced, "Miss Emily is going on a Twinning. Lydfield to Lydfield-in-the-Moor—sister villages. Just like twins, which is why it's called a Twinning. And look, we've got a set of towheaded girl twins right up front. Plus, how many of you have sisters of your own?"

A bunch of hands shot up.

"Yes indeed. So pose pretty, Miss Emily, and we'll scoot in before the tardy bell rings. Then Miss Emily will tell us all about her trip and what she's going to bring back for show-and-tell. And, as an added bonus, how she's going to take all of you on a hike up on the high meadow and compare our nice woodland trails with the wild moors when she gets back."

Checking her watch, Emily watched Babs snap away. She didn't know how to break it to her that not only was she not going to accompany the kids into the school, but she needed to get Babs on board with her strategy in time to get back to her car, drive to the airport, park in the long-term lot, check her baggage, go through security, and get in touch with Will. All before she got on the plane.

"Yes, I'll bring you some pictures," Emily said.

"And then what?" the towheaded twins shouted back.

"I'll tell you all about the wild, rocky moors."

"And then what?" all the others chimed in, catching on to the game.

Any other time Emily would have played along. But the blue sky and the overly cute kids were beginning to get to her. Like a Disney world where everything was sunshine and roses in contrast to all she was going through.

Luckily, Ms. Flustered piped in with a high-pitched, "Now, now, class. Have you noticed no more children have been dropped off? What does that mean?"

"We're gonna be late!" The line of children shot toward the entrance. Ms. Flustered was barely quick enough to yank open the glass-paneled doors.

Fumbling with her camera gear, Babs tried to elbow Emily inside. "Go on. Move it, missy, before this whole thing folds. Thanks to you, we've hardly got started."

Emily pulled away, but before she had a chance to explain, Babs said, "Okay, Ryder. Let's have it. What is going on?"

"The Curtises were scheduled to depart for Bath tomorrow but Harriet Curtis skipped town yesterday.

Her stay in London and who knows what-all might be underwritten by the GDC."

Babs's beady eyes locked. "Well, now. There's a story in it, right? Light years beyond this cutesy shtick. That's what you're finally, damn well telling me."

"Can't say exactly. First, I need to hear from Will."

"Oh, it's 'Will' now. No longer 'the guy working for my mom.' Since when do you play it so cagey? Talk to me, lady. Hear from Will about what?"

Emily checked her watch again.

"It's called a lead, pal," Babs went on. "Don't do this to me. I had Chris Cooper about to let on about some major loophole right before he—"

"What loophole? What are you talking about?"

"Never mind. I had this ace up my sleeve, but I wasn't ready to show my hand yet. So quit jerking me around."

Skip, the matronly crossing guard, came by to see what the fuss was about. When they both reassured her there was no problem, Skip nodded and returned to her post.

The morning sun continued to glare down on them as cars passed by along the main street. They both waited for Skip to look away.

Emily couldn't bring herself to tell Babs about Chris's passing. She would surely break down, losing her momentum.

Anticipating Babs's protests about the kiddie shoot, Emily handed her a brochure illustrating fun family outings in the moorlands of Dartmoor, plus a list of other spots Emily could take them and their parents to.

Babs grudgingly accepted the material with the usual

rejoinder. "This is really gonna cost you, pal. I am talking big time."

"Look, I'll give you a call right before the short hop to Kennedy Airport."

"A juicy call. One spilling over with implications."

"We'll see."

"We're talking proliferating developments and late breaking news."

"I said we'll see."

Emily left Babs shaking her head and hurried back to her car. Before long, she was on the way to the airport, taking the shortcut east through Paradise Valley. She failed to notice the dappled lanes with their gentle backcountry dips and curves, failed to even recall how carefree this ride was during this bright, late summer day. It may as well have been yesterday, under a veiled, low-hanging mist.

Chapter Ten

After Emily left, Will Farrow drove directly to the McMansion on North Lake Road. He parked in the circular drive, lowered the tailgate of his pickup and let Oliver spring free. "All right now," he called out. "But you stay close by this time."

Will watched as Oliver scampered around through the stone archway of the McMansion and back again, around the pickup and the circular drive, sniffing the grass on the verge and through the archway once more and on to the side of the building. Satisfied Oliver couldn't get beyond the fenced-in property, Will climbed up the aluminum ladder and took a closer look.

Several stories high, to his right, the slate ran across the main expanse of the roof as if it had recently been fired-up, polished, shipped from the factory, and laid down. To Will, the rest of the house looked pre-fab, including the copper flashing and gutters and the cone-shaped turret topped by a weathervane. The only thing that appeared well-crafted was the slate around the turret with its greenish oxidized cast.

He couldn't help wondering who would fancy this

mass of mock-masonry veneer, fake timber framing, cross-hatched windows, and overblown space. Somebody who wasn't affected by the fluctuations of the economy, probably. People who wanted to pretend they were still in England during the reign of so-and-so while enjoying all the modern conveniences as well. Or had this Miranda Shaw person had it built on spec, hoping to turn a quick profit and then got caught in the recent buyer's market?

Will had run into his share of her type from piloting ocean-going cabin cruisers. More often than not, it was a matter of what to do with all that spare cash. If this Miranda person had tired of hopping back and forth over the Atlantic, or if something else had turned sour while she was here, that might explain why she wasn't around to tend to this place.

High up on the ladder, Will still couldn't see anything amiss to explain why she'd made a fuss over a leak while she was all the way back in the UK. Or why somebody had come by, called her, and caused her to insist that her roofer rush right over. What's more, he'd gone down, found the front door unlocked, and assuming Chris or somebody had gained access, had entered, climbed the stairs to the eight-sided turret room at the top, and examined the hardwood floors, the oak writing table, and everything else. There was a faint watermark on a blotter, but that was all. No sign of any humongous leak from yesterday's downpour.

So what was this all about? What was somebody trying to pull?

He climbed down once again and moved the ladder left, to the extreme edge where the half-stone, half-masonry archway met the near side of a second story bedroom. From this angle, the octagonal turret formed a third story like a fairy-tale tower where the princess waited for her knight in shining armor. As Will braced the ladder and made sure it was flush with the cement walkway, Oliver came tearing around again and sat at Will's feet.

"No, Oliver. Not yet." Oliver didn't budge. "I mean it now." Will snapped his fingers. "No truck ride till this makes some kind of sense."

Will snapped his fingers and pointed this time. Oliver finally got the message and took off through the archway, back around the far side of the house. Truthfully, Will only wanted Oliver out of the way in case he came upon a loose slate tile that might tumble down.

Emily had said that she caught sight of Chris by the turret window. Seconds later, he shook like crazy and slipped or something. Maybe he'd made his way from right to left all the way across, got tired of skirting around the chimneys, and was just plain worn out. Maybe in all that rain coming down he had reached for the weathervane on top of the turret, lost his footing, and that was that.

But that version didn't cut it either.

Will took his binoculars with him as he climbed even higher toward the sill of the turret window. Emily had also mentioned it was a matter of pride that set Cooper off. A question of his workmanship. Fixing the slate just so on an eight-sided cone had to be really labor intensive. There sure wasn't another turret like this anywhere else around. And that must have been the real reason he ended up here at this particular point.

Will peered through the binoculars at a more difficult angle, one that Trooper Dave might have overlooked. He fixed on a spot where the power lines connected to the house, at a juncture above the narrow window to the far left. There he zeroed in on the connectors. Nothing different there, just your ordinary cube-shaped objects, bisected like a W and an M, split in two with the power lines fitted into the grooves.

But then something caught his eye. The copper flashing directly beneath the connectors glinted in an odd sort of way. It did so, Will realized, because it was misshapen and flanged. As if somebody had leaned out the window, dug under it with a crowbar and pried it up and over, bending it into a kind of trough. And something else didn't look right. A frayed piece of copper wire dangled from one of the connectors.

Puzzled, Will clambered down the ladder once more and whistled. But Oliver didn't come tearing back around the corner. Will called for him again and still no Oliver. Will drifted through the stone archway and down the side of the house between the walkway and the high wooden fence. He finally located Oliver at the rear by the far end digging furiously between some rhododendron bushes. Will tried to make him stop but Oliver was much too involved.

Sticking his nose deep in the loose soil, Oliver kept at it till he came upon a burlap rag. Clutching it in his jaws, he shook the dirt loose, proudly wiggled his backside, and brought it over. Will accepted the prize without question. He unfolded the damp ragged cloth and uncovered a rusty crowbar and a long, coiled strand of copper wire, so thin that from any distance it was virtually invisible.

Will swung by Roy's Barbeque Pit on the outskirts of town. Bracketed by an old garage on one side and a rundown convenience store on the other, the trio of rustic, one-story buildings were dwarfed by the looming, southernmost edge of the Berkshires—still a dark forest-green on the first of September, overlooking the gurgling Housatonic close by, running deep and fast after all the rain.

In a way, Roy's was a refuge, reminding Will of a dozen places like it from Cutler Ridge and Homestead down to Key Largo, Tavernier, and Islamorada. But that wasn't why he was here. It was the nearest place to call and get in touch with his pal Darryl, who worked for Florida Power and Light. As it happened, Darryl was on loan in Providence, Rhode Island, after the recent massive power outages from the electrical storm. Calling Darryl from Roy's also made sense because the strains of country music in the background, along with the buzz and clink of bottles and glasses, always got Darryl into a folksy, tell-it-like-it-is mood. Calling from the stillness of the B&B would set Darryl off asking a dozen irrelevant questions about where Will was calling from, had he been sucked in by some snotty Yankees, and the like. Besides, at this time of morning, the brunt of the working guys wouldn't be by for at least another hour, which left the phone booth free and clear.

Will asked the frumpy waitress to turn the speakers down a tad. At the moment, some husky-voiced country gal was belting out over the air waves, "I'm tellin' you, hon, better do me right; cuddle me close, all through the night."

It took Will three tries before he finally raised Darryl on his cellphone. A glance through the musty windows and calico curtains assured him Oliver was still okay, watching from the truck bed, enabling Will to focus on getting his facts straight.

The trouble was that, despite the muffled country tunes, the clink of glasses, and the patter between the waitress and two old-timers in the background, Darryl wanted to start off with some small talk.

"Come on, ol' buddy," said Darryl. "Don't cut me short. The truth now. That divorcée down in Lauderdale was a looker and came with a seventy-foot cabin cruiser with a cherry wood salon, a portside lounge, a mother of a flybridge, stern thrusters, and I don't know what-all. I say you tell her you really *can* be bought. 'Cause you can't have nothin' going for you up this-a-way."

"Mind if we get past this? I need some input."

"Don't tell me. More woman trouble?"

"Cut it out, Darryl. I am serious."

"Oh hell, the Will I know would let me tease him some."

"The Darryl I know would figure this is not the time."

"Okay, hold on." Darryl shouted to somebody he'd be right there soon as he helped out a no-account buddy stuck in New England, down on his luck. Returning to the line, Darryl said, "All right, what can I do you for?"

Will quickly ran the facts by him.

Darryl was just as fast handing Will the verdict. "Was the ol' man sweatin'?"

"All I know was he was caught up there in a downpour."

"Well, hell, that ties it. It only takes fifteen milliamps to do the trick."

"Meaning?"

"Meaning, the second he touched that copper wire, he completed the circuit. He became the switch."

"You're saying—"

"I'm saying some clown shut off the power, rigged the dang thing, and then hit the circuit breaker. Knowing as soon as anyone spotted and examined the busted flashing, he'd take the charge. Add it up. Downpour, slate roof, soaking wet old man, power line, copper wire, and copper flashing."

"So it wasn't the fall."

"It was the jolt and the heart attack. That's why your girl saw him jerk back like that. The fall was extra. No charge there, if you pardon the pun."

Will found Resident Trooper Dave Roberts's cruiser parked outside the regional high school by the gym. The bell had rung for the next period, but Roberts had a scrawny-looking teen with thick glasses by his side and wouldn't let him go as though he was some kind of culprit. With his eyes darting back and forth toward his fleeing classmates, the boy eventually slipped away and sprinted through the central glass doors. The doors were covered with tape but rattled anyway.

Will got out of the pickup, told Oliver to stay put, and intercepted Roberts as he slid behind the wheel of the cruiser.

Roberts yanked down the visor and peered up behind his oversized sunglasses. Instantly, Will knew what he was dealing with. After Will mentioned what he had come across, it became impossible for Will to get another word in edgewise.

"I'll tell you what's suspicious," said Roberts. "I no sooner check into the accident when along comes a drifter with his dog offering me some handyman special. I have vandalism and breaking and entering to deal with at the moment. And I have neither the time nor the patience to put up with the likes of you."

"What are you telling me?"

"What are you trying to wangle is the question. This your way of showing Emily you're sharper than me? Or are you so bored you got nothing better to do? And even if you did get permission from the owner, planting stuff is not the way you want to go, believe me."

"That's not what happened."

"Look, I think Emily has had enough."

"So you're brushing me off?"

"No sir. I'll call Troop L right now. Tell my lieutenant what we need here is not a resident trooper. What we need is a deadbeat who can stir things up. Let's face it, we just don't have enough on our hands."

Will pulled back. His intention had been to pass the ball, get Roberts on the job, and keep Emily posted. But Roberts was buying none of it. Maybe because he was sweet on Emily. Maybe he didn't want to appear careless and sloppy. Or maybe he was locked into the cracked glass doors of the high school and juvenile offenders. It wouldn't surprise Will if Roberts's next move would be to cite him for criminal mischief and claim Will had no business letting Oliver dig up Miranda Shaw's shrubbery. And then, likely as not, decide to plant false evidence in a burlap bag.

Holding his temper, Will said, "It was just that Emily mentioned you wanted a shadow cast. If the copper wire and all won't do it for you, what will?"

"I never told her I wanted a shadow cast or for somebody to dig something up. I said I could do something if there was something like a statement from an eyewitness. Or somebody who didn't have an ulterior motive. You follow?"

That did it. Will stepped away from the cruiser.

As if covering his tracks, especially as Emily was concerned, Roberts added, "You see, the thing of it is, there's nothing she can do about the developers. That's up to Brian Forbes and the Planning Commission. There's nothing she can or could've done for Chris Cooper. Which leaves her with getting through the stupid Twinning thing and getting back here and on with her life. With a business that makes some kind of sense."

Will didn't respond.

As he headed back to his truck, Roberts called out, "Oh, in case you've got any further ideas, I'm going to put in a word at the station. The dispatcher hates nuisance calls.

But if something comes up that has no tie-in with Emily, you be sure to run it by me and I will surely take it under advisement."

"I will keep that in mind," said Will, mostly to himself.

Will drove off and arrived back at the B&B with a few minutes to spare, but still wasn't sure how he was going to break the news to Emily when she called. He couldn't lie to her, but he didn't want her spinning her wheels over this either. In the end, he decided to tell her what he'd found and, as offhand as possible, relay Darryl's notions. They could deal with the ramifications when she returned to the states.

He got out of the pickup, still thinking about what to say to Emily, when he was confronted by first one visitor and then another who, doubtless, were about to throw another monkey wrench into the works. While fending off each in turn, he worried about how Emily was going to handle what she already had to deal with on her tour and all, not counting his news about something iffy he'd just come across back home, and now more troublesome stuff that just wouldn't quit. Including this pushy guy and this broker lady.

Emily found herself in familiar surroundings in the sprawling waiting area of Bradley Airport north of Hartford. It was now only minutes before her scheduled short hop to JFK and her flight to Heathrow.

She rang the B&B but there was no answer. Assuming

Will wasn't back yet from checking out Miranda's roof, she decided to touch base with Babs.

At this point, two more people joined another couple chatting away on their cellphones sitting opposite her. She moved to a quiet corner and turned away from the pulsating cell conversations of a half-dozen others as Babs picked up almost immediately.

"Hold it, okay?" Emily said, set to avoid the usual overlapping static on Babs's part. "This is the deal. You get two minutes to pass on Chris's disclosure about the regulations loophole and then back off for a second. I follow with a capsule version of a cellphone call by a guy named Doc from the GDC up in the high meadow on the morning in question, possibly leading to a second call that sent Chris racing to Miranda's."

"That's pretty cut and dried, Ryder."

"You hear all the background noise? You recall where I am? We'll be lucky to get that much done."

"Boy, you sure are full of some attitude. Okay, but get it straight. I am the pro. You are a shook-up bystander poking around the edges. Get it? Okay then. It seems Chris was pressured by Brian Forbes to follow to the letter the zoning regulations that 'development shall be permitted on the high meadow tract in view of economic circumstances.' Chris goes to the town clerk's office. He comes across the exact wording, to wit, that 'development *may* be permitted . . . in view of *present* economic circumstances.' The way Chris saw it, 'present circumstances' referred to the days of the Great Depression when there was a need for housing to accommodate factory workers in a factory that ultimately never got built. And the word 'may' was a far cry from the word 'shall.' So he told me he'd outline all this in a statement for the public record. But in that open and above-board way of his, he may have also made this known to good ol' Brian."

There was silence while Emily tried to take this all in. "Hold on," she said as she fumbled for a pen and made some cursory notes on the envelope holding her tickets.

Back on the line as the noise level picked up another notch, Emily said, "All right. So, for whatever it's worth, Doc, this streetwise sounding older guy obviously fronting for the GDC, told somebody over his cell he'd 'take care of it right away.' Maybe it's the way streetwise guys talk, maybe it's just because we were just talking about Chris. But taking into account what happened right after . . ."

Starting to get choked up, sensing other passengers were looking at her, Emily quickly broke it off. "Tell you what. I'll relay the gist of your information to Will when I get to the British Airways lounge at JFK. Right now, I've got barely enough time to touch base with him before boarding the shuttle."

"And I'm left to decipher what street guys mean when they say they'll take care of something."

"I guess. Got to go."

Despite Babs's sputtering attempts to keep her on the line, Emily hung up then hit her primary speed-dial number. She fell silent as Will mentioned what he'd run across at the McMansion. Will also slipped in the news about Dave Roberts's stonewalling. All along, Emily had expected a dire outcome in some shape or form the moment she saw

Chris shudder and fall. No matter how gingerly Will was attempting to couch it, taken together with what Babs just told her, Emily was convinced that someone deliberately set out to do away with Chris.

The noise level grew as more and more passengers filed in.

"Will, I think you're holding something back."

"Well . . . maybe."

"Don't."

"Hey, it's not like some done deal. Besides, like Trooper Dave put it and I'd sort of have to agree, I sure don't want to burden you any further."

"Look, Will, the truth is, I've been gearing myself up for some drastic disclosure. All I want to know is what really happened up on that roof. Chris didn't have to die! And besides, I'll have hours on the plane to digest whatever else you've got to add to my list."

"I don't know, Emily."

"Please, don't make me guess. With the way my mind has been running, that'll be a lot worse."

Hemming and hawing, he relented. "All right. But first, I almost forgot. Your mom called right after you left. She was kind of upset she didn't catch you and wants you to call before you take off for England. Let me give you the number." While fumbling for it, Will added, "Seems like she's given up on a tower ever coming here and doesn't want to mess with a cell phone anyways."

Emily jotted down the number where her mother could be reached as two harried businessmen sat down directly behind her, arguing over shipping orders. It made hearing

Will that much more difficult. Growing more impatient, Emily said, "Come on, Will. Let's have the rest of it. It's getting hectic and people are lining up."

Will told her that after sharing his findings with his old buddy who worked for a power company, it seems that what happened up on the McMansion roof was no accident. He also told her that realtor Martha Forbes had just been by to let Emily know of a possible generous offer from the GDC that she could pass on to her mother. Then she had scurried back to her car and just stood there.

"Go on," Emily said, girding herself for the rest of it.

"Well, this short, stocky guy pulls in right behind her and hops out. Martha takes an envelope out of her glove compartment, hands it to him, they shake hands, and she drives off.

"And then?" asked Emily, as the attendant behind the desk announced her flight was now boarding. Emily grabbed her travel bag and scooted in front of a few sloppily dressed slackers, making hand signals and dragging their feet. "Will, the line is moving and I'm handing over my ticket. Is that it? Or did Doc do or say anything else?"

"Doc?"

"The short, stocky guy."

"Well, the thing is, he walked right to the front door and asked about you. I told him you'd already left."

"And?"

Heading down the ramp toward the beaming flight attendant with the plane engines revving, Emily barely heard the tail end of Will's report. All she could make out was that Doc had booked a flight across the pond.

The drone of the cramped shuttle and the complaints of the frumpy woman next to her about cost-cutting schemes didn't keep Emily from realizing she couldn't go on like this. She was on edge and depressed. She had to juggle a tour while fending off developments that had killed her friend. She didn't know how she was going to get to the bottom of things.

She thought of her college soccer-playing days as a striker. She had to know when to go for a header or a shot on the far post and when to slough one off that had little chance of getting by the goalie. Or, as the coach always put it: *No regrets. Stick to it, read the situation. The game will tell you what to do.*

But a striker was a position, an assignment, a definite job with a rule book. Dave Roberts was a trooper, locked into prescribed criminal procedure. In those mysteries coming out of the BBC, each character had a definite role to play: chief inspector, his assistant, the superintendent, constables, prime suspects, witnesses, and so forth. PIs and amateur detectives had their place. She was not part of any outfit, had no idea of proper procedures, and had a fuzzy backup in place, if you counted Will and Babs.

Which was yet another conundrum. If she confided in Babs, Babs would want to take over and insist on a long explanation, which would put all Emily's efforts at a standstill. And, as far as she could tell, Will would want to make sure she kept out of trouble, especially with Doc on his way. He'd already made clear that he felt she had more than enough to deal with as things stood.

All things being equal, it still meant stepping in for Chris. Jockeying for position until she was able to hand the ball off to some authority in pursuit of putting things right. At the moment, that was the only pure mindset she could come up with. So she nodded to herself and let it go.

On the call to her mother in Vermont from the British Airways travelers lounge, Emily was inclined to just pull back and listen. It seemed her mother had decided that only if the GDC application fell through, and the B&B was booked solid for the fall foliage season, could she weather another year. If, as she feared, the development of the tract was imminent, she would pull up stakes and open another place in Woodstock, New York, or as far from the travails of the past few years as she could get, which included a fly-by-night husband, keeping the B&B going with no prior experience, raising Emily on her own, and all the rest of it. As Emily's mother became more despondent over the phone, she recounted how she had used the B&B to distract herself. Then got so lonely she couldn't stand it till the annual retreat and redecorating cycle started all over again. She just wanted Emily to know where things stood so Emily could plan accordingly.

For her part, as usual, Emily placated her mother, leaving out most everything and steering the conversation away from any link to Chris or "that coarse, pushy man taking soundings for the GDC" she'd fended off over the phone while Emily was away a week ago. The way Emily saw it, the last thing her mother needed was any inkling of how things were going to pieces back home. Given her nervous condition, all alone up in Vermont, it could very well just do her in.

"Mom," Emily said, continuing to wing it, "I have to tell you, Will is doing a marvelous job. He knows exactly what to look for. What to fix and what needs shoring up. He can spot leaks and cracks others would overlook."

"That's all to the good, dear. But Martha Forbes was pestering me before I left. And that husband of hers, that Brian, head of the Business Association, hammering away at the long-term boost to the Lydfield economy and the grand list as soon as a development comes in here and gets rolling. I tell you. Oh, by the way, have you heard from Chris about all this pushiness?"

Emily deflected as best she could, said the topic hadn't come up as they played phone tag in the short time she'd been back, and broke it off with, "Sorry, mom, got to check on my frequent flyer miles and make sure they've got the change in my seat assignment. You try and relax, have a good time, and don't get caught up in all the static. That's what a getaway is for, remember?"

"I suppose. That's what you keep telling me."

"That's what I want you to believe. Okay? Your turn to promise."

The call ended with another "I suppose."

In the interim, as she began to consider keeping things close to the vest as something that now came with the territory, a nearby stand provided Emily with a Columbian coffee, fruit, and a granola bar. Luckily, the BA waiting area was practically deserted, offering her the added advantage of being the only cellphone user. Putting it down to the time of day and the fact that even the most intrepid tourists were back at work, their kids at school or whatever, she proceeded to call Babs, once again tossing things off as best she could.

When Babs started in by saying she only recently found out about Chris and understood why Emily was not herself lately, Emily countered with, "Let's say the jury is still out about what actually happened. Anyway, I just talked to my mom, and it seems Martha is still at her to sell and Brian is champing at the bit."

"Better known as the intimations of dirty tricks and shady schemes of realtors, bankers, and developers," Babs chimed in.

"At any rate, you can jot down the sweetener Harriet received from the GDC and how she skipped town, ditched her siblings, and way ahead of schedule, checked into a pricey London hotel that she could never afford."

"Gotcha. Hey, not bad, Ryder, not half bad. But why is Harriet playing run-sheep-run from her siblings?"

"Good question. Now on your end, I'll need you to act as proxy for me and my mom while we're both away and to touch base with Will."

"Like you didn't know, given the absence of anything male and remotely hunky in my life, I will jump at the latter. Lucky for you, I will throw in covering the GDC hearing at the town hall tomorrow night which, needless to say, is where this caper is really at. But just as an extended carrot on the stick, is it safe to put Will down as unattached, quietly macho, and on the slightly mature side?"

Emily let that one go.

"Now you leave solving this case to the professionals, not that I don't appreciate your help."

Emily ended the call and let that one go as well.

She called Will again. Predictably, he wanted to know if she was going to be okay and if there was anything else he could do. Emily let him know about the arrangement with Babs and the "may" versus "shall" hitch in the town ordinance that Chris was about to disclose before he was eliminated from the equation.

But instead of casually going along as expected, Will seemed thrown by the change in Emily's tone. "Have to say, I don't get how you're taking all this. I also don't like the looks of this Doc character and the fact that he might be coming after you. Maybe you're doing your level best not to let all this get you down, what with your tour obligations and all. But I got to insist you keep me posted."

Emily hesitated a moment before replying. "Look, I'm only trying to keep busy and on top of things. What else can I do?"

"Still and all, now that you got me involved . . ."

Registering the deepening note of concern in his voice, finding it comforting despite her resolve to remain footloose, she realized it was almost time to board her flight. She thanked Will for his concern and promised to check in with him again around noon his time.

After this third hasty goodbye, she was beginning to

note that for those on her suspicious list, the art of playing
it close to the vest was second nature. They'd had years
of practice. She was only beginning to get the hang of it.
Needless to say, it had even rubbed off when dealing with
those she knew and trusted.

After being bumped up to business class for frequent flyer
promotional reasons, Emily felt like she was ensconced in
a sensory deprivation chamber. She was alone by a window,
shade drawn, in a padded recliner, separated from the
scattering of others somewhere to the left of her fluted
divider. At cruising altitude, there was no turbulence to
speak of, only a distant hum. When she wanted to check
out the real world, all she had to do was slide the divider
all the way back and peer over the aisle to the couples in
the midsection or the singles over in the second aisle, all of
whom were either sleeping or finagling with their iPads.
Hardly anyone was conversing.

For now, within this parallel universe, she began to take
stock.

Babs's tip about the loophole in the zoning regulations
and Will's hint about stray copper wires and a charge of
electrical current by the slate roof merged and gradually
sent her thoughts back to that early afternoon less than
a week ago that had previously crossed her mind for some
mysterious reason.

She had recently returned from a stint shepherding
a docile middle-aged couple around the Cornish coast to

smugglers' coves, old tin mines, and art galleries tucked away in St. Ives and was still dealing with jet lag when her mother sent her on a last-minute errand. A gaggle of lady guests belonging to a red-hat society had asked to stay on an extra day and had requested a special fresh-fruit-laden diet brunch. Always trying to appear amenable no matter what, this special request had sent Emily's mother into a tizzy. After all, she'd assumed she'd be using the opportunity to leisurely pack for her own holiday. So off Emily went to Chris's place to pick some peaches to tide the red-hat ladies over.

At first, this errand under the fluffy billowing clouds and noonday sun was only an extension of the easy time she'd been having for well over a fortnight. Up the dirt drive she went, flanked by a wall of verdant corn stalks. She pulled in past Chris's old station wagon and parked directly in front of the rustic cabin. The door to the attached greenhouse and potting shed was wide open. Assuming Chris was inside along with the baskets and cutting knife she'd need, she entered but found no sign of him. Instead, the first thing that met her eye was a hot plate on a rickety table against the far wall. Next to the hot plate were a pile of charred conservation magazines. The sheetrock was scorched all the way up to the skylight, which was covered with a smoky film. The smell of soot, water, and ash was everywhere.

She stepped back outside, reached inside her car window, and honked. Presently, Chris's gangly form appeared through the peach groves with a basket filled to the brim. Waving, cutting through the gap between the vegetable beds, he was soon by her side smiling and patting her shoulder, which was as close as he ever got to an open display of affection.

"This should do you for a start," Chris said, loading the peaches onto the passenger seat. "You can also pick the blueberries, blackberries, and whatnot. I'll finish with the drainpipe and ridge vents on that cape on Clark Road. And everybody'll be happy."

"Thank you, kind sir."

Clasping his hands in mock humility, Chris added, "No, ma'am, no trouble at all. Seeing that it's the red-hat gals, I am more than glad to interrupt work for a worthy cause."

Which was as close as Chris ever got to making a joke.

Brushing by her, Chris walked back to the cabin, pulled the door closed till it clicked, tugged on it a few times to make sure, and hid the key under a flower pot brimming with petunias. As he did this, he said, "I want to hear all about those typical English seaside resorts and how you made it all untypical. And how in the world you now got yourself saddled with the Curtises. Now that is what I call true grit."

Emily still hadn't responded, her mind fixed on the fire that must have recently broken out close to his cabin.

Moving across to the attached greenhouse, he went on. "Listen, tell your mom I'm going to look into those airtight zoning regulations. Not so sure they're all that airtight. A notion that doesn't sit well with some folks, not to mention any names. But nonetheless."

Emily nodded, not paying much attention. She was weighing ways to bring up the subject of short-term memory loss and the possible need for a caretaker. This was especially hard as she was dealing with a man who quoted Thoreau and Emerson about self-reliance. Someone who didn't ever want anyone fussing. How would he feel to have someone looking in on him, overly concerned that at his age he was finally starting to lose it?

Chris came out of the greenhouse with the extra pails and baskets she would need, saying, "And, oh, did that fellow show up yet, that Will Farrow? Comes highly recommended. Not bad looking either and just the right age. Best of all, takes everything easy and lets all the folderol pass right through him. Call it a through-me kind of guy."

Putting everything down, he said, "Besides, the break will be good for your mother too. Help calm her down."

"Chris—"

"Now don't go giving me that look. I'm only halfway serious." He pulled out a skeleton key, secured the greenhouse door, and tugged on it as hard as he'd tested the front door, and pocketed the key.

"That's not what I mean," Emily said as Chris walked past her and got behind the wheel of his old station wagon.

Tromping on the accelerator as he turned the ignition switch, he looked up at her and said, "I know, I know. Didn't mean to jump the gun about you and a possible beau."

The motor caught and then stalled.

Pressing a bit harder, Emily said, "What I'm trying to say is, you tend to your crops, the roofs, and all that village business. But maybe it's time you . . ." Emily stopped herself short, still unsure how to broach the subject.

Holding the pedal to the floor, Chris managed to bring the old engine sputtering to life.

Trying again, Emily said, "The fire in the greenhouse, Chris. What's that all about?"

Reaching out and patting her arm, Chris said, "Soon as I get a chance, I'm going to look into it. And soon as we both get a chance, you owe me a full report about those West Country English rambles." With that, he drove off, the undercarriage and exhaust pipes rattling as usual.

Focused on getting her mother squared away, final arrangements for the mini-Twinning, and catching up on her sleep, she assumed he had meant he was going to ask his doctor for some pills to help him remember details, like shutting off a hot plate before he went to bed and locking the doors.

Now, on this extended flight, it dawned on her that wasn't what he meant at all. When he was locking and tugging on the doors, he wasn't making sure he remembered. He was making sure no one broke in again till he could come up with a better safeguard.

And figure out exactly who might be after him.

As she kept mulling this over, all that was fueling her was tinged again with anger. So much for keeping her feelings in check.

With her fluted divider fully drawn, and armed with a notepad, she took stock but much more pointedly this time.

Up till now, what did she know for certain? How far did it go? What could she do to catch up and still stay on schedule? Keep playing both ends against the middle? No. She had to intercept Harriet Curtis in London before she flew the coop again. That was the first thing.

In the back of her mind, she recalled things Harriet had

said about her need for time and space and being under the gun, but hoped, in due course, to come to terms with all that.

It occurred to her that what passed for normal during her private tours was everything being more or less in place. Never before were couples, close friends, or what-have-you at odds with each other. Instead, everyone was generally relaxed and more than happy to be together on some big adventure. Never before did she have to round them up or wonder what they were up to. Perhaps she should never have assumed that three eccentric siblings she'd known in passing would ever form a doable trio, let alone stay put. Though her business prospects were hanging by a thread, she should have been duly forewarned and fore-armed.

She decided that after about six good hours of sleep at the discount hotel near Victoria Station, she'd get an early wake-up call, walk the few blocks to Warwick Way and make a concerted effort to find out what else Harriet had been up to. Harriet had waved the e-mail confirmations of her hotel in Emily's face and cut her losses in exchange for a pricey last-minute flight and private accommodations—all under the assumption she could do anything and take it all back. The least Emily could do for starters was put that notion to rest.

Bright and early the next morning, Emily walked six blocks to Warwick Way and down another three to the

Warwick Hotel, the only stopover she'd mentioned the other day that definitely got a rise out of Harriet. People were bustling around as she passed the tiny shops and the Sainsbury's market; the Mini Coopers were parked like toys down alleyways, and the sky was pearl and a faded blue. There were no insects or aromas suggesting anything growing wild. There was not even a hint of heat in the air. No screens in the open windows or fans or air conditioners as a matter of course.

At the corner, she passed by the Marquis of Westminster Café with its red-and-white striped awnings and lacquered billboards heralding "Homemade Beef Wellington and all Manner of Traditional English Food." As usual, Emily soon found herself adjusting to the distinctively English ambiance and urbane rhythm.

She made a beeline for the muted "Pimlico Room" sign, over to the chalky façade of the once-private Victorian dwelling, and hurried into the Warwick's cramped foyer. An immediate left took her into a cramped room that served as both office and lounge consisting solely of a mahogany desk and chair, a chintzy sofa, and a magazine rack filled with sightseeing leaflets.

In pursuing Harriet here, Emily had a few advantages. The boutique hotel had such limited space, ungainly Harriet had little or no place to maneuver, let alone hide. Emily had recommended the Warwick to all her touring clients and was owed a favor or two and a little cooperation. Lastly, the advantage of surprise. The only disadvantage at present was the baldheaded bloke giving Mavis, the concierge, a hard time over his bill. Which meant Emily had to stand by and keep her eye on the only access in or out.

"You know, darlin'," the man went on, leaning over the desk and thrusting his bloated face as close to Mavis's as possible, "for these prices you should have thrown in a fancy woman from Belgravia. Along with a few up-market tarts from Notting Hill."

Mavis responded with her customary "Yeh?" and let him carry on for another minute or so. Finally, she raised her bleary eyes and said, "Since I don't set the rates, this item you have in hand is your final bill, yeh?"

After some more sputtering, the man plunked down a handful of fifty-pound notes, snatched up his receipt, and shoved it in his vest pocket. Dragging his bulging leather suitcase past Emily, he got in the last word. "In Belgravia you get value added and great bloody service for the quid you're overcharged."

"I'm looking for Harriet Curtis," said Emily, the second the irate bloke was out of earshot. "I'm Emily Ryder, remember? I do private tours."

Barely lifting her long, tired face, Mavis said, "Harriet Curtis scarpered at half-six without so much as a by-your-leave."

"That early? Why?"

"Not a mind reader, love."

"Could you take a guess?"

"A call from the States might have done it. I rang it through to her room."

Emily assumed it was a call from Silas announcing

that he'd pawned his prized flintlocks and the three would rendezvous with Emily in Bath as planned.

"How did she act when she left?" Emily pressed. "Comparatively, I mean."

Instead of answering, Mavis said, "She done a runner, yeh?"

"In a way."

Mavis slipped an unlit cigarette in her mouth letting her jaw go slack. "Not that we're beholden to you, mind."

"I realize that."

"But for future considerations, you might say. And for what you've sent our way before this lot."

"You mean Harriet. As it happens, I didn't send her. She only heard me mention this place as a nice, handy alternative. Look, if you could just give me a general impression of how she was acting or some hint as to what she might be up to."

Mavis stopped pecking at her keyboard. "It's a general impression you want? Right. A big lump of a woman, stroppy, all thumbs and knobby knees. As for what she's about, she'll do herself in or someone else, I shouldn't wonder. Popping in and out and down Warwick Way and thereabouts."

"At sixes and sevens?"

"If that's your word for it. Much the worse when she left, I'd say. Chatting away."

"To whom?"

"Herself."

"Oh? What did she say?"

"Told you. Not a mind reader, love."

"But you must have caught some of the words."

Mavis's eyes seemed to lock for a second as she looked up at the plaster ceiling. "She might've muttered something about 'accessorize?' . . . no, 'accessory' more like, whilst shaking her head a lot. 'Must scurry,' says she. A bit daft, if you take my meaning."

Emily held still, taking this all in.

Then she said, "How about other calls? Ones she received or ones she may have made."

"Right," Mavis said, "now there's where you do for me."

The upshot was that Harriet had paid for her accommodations, but she'd snuck into an empty adjacent room and used the phone a dozen times.

After studying the sheet Mavis handed her, Emily asked for a copy. She was familiar with two of the local exchanges and Miranda Shaw's old number in Bovey Tracey. Knowing Miranda, there was no way she was going to ruin her beauty sleep and put up with Harriet Curtis at the ungodly hour listed. The only overseas number Emily was familiar with was the one to the Sharon hospital in the Connecticut hills, obviously checking up on Chris's condition.

Pocketing the printout and promising Mavis she'd look into it and get back to her, Emily asked if she could take a peek at Harriet's room.

"It's being cleaned," said Mavis, pecking away again. "That's the custom as soon as it's vacant. The custom everywhere decent."

"How about the empty one she'd been sneaking into?"

Mavis stopped her pecking, gave Emily a peevish glance and said. "Some other line of business you fancy going into?"

"Just humor me. I'll only be a minute."

"Low marks for a tour guide who loses track of her people, yeh?"

"Please? Just give me a break, okay?"

Giving in with a shrug, Mavis pointed out the room at the top of the landing to Emily's right. "And you'll make good on the charges, mind."

"Absolutely."

One flight up the narrow stairway, a quick turn to the right, and Emily was through the doorway. The walls were covered with a faded teal-blue rendering of a jolly fox hunt, the two open windows looking out on the hurrying passersby and the intermittent street traffic below.

At first glance there was nothing of note, only the standard chintzy couch, a wing chair on spindly legs, and a bed with knurled posts. Nothing in the room seemed out of place—except for a wastebasket, tipped on its side and shoved beneath the mahogany writing table that held the phone. Torn bits of hotel stationary were scattered inside the basket. It was understandable that someone like Harriet might scribble a few notes or doodle, especially while calling the hospital and being put on hold. It was also conceivable that in her haste, afraid of being caught sneaking into an empty room, Harriet had tossed the scraps of paper away. But why would she go to all the trouble of ripping them up, tip over the wastebasket, and push it that far under?

Retrieving the scraps, Emily sat at the desk rearranging and smoothing the pieces until they fit together.

Doodles of neat floral arrangements took up all the space on the first sheet—obviously Harriet in her flower-judging mode. The doodle on the second sheet was much different. Flowers were strewn every which way at the foot of a looming, warped gravestone.

Chapter Fourteen

Ordinarily, Emily would have enjoyed the train ride from Paddington station. Rolling west, she was seated comfortably next to a wide picture window, a smiling young mother holding her sleeping baby across the way, a gaggle of passengers behind her chatting amiably, the deep-green landscape dipping and rising. Moreover, each expanse was marked by neat, coloring-book hedgerows—all of it ideal for a tour guide headed west for the center of Bath on a pleasant, early Wednesday afternoon. Just a short cab ride to pick up her rented Vauxhall station wagon and she would be lazily wending her way to Darlington House to meet up with her clients.

Ordinarily, Emily would have also been looking forward to going to the market to pick out her trip snacks of fruit, nuts, and assorted biscuits followed by a leisurely exploration of the ancient city. They could have had a pleasant early supper at a favorite spot near the Roman Baths, going over plans for the upcoming mini-Twinning and fete; talking to Harriet about the flower judging, Silas about his lecture on the Lydfield and Lydfield-in-the-Moor heritage, and humoring Pru about her storytelling stint and foraging for authentic tales of the mist-sodden moorland.

Ordinarily, Emily could have settled back into her role as a seasoned rambler and guide.

But as things stood, there was nothing remotely ordinary in the offing. And Emily could not shake off Harriet's gravestone doodle. Once again, Emily reviewed the calls Harriet had made.

Though the other overseas numbers didn't register, there was a strong possibility the call to the Sharon hospital was made to see if Chris still had a pulse, or to make certain Chris was no longer in the way. The calls to Heathrow and Paddington Station must have given Harriet an inkling of Silas and Pru's arrival and when they could be expected to converge in Bath. This coincided with Harriet's demand that Emily arrive exactly on time so they could move on. Which meant that Harriet had anticipated the possibility that Silas would barter his way over, and she'd have to be at the ready to skip out again, keeping one step ahead of the game. Which was exactly why she'd muttered "must scurry" to herself.

But why, exactly, was she avoiding her siblings? Did it have something to do with finagling something with the GDC and then cutting them out of the transaction? Or did being "under the gun" mean getting as far away from Doc as possible? And what did she hope to accomplish during her retreat?

Accommodations had been booked for the three of them that night in Bath. Emily had originally been contracted to explore Bath with the trio before carting them to the four-day stopover at the fete followed by visits to points in Cornwall as planned. All this was in writing whether Harriet liked it or not. All of this had been confirmed.

But under the circumstances, reiterating the contracted arrangements wasn't going to change a thing. She could only keep them in mind.

Emily kept to her basic plan. As soon as anything cropped up concerning Chris's undoing, Emily would notify the proper constabulary and let them take it from there, exposing Harriet as a person of interest in a possible criminal investigation. An "accessory," in Harriet's own words. In the meantime, Emily would handle her duties and avoid getting into trouble with the British Tourist Authority for noncompliance. For the moment, all she could do was get the rental car, zip over to Darlington House before Silas and Pru spilled onto the drive and, once again, try to confront Harriet.

She spent the rest of the train ride gazing out the window at the hedgerows and the endless rolling green, trying once more to give her rampant thoughts a deserved rest.

Approaching the Bath station fifteen minutes behind schedule, Emily carted her luggage out of the station and made her way to the taxi stand. She missed out on the first taxi in line but managed to flag down a curly-headed driver with a fixed grin who slammed on his brakes, hopped out, said his name was Alistair, and announced with the brassy voice of a music-hall entertainer that he was at her service.

As they sped off, he informed her he'd driven a black cab all over London for the past fifteen years. He failed to mention that although he knew every inch of London's West End, East End, and Southwark, he was only learning his way around Bath. As a result, he took off the wrong way and headed smack toward the center, Old King Street, the bottleneck at Grand Parade and the Putney Bridge, all the while grinning away. It was only by promising to listen to his silly tales about American tourists that he slowed down and permitted Emily to redirect him up Brock and past the Royal Crescent to the Kemwell Holiday Auto Rental Office.

"As I was saying," Alistair went on as if nothing was amiss, "first off, most of you lot—present company excluded—want to know what the weather's going to be. Then it's questions about this ruddy statue, that lovely monument, this park, and on you go. Now I don't know all them answers, now do I? So for a starter, I say, it's going to be right fair with cloudy intervals, periods of occasional brightening, and a chance for a spot of rain."

Emily reminded him he wasn't in London and the roundabout was coming up in a few blocks.

"Fair dues," said Alistair, continuing to glance at the rearview mirror to see how Emily was taking his comedy act. "As for the statues, I say, there you have Lord Nelson peeking out to make sure his ships are neat and tidy-like. And those there are in honor of young Elizabeth whilst frolicking about as a maiden. Regents Park, you ask? Well, it's because it's where all them regents went larking about."

"You passed it."

"Beg your pardon?"

"The auto rental office. It's next to the cobblestone mall. You'll have to turn around again and hang a left."

When Alistair hit the brakes, followed her directions, and became withdrawn, Emily told him his silly Yanks routine was pretty clever. She just wasn't in the mood. In truth, not only was she not in the mood, she was going over her tactics in preparation for Harriet. Being behind schedule, the imminent arrival of the other two, and Alistair's messing about wasn't helping in the least.

After more blundering, Alistair dropped Emily off at Kemwell's. There she encountered more hassle, dickering over the frequent-flyer discount while being hit with the 17.5 percent value-added-tax and the rate of exchange.

Once she'd adjusted to sitting behind the wheel and driving on the right, she took the mile-and-a-half route west at a steady clip. In virtually no time, she pulled up to the private car park fronting a Georgian country house.

At the outset, the ochre stone building seemed deserted. There was no sign of movement behind the elongated windows on the first or second floor, as though it hadn't been occupied since the early nineteenth century when the Duke of Wellington had it built for his mistress. The current proprietor, Clive, hadn't done a thing with the scruffy grounds or any aspect of the weathered façade since the former owners let it go to seed years ago.

But any concern over this additional annoyance was quashed the second Harriet Curtis shambled through the portico and barged straight toward Emily. "You're late," Harriet said. "Extremely late."

"Just a minute," said Emily, intercepting her before she took another step.

"Sorry?"

"First of all," said Emily, starting to lose it despite herself, "let's get a few things clear. I'm a tour guide, not a flunky or a taxi service. And, as I pointed out before you ran out on us, the contract for this tour also includes your brother and stepsister. Plus, it has provisions that take into account all four of us, which, again, you know full well."

Harriet was obviously taken aback as Emily added, "This means that somehow or other, we all have to try and get along."

While Harriet remained speechless, Emily was surprised at her sudden outburst. She'd always been deferential to her elders growing up, especially those who possessed a lineage like Harriet's that could be traced way back.

Regaining her composure, Emily reached into the inside pocket of her windbreaker and handed Harriet the bill from the Warwick Hotel. "In the meantime, this came to my attention."

Still at a loss for words, Harriet retreated a few more steps, stumbling over the loose gravel.

"It's from your stay at the Warwick, Harriet, something else you seemed to have skipped out on. I promised Mavis I'd help her collect."

Harriet didn't question the fact that Emily must have gotten an early start to track her down from Victoria all the way to Paddington station. All Harriet could say was "I don't see that it's any of your concern. And I certainly don't like your tone."

"Fine," Emily said, determined to remain on a professional, even keel. "Except that it reflects on me when my clients sneak into empty rooms and make long distance calls without paying."

And it especially concerns me when my clients make doodles of gravestones and secret calls to the Sharon hospital, along with muttering about being an accessory, she desperately wanted to add, but kept it to herself. If she knew anything about entrapment, she certainly didn't want to make unsubstantial accusations and put her suspect on guard.

Harriet's hawk-like features twitched as she floundered for a reply. "As you well know, or should certainly be aware, I was overcharged for those accommodations. Just a few international calls or even a simple call from London to Bath, and you're charged an arm and a leg unless you prepay."

Harriet crammed the bill into her bulging shoulder bag, told Emily she would see to the phone charges in her own way and in her own good time, backed off a few more feet, and almost lost her footing again.

Under the fickle sunny intervals, Emily spent the next few minutes trying to eke out a few telling replies, but Harriet kept changing the subject. Then and there, Emily had to come to terms with the fact that she had no authority to get a statement on or off the record from anyone. So she eased off. Moments later, a taxi pulled up alongside her rented wagon.

Harriet's fretfulness became more pronounced as Alistair slid out first, followed in turn by an ever-rumpled-looking Silas and a flouncing Pru in a mock peasant blouse and long skirt.

"Well, I never," announced Alistair, yanking out their bags from the trunk while Pru took in the surroundings. Silas held still and peered over his bifocals at Harriet.

"I says to myself," Alistair went on, "I am doing a proper deed, reuniting a brother and sisters, now ain't I? Lovely, I say to that. And hello again, Miss Emily. See you made it here without my assistance."

Getting no response from the quartet, Alistair tried a little harder. "Would you fancy a sightseeing tour of what's known hereabouts as a world heritage city? Been here since the Romans, even longer than me."

Yet again, Alistair failed to get a laugh.

"Oh, I'm sure Emily will take us where we want to go," Pru said. "It's all been arranged. You see, she's our guide. Knows all about this area and the moors and Cornwall and you name it."

Glowering at Harriet, Pru added, "And if we try real hard, perhaps we can still make the best of it."

Undaunted, Alistair chipped in with, "Well, if you change your mind, or your Emily needs a break, all you have to do is ask for Alistair and Bob's your uncle."

"Bob?" Pru said.

"It means that I'm at your service." Alistair bowed and scraped a little before shuffling back behind the wheel. It wasn't until Emily nudged Silas and indicated Alistair was waiting for a tip that Silas complied.

Alistair let out a hearty "Lovely," and presently the foursome found themselves alone.

Continuing to peer at Harriet, Silas lapsed into one of his mumbling, running commentaries under his breath which ended with "Didn't have to . . . wasn't necessary. Not good, not good at all, Harriet."

During the few times Emily had had any dealings with all three of them, there had always been an undercurrent of tension between Harriet and her siblings. This time, given the volatile, mysterious rift, Emily truly had her work cut out for her.

"Look," Emily said, fully resigning herself to the awkward situation, "we're going to have to come to some understanding. And it looks like it's going to depend on Harriet."

"Well," Pru said, as if scolding a misbehaving child, "if she would stop worrying us and if she would promise on her word of honor—"

"Oh, shut up, Pru," said Harriet in a feeble attempt to reassert herself.

Clive, the proprietor, peeked out past the thick stone walls of the portico and beckoned to Emily. With his weak chin, diminutive frame, and receding hairline that went with his subservient manner, in Emily's mind, Clive only added to the charade.

"Just give me a minute," said Emily to the trio, hoping that the siblings would just manage to keep still.

Following Clive into the airy, high-ceiling alcove, Emily did her best to convince him she had the situation in hand. Nevertheless, Clive kept waffling. "But, if I may presume to say, now that the other two have indeed arrived, the situation is, to say the least, rather a muddle. First, I'm told there is only the one and she must make haste. And suddenly it's ever so different."

Reaching for some way to keep things from unraveling any further, Emily said, "You have to understand, Harriet Curtis has never been abroad before. And she has a big responsibility judging the flower show at the fete."

"But I simply don't follow. Whatever does that have to do with the reservations?"

"Well, if you consider the logistics, it's no wonder she got her dates mixed up and didn't realize we're leaving tomorrow."

Still perplexed, Clive said, "But you see, I've been receiving inquiries as to availability. For this evening, that is. And when she insisted she was departing immediately . . ."

"She was confused."

"And the tour of the Jane Austen Centre and the Museum of Costume I arranged for Pru Curtis? May this go ahead as scheduled?"

"Give me a minute."

Emily glanced out the French windows to make sure the three of them weren't at each other's throats. Clive went on to mention the gardens at the Royal Crescent and the antique shops by the cobbled North Parade, also prearranged.

"We'll work it out," said Emily, hoping, for the time being, all four of them could actually fake their way through this.

Emily left Clive standing there, still wringing his hands.

She rejoined Harriet, Silas, and Pru and found that no one had moved an inch and nothing had been resolved.

Sidling over to Emily, Pru said, "I don't know, Emily, I just don't know. I hate to think we've come all this way only to find Harriet still being impossible."

"I don't have to answer to you, of all people," said Harriet. "As if things weren't bad enough."

"Listen," Emily said, "I just told the owner there was a little mix-up over the reservations, but everything was going according to plan."

No one spoke or changed their positions. Breaking the standoff, Silas said, "Yes, maybe we could give Harriet a second chance . . . the benefit of the doubt. As long as we're able to . . . a trial run, that is."

"A kind of wait-and-see," said Pru.

"Oh, really?" said Harriet.

"What then?" Pru answered back. "Let you do your worst? Is that the choice?"

"Enough." Feeling more like a nanny than ever, Emily said, "Let's all back off, okay? It's been a long day, and I'm sure everyone's just overtired."

Harriet picked up her suitcase in some kind of defiant display of independence, wheeled around, and made her way back to the portico. "Very well," she announced. "We'll go on with this untenable situation for the time being, until . . ."

"Until what?" Pru called out as Silas shuffled past her, following Harriet.

"That's for me to decide, thank you very much."

Tugging on the sleeve of Emily's windbreaker, Pru said, "I am so worried, absolutely exhausted, and thrilled to be here all at once."

"Like I said, Pru, the best thing right now is to give it a rest."

Dissatisfied with this answer, Pru said, "Did you know that right before we left, Martha Forbes, the realtor, came by? She asked about Harriet and what her plans were. When I told her I wasn't sure, she asked about Brian, her own husband, and his dealings with Harriet. As if Brian and Martha kept secrets from each other. Now what do you make of that?"

"I have no idea."

Pru dawdled a little while longer, snatched up her suitcase, and excused herself.

"Well, you think about it. As for Harriet, it all hinges on what's going on in that brain of hers." Pru let out a big, storybook sigh and began traipsing after her siblings. "At any rate, I might as well lie down for a bit. That's always best if ever you feel yourself getting out of sorts."

Assuming Clive would show them to their rooms, Emily circled the premises until she found a wrought-iron bench. She took in the deep-green, rolling hills in the far distance and basked in the shimmering afternoon sunlight, more than grateful for a break from all the trepidation. More than grateful for a chance to just hold still for a moment.

Chapter Fifteen

In contrast, Babs was champing at the bit. After all, the GDC was a major developer from New Jersey. And since it was a New Jersey chain that had swallowed up the paper she was writing for, what better way to get a leg up and some notoriety too? Move forever from cutesy features and, at the same time, boost circulation by giving the locals what they wanted—juicy leads and sidebars that would make them beg for more. If she could shake things up, she'd be a force to reckon with for once in her life.

On that breezy Wednesday in the Connecticut hills, Babs found her opportunity. From the way Emily had been acting and the way she sounded over the phone, she'd made the right move in handing the ball over. No matter how you looked at it, it would be hard enough for Emily to pull off this latest tour with the wacky Curtis trio, much less handle the fate of her mother's B&B and the shifty tactics of the GDC while she was way across the Atlantic.

Babs lingered just for a moment on the Green, gave her bib overalls and bright-yellow top a once-over, and smirked. Right, she would keep him guessing. Let Brian Forbes think one thing and hit him with another. Keep him off-balance, just like Woodward and Bernstein from *The Washington*

Post in that old Watergate flick when those two were really clicking and bringing down the White House.

Clutching her steno pad, Babs hurried across the street, climbed the stone steps of the bank in stride, and passed through the white colonnades and foyer. She whisked by Chuck the security guard, brushed aside the wooden gate, and plunked herself down directly in front of Brian's polished, maple desk.

Sporting a powder-blue suit and candy-striped tie, Brian faked a plastic smile before looking out into the lobby as if seeking help. Then he smoothed back the temples of his grayish-blond hair and straightened his posture.

Babs figured she had Brian positioned right where she wanted him. In his corner niche, only a few feet beyond his low-hanging swing gate, he was in full view of every bank customer at each and every teller window. That, of course, was the whole point of Iron Bank's policy of homey accessibility. That also accounted for Brian's fixed smile and smooth delivery. He couldn't afford to get upset or allow Babs to raise her voice and draw any kind of attention. That would ruin his image.

"Well, well," said Brian, looking askance, "it's been quite a while, Miss Maroon. So what brings you here? Don't tell me. Some human-interest story about our helpful services? Have you finally decided to include our own venerable village bank in your reporting?"

Fully enjoying this moment of one-upmanship, Babs said, "No, Brian. Good guess but no cigar."

Brian kept up his smile, but from the way he kept glancing about, Babs could tell she definitely had him off guard, especially in calling him Brian instead of Mr. Forbes, something she never would've done with any other bank vice-president who was her senior.

Obviously attempting to disarm her, Brian said, "You know, we still talk about the comments you made when you had that trouble with your checkbook. Remember? All those overdrafts? And I said, 'Did you do your statement?' And you came back with, 'What statement? I believe in the constitution and the Bill of Rights.' And then I said, 'But surely you've looked at your outstanding checks.' And you said, 'Well, my most outstanding check is the one I made out to the Oklahoma tornado relief fund.' Let me tell you, we still get a chuckle out of it."

"No chuckles this time, Brian. I wanted to get your side of it first. I'm talking something along the lines of conflict of interest."

Fingering the knot in his tie, Brian hung onto the smile and said, "Now, now, Babs. If you've come to play games, I happen to be very busy."

"No chuckles and no games. Where would you like to begin? We know that just before she cut out of here, Harriet Curtis accused you of starting something, yelling so loud everybody could hear. Then we've got the check to Harriet from the GDC, which you gladly okayed so she had the funds to suddenly take off. Plus the fact that Chris Cooper is permanently out of the picture after telling me about the loophole in the zoning application."

Noting the dumbfounded look on his face, Babs said, "You know about the loophole, right? The one that could very well put the kibosh on plans for gutting the highmeadow tract? The one the GDC is slavering over? And we've also got you in the catbird seat for tonight's hearing, taking over Chris Cooper's place as chairman. At the same time, your role as head of the Business Association means you're dying to see this thing go through. You still with me?"

"You print any of that and you and your paper will face the biggest libel suit you ever saw."

Scribbling away, Babs raised her voice and said, "Is that your answer? Is that really what you want plastered all over the next edition? About the conflict of interest issue, I mean? Oh, and I forgot to mention the pressure on your wife to foreclose the Curtis property. At the suggestion of your pals at the GDC, of course."

A portly couple were leaning over the bank counter, straining to hear more. Noticing them, Brian rose to his feet, held the swing gate back and said, "If you'll step this way, Miss Maroon, I'm sure we can clear this up."

Waving to the eavesdropping couple, Brian ushered Babs behind the tellers' counter, up a flight of stairs into a wood-paneled conference room, and closed the door. Babs seated herself in one of the ladder-backed chairs on one side of the long table. Brian positioned himself directly opposite.

"Now hear me out," said Brian, "and don't interrupt. All right?"

"All right, shoot." Babs flipped open her steno pad again and held her pen at the ready.

Brian immediately began carrying on as though he'd rehearsed this speech and was trying it on for size. "In the first place, it was the elder Curtis, now deceased, who was responsible for the second mortgages and the non-payment of taxes, which is all a matter of record. All I did was inform him that the low rate of interest we were currently paying was unlikely to change and he'd have to look elsewhere for a higher return. But even so, that wasn't going to prevent the inevitable loss of his property or keep his two children and stepchild Pru solvent."

"So," Babs cut in, "you waited till the very last moment, with the axe hanging over her head, to tell Harriet that, as the oldest and the one her dad left it all to, her option was to either sell out or wind up on the street. Herself, Silas, and Pru, that is. However, if you had let them know much earlier, they all could've—"

"What? Gone to work, paid off the debt, and made enough to live on? Or relied on Silas's flaky antique trading? Oh, please."

Brian continued to twiddle with the knot in his tie, loosening it, straightening it, and loosening it some more.

"Still and all," Babs said, "Harriet sells out at your suggestion."

"Signs a letter of intent."

"Signs her life away to the GDC at your suggestion."

"I want you to stop saying that."

"Why? You think my readers are going to buy the idea this all just happened? That Harriet wasn't feeling so much pressure that she blamed you and skipped town a day earlier than scheduled? That you weren't counting on Chris Cooper being out of the way so you could railroad this thing through?"

"Now, wait a second."

On a roll, Babs raised her voice and said, "You think you and your cronies really care about the environment and aren't licking your chops over the revenue and new businesses to come and whatever else you guys lick your chops over? Not to mention where your realtor wife Martha comes in."

A troubled look fell across Brian's face for an instant. Securing the knot in his tie, he rose slowly and reverted to his usual plummy tone. "Good try. Naturally you're out of your league, but not to worry. Tonight at the hearing, you will learn how things actually work. In any case, I'm sure you didn't expect me to throw up my hands and say, 'Gosh, I guess you found me out.' I'm also sure you'll excuse me while I take a much-deserved lunch break."

Babs reached for another comeback but came up empty. She had no recourse she could think of but to pocket her steno pad and follow him down to the main lobby.

From there, an over-eager Chuck nodded and attempted to escort her out the door. Babs took his arm instead and said, "Come on, Chuck. It's high time we switched places."

Pulling back, Chuck said, "Now, now, Miss Babs. Don't want Mr. Forbes to get any funny ideas and think of replacing me."

"No way, man. Unlike me, you're as safe and predictable as clam chowder."

She left Chuck scratching his shiny bald head and shrugging off a disapproving glance from his boss.

Bounding down the steps, Babs felt pretty good about how the first round went. Tonight she might do even better.

She was on the way to getting closer and closer to the bottom of this fiasco.

Babs knew from experience that hardly anyone attended Lydfield Planning Commission meetings. The agenda usually consisted of someone requesting a variance so they could put up a shed or extend their driveway beyond the setback regulations. In terms of sheer dullness, meetings could get bogged down over the location of a grease trap for a hamburger stand that straddled the village line. Therefore, it was highly unusual to see an army of people in attendance, the majority of whom sported a gold GDC logo on the breast pocket of their navy-blue jackets. As a result, it was standing room only in the little meeting room at the back of the village hall designed to seat, at most, thirty-five people.

The only ones not clutching plans, charts, drawings, and displays were the seven members of the commission seated up front around an oblong table under the fluorescent lights. Also in attendance were an assortment of onlookers, Babs herself, and three ladies wearing safari jackets, walking shorts, and hiking boots. In addition to their outfits, all three outdoorsy women had weathered faces and gray, cropped hair. Before the meeting started, they pumped Babs's hand and reminded her they were longtime advocates of the free migratory patterns of birds and mammals. When they asked why in the world her friend Emily wasn't present, all Babs could answer was, "She's away again, but I'm her proxy. Except, as a reporter, I can't speak out and take sides. But I'm still onto it, you bet."

Her reply prompted the wildlife champions to bristle and move to the other side of the room. Nonetheless, aside from zeroing in on some supporting data as an investigative reporter, Babs also had it in mind to score some points through Will's testimony. From what she understood, he had the opportunity to bring up the loophole in question. In the back of her mind, she also entertained the notion to make a play for Will, provided he was as promising in person as he sounded over the phone. Why should Emily get all the action on that front? Why shouldn't there be a bonus in it for Babs for once in her loopy life? Juicy revelations and sultry prospects to boot were just what the doctor ordered.

As the time drew near, however, she began to worry that Will might not show up at all. No one else could bring up the issue that the regulations read "may" not "shall" with regards to selling the tract on the high meadow for development. No one else was prepared or even knew about it. No one else was outside the usual wrangling village politics to mention their now-deceased chairman's discovery and afford the few moderates on the commission the impetus they needed to raise a few objections. Or, failing that, casually call for a referendum establishing the tract as a sanctuary or who knows what else she could get Will to do. As a reporter, Babs was prohibited to even broach the subject, but perhaps she could get Will to do something.

When the hearing was promptly called to order, and still no sign of Will, things didn't look promising. The lead attorney for the GDC, a tall, bony man with a mop of dyed black hair, began to lay out the ground rules. He advised the commission that their charge was to approve the site plans only. Now was not the time for deflections about animal rights or complaints about alterations to the historic nature of the village.

One of the three lady conservationists objected on the grounds it was supposed to be an open hearing and residents and taxpayers had rights. A few onlookers murmured their approval.

Brian Forbes banged his gavel, waved the lady wildlife champion down, and said, "Yes, yes, Ms. Trumbull. All in due time."

From then on it was one suited "expert" after another. And each suit had a presentation longer and more laborious than the one before. At one point, a soil engineer went on and on in a low, garbled monotone about projected sediment loss and recovery ratios that would be handled by his state-of-the-art converter system. By the time he had flipped over diagram number fifteen on his portable easel, Babs couldn't help but feel useless. The only saving grace was the fact that Ms. Trumbull had also had enough.

"This is ludicrous!" shouted Ms. Trumbull as she shot up out of her seat. "You call this an open hearing, Brian? When does the public get to speak?"

"Excuse me," said Brian. "But we have an agenda."

"Wonderful. How long does this filibuster go on? Do we get equal time? And even so, we don't have an endless bunch of hired guns. We don't have a slick lawyer. What are we supposed to do?"

Babs jotted all this down as the GDC lawyer took exception to the "unprofessional mudslinging."

Brian assured Ms. Trumbull that after the GDC had presented its case, the public would have its turn.

"And when will that happen?" hollered Ms. Trumbull. "How old will I be? I know for a fact that the fifteen-minute break is coming up. At the rate this is going, we will never be heard. And what about equal representation?"

More murmuring agreement by the same few onlookers.

Babs glanced back over her shoulder and spotted a tall guy in Levi's leaning by the doorjamb who, by all accounts, had to be Will Farrow. Babs also spotted Martha Forbes slipping into the meeting room and gazing directly at her husband.

Everything came to a halt. Babs couldn't tell whether it was Martha's sudden appearance or Brian's loss for words over Ms. Trumbull's allegations that brought proceedings to a standstill. She also wondered why the other six members of the commission hadn't so much as batted an eyelid during this altercation. Perhaps Brian had them all in his pocket, or they had been paid off by the GDC, or they had never run into a team of high-powered operators and were flabbergasted and cowering over the prospect of using tax payer money to hire legal consultants.

Brian came up with the slick rejoinder that Ms. Trumbull and her cohorts could file for intervener status, hire their own lawyers and experts, and present their case. When asked where they were supposed to get the money to compete with the GDC's bottomless pockets, Brian signaled for the break.

Without Chris Cooper at the helm, it seemed to Babs that just about any corporate scheme could be steamrolled through. Antsy as can be, she got up, hoping to see what she could wheedle out of Martha and then find out what was going on with Will. But Will became the first order of business as she spied him ambling toward the exit a few yards behind Ms. Trumbull and the others as they proceeded to barge out in sheer, powerless frustration.

"Hey," said Babs, catching up to him. "I'm Babs. You're not really going, are you?"

"Looks that way."

"But you can't. What about the 'shall' and 'may' business? What about doing some good?"

Most of the onlookers brushed past them on their way out, including Martha Forbes with a self-satisfied look on her face, doubtless realizing it was all a fait accompli, leaving Brian, the rest of the commission members and suits in the meeting room, and Will and Babs lingering in the hallway.

"No point that I can see," said Will.

"You can't mean that."

Babs kept looking up at Will, hoping for something positive. She liked his lean looks but didn't at all like the way he was sloughing her off.

"Looks like a stacked deck to me."

"Fine. The whole thing is rigged. The B&B goes belly up, Emily's mom has to pack it in, and you're out of luck."

"Could be."

"Come on. How can you show up and then back off one minute later?"

"Let's say I'm just not up for this kind of thing."

"Then what are you up for?"

After thinking it over, Will said, "Tell you what. Meet you at Roy's. I could use a couple of cold ones, and I guess you could use a little advice."

Will gave her a nod as he exited the hallway. As an afterthought, he said, "Look for the pickup with the friendly dog. Name's Oliver, but don't give him any ideas."

"Okay. Be with you in a minute."

Babs watched him move out of sight. Looking for some way, any way to regain the initiative, she slipped through the exit and spotted Martha Forbes shaking hands with the lead attorney. Martha abruptly moved off and cut through the gap between the laurel bushes. Babs followed until they were both blocked by a high, wooden fence. It was pitch dark now and there was a slight chill in the air.

Avoiding the haughty look that went with her tailored suit, Babs used the same ploy she'd used earlier with Martha's husband.

"Look, I only need a few seconds to make sure I've got this right."

"Some other time, all right?" said Martha in her crisp saleswoman tone. "Now if you'll kindly step aside."

"Sure thing. But I only wanted to give you a chance to dispel the rumors."

Martha stepped back the few remaining feet, keeping her distance. "Listen, I don't know what you think you're doing, Babs, but the hearing is about to resume. So let's drop this nonsense, shall we?"

"Okay. I'll just note you're very chummy with the

GDC and, given your iffy track record as a broker, have everything to gain from all this."

"I beg your pardon?"

"I'm saying, instead of little or no sales in living memory, you've got prospects here for commissions on a bunch of upscale condos. If you want to add it all up, it goes something like this. For starters we've got Miranda Shaw's white elephant that you can't unload. But now, with Chris Cooper out of the way, Brian at the helm of the committee, Harriet Curtis in the GDC's pocket, and their steamroller in high gear . . . you see what I'm getting at?"

There was a strained look on Martha Forbes's face that registered even in the deep shadows. Dispensing with any hint of civility, Martha said, "You print any of that and I'll sue you."

"Funny. That's exactly what your hubby said."

As Martha edged past her, Babs added, "Hey, while we're at it, how high up does this go? To Hacket, the guy who moves in after the GDC does its hit-and-run?"

Reentering the glare of the hallway, Martha said, "I'm going to forget this ever happened. And I'm sure you'll do the same."

Answering just before the door clicked shut, Babs said, "That's what's called a non-denial denial, Martha."

Feeling a tad better about things, Babs drifted over to the parking lot clogged with shiny cars with out-of-town plates and slipped behind the wheel of her beat-up Chevy. She proceeded onto the main road into the darkening stretch that took her out of the historic district all the way to Roy's Barbeque, its glowing lights the only sign of life by the dark, rippling Housatonic and the shadows of the burgeoning hills.

She figured this whole thing went all the way to the top of a huge realty enterprise. Brian and Martha were simply cogs in the wheel. If nothing else, she'd latched onto something not as big in scope as Watergate, but around these parts, pretty damn big indeed.

Pulling in outside Ray's Barbeque a few minutes later, she spotted the pickup with the chunky golden retriever perched by the rail of the truck bed. Eager to greet her, the dog wagged its bushy tail while letting out a deep-throated bark. Babs hoped the dog's amiable mood had rubbed off on his master and that Will had something positive to offer.

In the smoky haze of the bar, the speakers blared the sentiments of a throaty female vocalist declaring that "Looks, sugar, without the touch, don't cut no ice, won't get you much." Babs recalled a time when country gals declared they would stand by their man. Evidently, they'd been replaced by hot babes holding auditions in the bedroom.

Easing into the pine-paneled restaurant, she spotted Will in a booth in the far corner. Sliding in across from him, she was about to share her observations about the raunchy singer when she noticed his mood had apparently gone downhill. As he drained his Corona, Babs began to get the gist of what was on his mind.

"You see," Will said, ever so slowly twirling the neck of the empty beer bottle, "I don't know anything about this site approval business. All I'm trying to do is keep Emily from any more grief. If I could just show her that there was nothing she could've done and how she's better off steering clear of any trouble."

Though it went completely against her get-with-it style, Babs didn't interrupt. She sat still and waited him out.

Putting the beer bottle aside, he said, "If I could get this state trooper, this Dave Roberts, to take over, it'd be on him. But now we got this Doc character."

When his train of thought broke off again, Babs said, "So? Hey, I'm listening, I swear."

Will peered at her as if he was unsure whether to go on. Then he added, "Not that long after Emily left, he came looking for her at the B&B."

"The guy from the GDC?"

"I guess. I brushed him off about how to get hold of her. He shoved Oliver out of the way, walked off, and says, 'How the hell do you get to the Brit boonies and kill two birds with one stone?'"

"So you're saying there's a lot more to this GDC land grab," said Babs, thinking about Emily's remark about Doc's cellphone call on the high meadow to get Chris "taken care of."

"The way things are shaking out . . . how do you make her steer clear, is all?"

"Steer clear of what?"

"That's the point. I don't rightly know."

Will looked at Babs and shook his head, perhaps indicating that confiding in her had been a bad idea or that he was bone tired and wanted to call it a night. He excused himself, paid his tab, and left her to draw her own conclusions.

The first, and most obvious, was that there was no future in her notion about hooking up with an older guy, at least not in this case. He was solely interested in Emily, and Babs's sense of humor and availability were worth zilch.

But more importantly, it looked like this guy Doc had a lot more on his plate. Which meant at the end of this day's work, either Babs was on the mark, ensconced where the main action was, like she said or . . .

She shut her mind to the alternative. She was a whiz at this sort of thing, given half a chance. The ball was in her court. Emily was understandably saddened over Chris, not at all herself, and was far better off out of the picture.

Looking at it another way, however, given this Doc character's connection with the GDC, despite Will's efforts to shield Emily, something might be closing in on her over in what Doc called "the Brit boonies."

Chapter Sixteen

By Thursday afternoon, heading southwest on the M5, Emily had decided to ignore Harriet's standoffish routine. The elder Curtis, in the front passenger seat to Emily's left, hadn't exchanged one word with Pru and Silas who, along with the picnic basket of snacks, occupied the back seat. Babs's phone message about the stonewalling at the hearing wasn't at the forefront of her mind either.

As she passed Wellington, moving closer to the switch-off to the A38 and echoes of Dartmoor, Emily mulled over the "two birds" Doc was going to kill with one stone, which Will had divulged during Emily's quick call to him that morning. In his trademark style, Will hemmed and hawed and asked her to let it ride, and remember to stay clear of the slightest sign of trouble. To placate him, Emily had replied she would do just that as soon as he owned up to what sign of trouble he had in mind.

In Emily's mind, the first bird was probably Harriet or something to do with her. There was Doc's reference about "taking care of things" and Harriet declaring she was "under the gun" and muttering to herself back at the Warwick, shaking her head about being an accessory. Emily kept wondering when Harriet would be at it again, giving off even stronger signals or making some telltale maneuver. Would it be when Emily turned off at Bovey Tracey for the scheduled cream tea? It stood to reason that Harriet was somehow in cahoots with Doc before she suddenly turned on him and prompted his hot pursuit. In any case, no one except Emily knew the location of their new lodgings, or the fact that the secluded manor house went by the name Penmead and had a hidden track that led to its front gate.

But the prospect of Doc and Harriet running into each other complicated matters, as if they weren't already as twisted as could be. Emily had tried keeping her tour on track while keeping her eye out for any telltale slipup on Harriet's part. Something absolutely "tangible." But now even that seemed problematic.

Emily's thoughts dovetailed to those British mysteries on the telly, confined to a small locale and a limited window of time. The opening shot always consisted of something untoward happening in the shadows to the first victim. Soon enough, the inspector had the handful of suspects nailed down. Given the present circumstances transposed to the BBC show, there would be some graphic link between Martha Forbes paying off Doc, a connect to Miranda, whose McMansion Martha was trying to unload, and then over to the local developers. Everything highly efficient as the inspector's team ran down all the leads and the inspector was enabled to have a sudden brainstorm just before the closing credits.

Emily caught herself and shook off this daydream before it started to get the best of her.

Wiggling around, Harriet dipped into another tin of

biscuits and chocolate shortbread she had at the ready, sipped some more of her bitter-lemon drink, rustled her map, and pulled it up close to her eyes. Pru, seated directly behind Harriet, shrugged off Harriet's restlessness, sighed and gazed out the window in predictable wonder.

In turn, Silas remained scrunched up in the seat behind Emily on the driver's side, his lips moving as he scanned his clipboard. Off and on, he had tried to gain Emily's help in coming up with the most compelling itemization of shipments of arms, contraband, and trading goods, apropos of the War of Independence to display in his information booth at the fete. What should be the first order of business? How much supporting detail? That sort of thing. Off and on, he'd muttered and protested that he'd had no experience holding the attention of a gathering of people, let alone Brits in the West Country at a fete. Emily thought it doubtful that Silas could hold anyone's attention. But rather than hurt his feelings, she suggested that whatever order he came up with would be absolutely fine. Everyone residing in Lydfield-in-the Moor and visitors from miles around were always very accommodating.

As Silas's mutterings began to compete with the steady drone of the Vauxhall's motor, Harriet broke her silence. She crinkled her map, shoved the biscuit tin and drink aside and said, "I suppose, Silas, you won't tell me what you were doing in that musty antique shop?"

Silas's reply was a muffled "Ah, yes."

"Down that dark alley," said Harriet, turning around and facing him. "Late yesterday afternoon."

"What alley?" Pru asked, cocking her head. "In Bath,

you mean? Down the Parade Passage with those old-timey shops like in Shakespeare's day? Is that what you're going on about?"

"No, you ninny. It was on Molson Street. Right after Emily picked me up at the botanical gardens and we had to go back to fetch him. And there he was, scooting out and clutching his leather satchel."

"Molson Street?" Silas said. "Or was it Milson Street?"

"Answer me. What were you doing there?"

"You stop it, Harriet," said Pru. "I thought we'd come to a truce."

"We had come to no such thing. It was strictly an impasse."

Emily tried to ignore the renewed bickering. She was much too busy contending with the merging traffic and making sure she didn't bypass the A38 and have to double back.

Yet, at the same time, she had the oddest feeling she might have missed something. It was like that puzzling sense of unease she had felt when she was down in Silas's vault.

After more bickering, more unanswered questions, and more protests from Pru, Silas put his clipboard aside and said, "Can't concentrate. Too much confusion. Time is drawing near, you know. Have to be prepared." Silas retrieved his clipboard, lowered his curly head, peered over his bifocals and carried on, muttering once again.

"That's right," Pru chimed in. "Stick to why we came, what we have to do."

With an exasperated moan, Harriet turned back around,

unfolded her map and attempted to chart their progress, but not before reminding Emily they had a scheduled stopover for cream tea at Bovey Tracey.

After voicing her displeasure over any stopovers, Pru returned to her favorite subject. "Where is it we're staying exactly, Emily? How close to the moors? Close enough to check out the witch hut? And her stories about tricky Devon pixies? And the dreaded wisht hound in league with the Devil? Faithless wives and fickle maidens forced down the banks of the river? You said we could hike there, remember?"

Humoring Pru for a second, Emily noted that the manor house was close to the village in Dartmoor, which was famous for its 365 square miles of high moorland, valleys, and a scattering of quaint little villages. In the area, there were also Stone Age granite tors and circles, bogs, farms, boulder-strewn rivers, and streams. As for the witch's hut, if it existed, Emily would have to ask around.

Emily recited this cursory information while keeping her eyes on the road and watching for Harriet's next move.

Sure enough, as they drew close to Bovey Tracey, Harriet became agitated once again. Staring directly at Emily, Harriet said, "How much longer till we're there? I need to know."

"Any minute, Harriet."

It was now obvious. Harriet had no need for a Devon cream tea and gooseberry folly. She was anxious to make another call. To Miranda Shaw, perhaps, the owner of the ill-fated Tudor McMansion, who lived close by, perhaps in some attempt to get their stories straight, or who knew what? How she got hold of Miranda's number was anyone's guess. At any rate, this was Harriet's opportunity to bolt again.

Sitting stiffly upright, Harriet said, "Exactly how many more minutes, how many miles?"

That did it. Before Harriet knew what was happening, Emily swerved onto the 382, cut past the turn to Bovey Tracey, passed Lustleigh, and continued driving deeper and deeper into the outlying moorland. She finally slowed down, found an ideal spot by the side of the road and parked.

Gaping like a tourist, Pru jumped out of the car, not seeming to mind the careening drive a bit. Silas was glad for the chance to stretch his lanky legs and actually thanked Emily for getting on with it. Harriet was livid.

Unable to hold back any longer, Emily peered into the front passenger seat. "Look, Harriet," she said. "I passed the stopover to make sure there was no way you could skip out again. Sooner or later you're going to have to face whatever is eating at you and own up. But in any case, the villagers and neighbors are looking forward to this bankers' holiday. If you start taking it out on them like you've been taking it out on Pru and Silas or keep scampering here and there, the Twinning portion of the fete could very well get cancelled. Because there is no way the organizers will put up with any unpleasantness. For your information, the Twinning portion is just an afterthought for old times' sake. You go off on a tangent and just guess what'll happen to your flower judging, not to mention Pru's little storytelling stint, let alone Silas's meanderings about Lydfield's historic beginnings. In short, you're going to have to come to terms about being under the gun or whatever."

Harriet had no retort, as surprised as ever at Emily's newfound feistiness. She became withdrawn again and stayed in the car while everyone else took in the view.

"Oh, Emily," said Pru, "I'm getting story ideas already. It's just like you said, so wondrous and mysterious all at once."

From Pru's vantage point, there were nursery rhyme brown cows sprawled in the spongy grass in the foreground. Past the cows, the land fell away in greenish swatches until it came to rest by the granite turret of the ancient church, the remains of the old castle, and a corner of the village green. There the land began to roll up again until, at the very top, running east and west as far as the eye could see, the moor took over—purplish, stretching itself out under a slate-gray sky.

Spotting the verge of the moor, Pru said, "That must be it. The beginnings of all those pixie and ghost stories, and getting lost and coming across a mad hound. It's perfect."

Emily had no comment. She didn't recall telling Pru how wondrous it was all going to be. Gazing out at the verge and moorland shadows, only that same sense of uneasiness seemed apt.

Chapter Seventeen

A short time later, Emily pulled into the hidden track bracketed by hedgerows, and up to the circular drive fronting Penmead. They all got out; Emily went around and flipped open the trunk of the Vauxhall.

As if hearing a signal, Tinker, the loopy Irish setter, came tearing around the corner. Pru screamed as Tinker cornered her by the garden gate. It had slipped Emily's mind that Tinker was probably on the loose, seeking out any kind of mischief that, more often than not, included knocking over urns and gardening tools, ripping down hanging washing on the line, chasing scurrying critters and, if given the opportunity, snaring a small, childlike person. His feathered red forelegs rested on Pru's chest while he slavered and wagged his tail in sheer joy.

Silas muttered something unintelligible. Harriet turned away.

Emily was about to go to Pru's rescue when a series of claps and an amused "Do get down, Tinker" ended the sequence. The familiar, affected tone belonged to Trevor Eaves, the self-styled squire of the village and owner of the manor.

Tinker released his prey and was off on another spree. Pru still hadn't moved an inch, despite Trevor reassuring her that Tinker was incorrigible but harmless. Even after Trevor explained where their accommodations were located "below stairs," Pru remained frozen against the gate. When she spoke, all she could say was, "It was scary devilish. Like a wisht hound."

Offering Pru his arm, Trevor said, "No, no, not Tinker. It's all a lark, I promise you."

Perhaps it was Trevor's nonchalant manner, tweed suit, and trim mustache that did the trick. Perhaps he reminded Pru of some English storybook character. Whatever the reason, Pru nodded and dusted herself off.

All Emily could offer was "She's afraid of dogs. Guess I should have warned her."

"Nonsense," said Trevor. "Good to see you, Emily. You're looking fit as ever."

Emily countered with the usual pleasantries, reintroduced Harriet—whom Trevor had previously met during a trip to the Connecticut hills—and introduced Pru and Silas. Pru curtsied and thanked Trevor for coming to her rescue. Silas nodded and made some vague historical reference to the sister village across the pond. Harriet barely nodded. Trevor seemed to take note of Harriet's reserve but disregarded it.

The little incident over, Trevor escorted Pru past the formal gardens around the side of the country home. Emily helped with the luggage, took Pru off Trevor's hands, and got her settled. After making sure Silas and Harriet were accommodated at opposite ends of the long narrow hallway in the old servants' quarters, she went to speak with Trevor outside.

While waiting for him, Emily reacquainted herself with the layout and the contrast of textures that made up the eighteenth-century structure; hard and soft weathered stones of different hues—honey, golden, creamy-white, greenish-blue and slate—very unlike Miranda's makeshift facsimile back home.

Thoughts of Miranda's McMansion set Emily's mind off and running again as she strolled around to the rear of the property. She sat on a stone bench, taking in the soft air, heavy with the scent of hawthorn, larch, and beauty-berry shrubs, grateful once again for a diversion to break the tension.

After a time, Tinker returned, racing at full clip. Emily watched him bound through the concealed garden, down the slope, and across the stony outcrop. Then, changing direction, he ran up the rise, away from the manor house toward the folly, circled it twice and left the property altogether. Tinker's pointless chase seemed like a signal, especially the spin around the folly, that miniature replica of the village castle during Norman times.

"There it is," her old soccer coach used to say. "Confusing motion with action."

She allowed her thoughts to drift aimlessly into the hues of gray that smudged the late-afternoon sky. She did so even though she still had no inkling what in the world Harriet actually had in mind.

But hard as she tried, she couldn't shake the off-again, on-again sense of unease. Then, unbidden, the last words

Chris spoke to her over the phone crossed her mind. His by-me. *If this is ever going to get fixed, it's by my hand.*

Emily nodded. "By my hand."

Chapter Eighteen

After sitting by herself for a short time, Emily caught sight of Trevor ambling toward her.

"Odd lot you've brought us this time," said Trevor, gesturing toward the old servants' entrance. "That bit of a phone warning you gave me was spot on."

"About Harriet, you mean. I just meant it as what we call a heads-up."

"Precisely. Not at all the same person we'd met in passing at your Connecticut White Flower Farm. She appears to have gotten rather sullen. And, I daresay, a bit overbearing. She spoke harshly to her siblings and made a few uncalled-for remarks, if you like."

Trevor gave one of his subtle looks of disapproval. "Must spare my invisible Constance, you know."

Emily guessed his wife Constance still hadn't come to terms with the financial necessity of taking in lodgers. Though Trevor would often comment "Needs must," she left it to Trevor and the housekeeper and cook to ensure her path never crossed with the paying guests. If ever they did, she moved past silently as Trevor's "invisible Constance," leaving it to Trevor and the housekeeper and cook to come up with some pretext.

Getting to the point, Trevor said, "You see, only last week, a few below stairs confronted Constance with some trivial complaint or other. And now—given the festivities at hand and what with visitors from Newton Abbot, Dunsford, Okehampton, and all round—if what I've just encountered, and what Constance may also have been privy to, is any indication . . ."

"I know, Trevor. But you see, the Curtises have had a misunderstanding. I realize what it would do to your balancing act if Harriet continues to carry on and upsets Constance. I certainly don't want any of this to spill over into the fete. That's why I called you from Bath and why I spelled it out to Harriet only a short while ago. But evidently it still hasn't gotten through."

As if on cue, Constance emerged from the formal rose garden. Standing almost directly above them in her lacy summer frock, she beckoned to Emily. Emily complied, recalling that Constance was so shy that, when distraught, she was given to writing notes.

The moment Emily reached her side, Constance said in a half whisper, "I don't know what to make of this." Handing Emily a crumpled piece of Harriet's stationary, she said, "Perhaps, Emily, you could . . . decipher this. I found it among the roses."

The cryptic note read, *Can't go on like this. It's all about to come undone. By tomorrow. Believe me.*

Emily couldn't decide whether Harriet had had second thoughts about writing the note and threw it away or

Pru had come across it and tossed it at the roses as some pixilated counter to Harriet's threat. In any event, Emily had to come up with some way to defuse the situation.

Joining the two of them and glancing at the note, Trevor said, "Ah, yes. As I was telling Emily, this sort of thing won't do. However, my darling, Emily has given me reassurances."

"Yes," said Emily, repeating the excuse she'd given at Darlington House. "Put it down to nerves. Harriet has never judged a flower show this big before, let alone crossed the ocean and dealt with jet lag. I'll do my best to keep her contained."

At the same time, Emily didn't really want Harriet contained. She wanted to give her enough slack to expose herself. Apparently, Harriet truly was at sixes and sevens at this point. Leaving her siblings in the lurch and opting for a great deal of "time and space" hadn't panned out. And now it seemed that Doc was in hot pursuit. Harriet was getting cornered and would have to retaliate. At the moment though, the only option was to keep a lid on things and count on the possibility it really would all spill over tomorrow. Maybe, given Harriet's ego and more pressure on Emily's part, nothing really dicey would happen until after the flower show. In this way, keeping up the juggling act, Emily could fulfill the key element of her tour contract, remain in Trevor and Constance's good graces and, soon after, implicate Harriet with some "tangibles."

There was still no way, however, Emily could do this

on her own. Deciding then and there to set something up, Emily said, "Mind if I use your phone? I assume Maud is still pulling pints at the pub?"

"Indeed," said Trevor, flashing his supercilious smile to defuse any further unpleasantness. "Maud is still the publican. Still our loquacious innkeeper."

"Excuse me," said Constance, "but should things continue in this odd manner . . ."

Winging it, Emily said, "Remember when I escorted your contingent to the Connecticut gardening tour, and you found Harriet quite orderly and proper? Which was why, in your capacity as honorary chairwoman, you invited Harriet here and broached the idea of a sort of mini-Twinning, reminiscent of the days when the sister villages made a full-fledged exchange?"

"Indeed," said Trevor. "We offered to provide the accommodations, as it were."

"Exactly," said Emily, discounting the troubled look on Constance's face. "Now about the phone?"

"Feel free," said Trevor, flashing that affected smile again.

"Thanks. I appreciate it."

Making her way past the rose gardens and entering the glassed-in conservatory where they kept the coveted upstairs landline, Emily thought about handing the ball over by hooking up with Constable Hobbs. He should already be installed at the Village Green, keeping an eye out for undesirables like pickpockets at the fete. If the timing was right, Harriet would get caught red-handed pursuing whatever subterfuge she had in mind.

The call to Maud at the pub was nearly impossible due to the din in the background. All Emily could gather was that Maud was glad to hear from her but much too busy to chat on the phone. She did say someone was inquiring after her but would fill her in if Emily could "pop round." This meant Emily would have to make arrangement to appease Pru, Silas, and Harriet in the interim.

She returned to the formal garden and found Constance gone and Trevor strolling about. Getting Trevor to humor Pru while Emily slipped out for a little while was relatively easy. He'd taken a liking to Pru and would gladly take her on a few strolls to keep her occupied. As for Silas, Trevor suggested a walk on his own to the folly after Trevor apprised him of the rise and fall of the actual castle.

Next, Emily pulled Harriet aside. "Harriet, I hope you realize that now you've got Trevor and his wife on edge. She found your note all crumpled up in the rose garden. I don't know if you tossed it there or maybe Pru . . . In any case, you are cutting it really close."

Predictably, Harriet didn't answer. She just abruptly turned away. Nonetheless, to occupy Harriet's time, after talking it over with the staff, Emily suggested a cream tea to make up for bypassing Bovey Tracey, followed by a cook's tour of the hidden garden beyond the stone wall in the rear of the property.

Settled without a response from Harriet, Emily took Pru aside as well.

"Pru, I've more or less got Harriet squared away. I'm going out for a little bit to check out the lay of the land."

"Good," said Pru. "I've had quite enough of her, and I

certainly wouldn't mind some more attention from Trevor. With his tight-knit blond hair, graying temples, sharp little nose, and upright carriage, he reminds me of a queen's consort."

"Then it's settled. I'll be right back."

Granted some breathing room away from the worrisome trio, Emily drove off through the long stretch of hedgerows leading out of the estate. Ironically, and for no reason, her automatic e-mail response came to mind.

Hi, I'm off on another hidden UK adventure and will get back to you just as soon as I return. I can't tell you how much fun and excitement each day brings.

Chapter Nineteen

The smudged-gray pattern of the sky held steady. Emily took the meandering back roads with ease until she reached the triangular stonework around the traditional Green. Due to the number of cars, she had to circle back and park well short of the High Street.

Hurrying along, she soon found herself surrounded by villagers dressed in outlandish garb and greeted revelers who remembered her from previous jaunts. All were headed for the village hall behind All Angels, the ancient granite church with a spire that served as a landmark for miles around. Everyone seemed to be in good spirits, eager to take part in the final dress rehearsal for the annual parody, always a highlight of the fete. In fact, everyone she met remarked how it was going to be more of a lark than ever as men took on female roles in a spoof called *Chippy Chippy Bang Bang*.

One young lady even invited Emily to join in. "No problem, love. Even if you're hopeless, everything comes up trumps."

Giving her and her companions a "Thanks anyway," Emily promised to catch the show tomorrow night and continued on her way.

She strode past the familiar slate and granite of the

shop and post office, tea garden, and bistro to her right, and Moorpark garage and petrol station opposite.

At the point where the High Street became a bit steeper, more costumed players ran by, cutting across the path by the ancient gravestones and exiting behind the great stretch of the twelfth-century church. Beyond the church, she could make out the outline of marquees lining the greensward, all propped-up like huge party tents for tomorrow's festivities. The site would easily accommodate the mini-Twinning and, at the same time, swallow it up.

She kept walking toward her rendezvous with Maud the innkeeper. But as soon as she reached the ruins of the old castle, she hesitated.

It wasn't the sight of the stone mound and curtain wall around the remains of the castle keep. Nor was it the image of the open stone staircase that tumbled down to the basement of the dungeon four stories below. Not the steep slope of the earthworks on the other side either. She'd often taken her charges to this very spot and even described some of the bloody battles that took place during Norman times. What caught her attention was the figure leaning against the ancient wall, probably in his early twenties. There, in the deepening shadows, wearing a black hooded sweatshirt, he took slow drags on a cigarette. Just as slowly, he pulled his hood back and revealed the shock of his spiked red hair. Giving Emily a weird salute, he took another deep drag, turned away, and flipped the still-lit butt down the stone staircase. Pivoting back around, he gave another salute and pointed a forefinger directly at her.

Shrugging it off, Emily kept walking until the ground leveled off at the entrance to the Elizabethan Castle Pub. Inside, she spotted Maud behind the lamp-lit oak bar. With her beaming face, white hair tied in a bun, and sleeves rolled up her ample arms, she went about her business pulling pints under the bowed ceiling while cheerfully acknowledging Emily's presence.

"Ah, now there she is," said Maud above the noise of customers arguing over Labour's plight, caught between economics and Tory aspirations.

Emily cut between the debaters, raised her voice, and asked Maud about the message or whatever it was that she had received.

"Sorry, dear," Maud hollered back. "Can't hear above the chatter, now can I?"

Springing from behind the bar, Maud steered Emily through the crowd and around to the snug. The alcove under the hand-hewn beams offered some relief from the banter. An assortment of hanging ox yokes, eel traps, and framed stuffed pike covered the walls.

"Fancy a pot of tea?" Maud asked. "And a ploughman's plate with stilton and grapes, if memory serves? Glad you're here for the fete. Lovely, lovely." Maud wiped down the scarred, old table with a damp cloth. "And a bit of a Twinning, you say."

"Can you tell me about the message?" Emily asked, trying to get past Maud's nattering. "And I was also wondering about where I could find Constable Hobbs."

"Our roving constable is anywheres at present, but will

be by tomorrow for certain. Usual time, I shouldn't wonder, once it gets under way."

"Not till then?"

Maud paused mid-motion. "Why? Is there something dodgy in the offing? Perk things up? That's the spirit."

"Speaking of dodgy, Maud, what about the hooded slacker hanging around by the ruins?"

"Caught your eye, eh?" said Maud. "Bit of a tearaway, our Cyril is. Waiting for that party who was asking for you, I'll wager."

"Come on, Maud, talk to me. Who called? And how does this Cyril character figure in?"

Distracted by the voices from the bar reaching a higher decibel, Maud said, "There they go again. But you know the way of things during the fete, and me not wanting to shout out anyone's private business."

Emily's tea was unceremoniously plunked down in front of her as another group entered the bar and started clamoring for service. Maud dashed off before Emily could say another word.

When she returned a few minutes later, Emily pressed on. "So you were saying?"

"Right. The caller with Cyril in tow. The former sounding a bit worse for wear. Quite knackered, more like."

Again, Maud was called away to the bar. But no further description was needed as Doc's stocky form barged in through the throng and headed straight for the snug.

Chapter Twenty

"Hey, it's not like we got some moral dilemma here," said Doc, prodding his mincemeat pie with a fork. "I'm talking strictly business."

Emily scooted to the edge of the settle opposite him as she confronted Doc's blunt features and closely cropped gray hair. He was wearing a rumpled navy-blue parka over a thick polo shirt and was bearing in on her with no attempt whatsoever at being amenable. It wasn't enough that Emily was up against a cornered Harriet Curtis, who was clearly up to no good, but now, she had to factor in Doc and this newly acquired sidekick Cyril as well.

Taking another swig from his tankard of ale, Doc carried on. "I mean, here you are on your own. So you must've ditched the Curtises who, I know for a fact, have all hitched up. If you can do that, you can just as easy take me to Harriet. Then you can drop me at Bovey Tracey so I can take care of this other matter."

Emily's train of thought ran from Harriet to Miranda Shaw by way of Martha Forbes and possibly even Brian Forbes and back again as she continued to glare at him.

"And how about Martha?" Emily said. "And Miranda? How far does your 'taking care of business' go?"

"Never mind."

"Right."

"Hey, are you listening?" said Doc. "Don't tell me you still got it in for me. You need to skip the personal crap and start to wise up."

"Uh-huh."

"I mean it. So quit jerking me around about what I may have said or done or whatever else is rattling around in that brain of yours and stick to what I'm asking here."

Maud thrusted her broad face between them and asked how the "pair of Yanks" were faring. Emily shook her head, assuming Maud would pick up on the fact that Emily had been looking for Constable Hobbs and was wary of Doc and his dubious companion.

But Maud didn't pick up on anything. When she headed back to the bar, Doc gave up on the mince pie and dropped his fork on the plate.

"Okay. What's it gonna take?" Casting up his bleary eyes at the bowed ceiling, he added, "What with everything else, I gotta tell you, I really don't need this."

"Ditto," Emily said, doing her best to hold her own.

Shoving aside the tankard, Doc said, "Right, I get it, I got it. We each got a list, I'm on yours. Hey, give me a break. Things happen. Whichever way it shakes out, you use it."

"Like your new friend, Cyril."

"Absolutely like Cyril. I get to Bickington—don't ask me how—to find a place to crash. The landlady's flunky is hanging around. He carries my bag, he's hungry, he's available. He's from here, knows every inch, every angle, every corner."

"So you're all set."

"Get off it, will ya? The freakin' beer is warm, I'm starving, digging into some mystery-meat pie. On top of that, I got only a twenty-four-hour window. Which leaves me zip to play hopscotch here. So let's cut the tap dance, what do you say? Give me the skinny on where Harriet is hiding out. Don't drive me, I'll stick with Cyril's little crate. Whatever."

Rising from the table, Emily said, "Nothing has changed. So just cut me out of it."

"Oh, terrific," said Doc, blocking her way. "Fine, don't chip in, don't tell me where you got her stashed. She's got to show for the flower judging. I got the timetable on exactly when and where and that includes all three of the Curtis bunch."

"What do mean, 'all three'?"

"You're some piece of work, you know that? I tried making nice, I tried being reasonable. Forget about it. In this life you got your work cut out, you play it as it lays, and you don't take it personal!"

Doc shambled off, announcing to no one in particular that English food was lousy, which included fisherman's pie, sausage and mash, and bubble and squeak, "whatever in hell that was." After slapping some pound notes on the bar, he barged into the night as heedlessly as he'd barged in.

Emily lingered for a moment, taking in the notion of Doc's twenty-four-hour window. Subtracting a trip back to Bickington, food, sleep, and a hasty return, that would give him enough time to do what, exactly? Whatever it was, he would certainly start no earlier than the next morning at the opening of the fete.

Moving to the far corner of the bar, Emily ordered an Irish coffee and got hold of Maud the second she had a free moment.

"So what's the upshot?" Emily asked.

Brushing a hank of hair from her ample brow, Maud said, "Is it what our Cyril is capable of that you're wanting to know? Or is it, will our DC Hobbs leave off mucking about, which resulted in his present position? Which do you fancy?"

"I heard something about Hobbs's demotion," said Emily. "From detective sergeant to constable. Got it from Trevor."

"Too chummy by half, I'd say. Whilst not forgetting the last straw, up to the gills with a few pints, he was. Watching a rugby match on me own flat-panel telly when the sod was supposed to have been on surveillance in Brimley."

"But still, assuming he's learned his lesson, do you think he could handle a lady client who's up to something?"

Maud's shrug and roll of the eyes was not exactly reassuring.

"All right, how about this," said Emily. "When, at the earliest, would be a good time to run some police matters by our roving constable?"

"Well, seeing that it's yourself and not being at all like yourself, I will ring you as soon as I have word Hobbs is on duty and not larking about."

"That'd be great. But can I ask how you got hold of the number of the extension below stairs at Penmead? Given the fact that Constance wants little to do with the outside world?"

"And may I ask what dodgy business you've gotten yourself into?"

When Emily didn't bite, Maud smiled. "Ah, never you mind. So, my girl, we'll both keep our little secrets, now won't we?"

With nothing else for it, Emily nodded and let it go at that.

Outside in the damp evening air, Emily found no sign of Cyril and Doc. Except for the sounds of laughter coming from the village hall, the walk down the High Street past the castle ruins and the granite-walled Green was uneventful. So was the drive back under the darkened sky. Pulling in to Penmead, she found the old manor house to be quite still, a sign that perhaps everyone had turned in early. She shut off the engine, got out, closed the car door carefully so it barely made a clunk, and eased past the foliage by the formal garden. But after a few steps, Trevor appeared abruptly.

Steered by Trevor over to the trellised shadows, Emily could tell by the way he pressed his fingers to his lips that he was not too pleased.

"Did something happen?" asked Emily.

"Actually, yes and no. Amusing by some standards perhaps. Not to suggest that it wasn't a splendid idea for you to nip down to the village. However, you left me in charge, as it were."

Eventually, Emily managed to pry out of him that, first of all, he had no idea where this storytelling witch Pru had been carrying on about might actually reside. But he had drawn her a map, assuring her a horse and cart driver could take her past the crest of the High Street close to the edge of the moor where she might follow a well-worn path. He had suggested that perhaps she could investigate this dubious happenstance after her stint at the fete tomorrow morning.

"And need one point out," Trevor added, "it would be entirely your responsibility. As for brother Silas, he was quite vague, as seems his custom, but no bother. Be all that as it may, dame Harriet had commenced once again, threatening, according to what the housekeeper overheard, to take matters into her own hands by noon. This on the heels of my graciously putting up tomorrow's schedule below stairs, which was quite awkward enough, as it were. Constance's idea, actually, though it was posted all round the village. We thought it only fair that you and your charges should know the schedule beforehand. And with you gone, do you see?"

"Of course," Emily said, waiting for the upshot.

"But then to be privy to another of Harriet's tiresome threats. This time directly to her siblings."

"I'm so sorry, Trevor."

"I'm sure. But not to put too fine a point on it, this is not the Emily Ryder I've come to rely upon. Fit, unflappable, keeping everything quite under control. Perhaps, I dare say, a bit of the opposite."

"I know, I know. I'm working on it. I've even, just now, arranged for some backup. Thanks for your tip about Hobbs, by the way."

"Then you will see to it this nonsense does indeed end once and for all. And certainly by the time I take my customary stroll past the ruins, greeting all and sundry. And it's on into the snug where Maud will pour me a dram or two of Cragganmore to toast the festivities. The pungent, smoky maltiness, as it were, a topper to this time-honored ritual. You did intimate whatever our Harriet had in mind hinged on the flower judging, did you not? And that would be an end to it?"

"From all indications. She wouldn't be able to keep it going, now that she's put everyone on notice and announced a deadline."

"I see. Jolly good."

Obviously Trevor didn't see but had extended himself and didn't wish to pursue the matter any further. To Emily, the message was clear. Either she saw to it that the whole Harriet business was resolved by the conclusion of the flower show or Emily and her charges were no longer welcome at Penmead. Without another word, he proceeded back through the glassed-in conservatory at the front of the estate.

Emily continued to walk down and around to the rear. But, as she might have known, the day's activities weren't over yet.

A door squeaked by the old servants' entrance. Harriet appeared, paper bag in hand, heading toward the marble bench that sat above the path to the hidden garden. Just as she was about to plunk herself down and reach for one of her packets of shortbread, Tinker came flying out of the darkness, snatched up the bag and spun around, daring her to come after him. Harriet reached down, grabbed a stone and flung it. Tinker dodged the stone, wheeled around again, slinked in close, and waited for her next move. Lunging wildly, Harriet tripped over her own feet, fell onto one knee, and set Tinker barking.

Just as Emily came upon the scene, Pru and Silas opened the door by the old servants' entrance, catching sight of Harriet kneeling and wincing.

Tinker raced toward Pru, who ducked back inside. Silas followed suit, looking unsure of himself as always. As Emily offered Harriet a hand, Tinker flew off into the night, clutching the dangling paper bag prize in his teeth.

Pushing Emily away, Harriet righted herself and, in a voice uncharacteristically flat and cool, said, "Rest assured I shall fulfill my obligations at the flower festival. And then, finally, I can take matters into my own hands, no matter what the cost."

Not in the least interested in anything Emily had to say in response, Harriet went back inside.

Emily stood motionless until all was quiet again. She set off up the slope, well away from the manor house, headed toward the folly. In the past, a call at that elevation and at this time of night was good for at least a minute or two before the signal from her cellphone broke up.

She trudged along. As she approached the scraggly top of the rise, she hoped Will had absolutely nothing to report and would provide her with some much-needed small talk.

She paused close to the optimum spot, hit the primary number on the speed-dial, and waited. There was a strong enough signal but no answer. When she reached the crest, she tried again. This time she connected.

She was soon comforted not only by the easy Southern drawl, but the sound of folk music coming from an FM station in the background.

"Hi," said Emily. "I just wanted to check in to let you know I'm keeping my part of the bargain. Keeping a lid on everything, I mean."

"What time is it over there?"

"Oh, late. Don't worry about the time difference."

"Uh-huh."

"It's been a long day for me here, what with the trip from Bath to Devon. Tomorrow is the big day, so we need to start bright and early. This was my only chance to get back to you and find a high enough spot so the call could get through."

There was a slight delay before Will asked, "You behaving yourself?" as he stifled a yawn. "Has that Doc guy shown up there?"

"He has no idea where we're staying. Besides, a constable I know will be on duty the whole time."

"Well, all right then. I mean, you never know."

Some part of her wanted to tell him everything. She was tired of being independent and intrepid, a thoroughly modern gal since heaven knows when. At the same time, she was fully aware of what that might lead to.

Feeling a bit chilly standing there in the overcast darkness, Emily deflected again and asked what he was listening to.

"Some folk station that always puts me under. Right now, it's an old Eagles song. You know, the one about not letting the wheels spinning in your brain drive you crazy."

"Good tip," Emily said, relieved this was going no further, stifling a yawn as well. "Only so much you can control."

"So they say. Oh, and your mom called again. I told her a little white lie and said everything was going just fine. Leaving out the development stuff and all."

Emily nodded to herself. Little white lie was a good way to put it.

Oliver let out a barely audible bark and Will excused himself to let Oliver out.

A damp breeze kicked in, mingling with a few rustling sounds. The signal began to break up when Will came back on the line. He bid her good luck with "the Twinning thing" before they said their muffled goodbyes.

Emily drifted back down the slope, still basking in the sweet, uneventful exchange. She stifled any notions about what Doc and Harriet had in store as her thoughts dwindled to a single wish—*if only tomorrow morning would come and go.*

Perhaps she was being as childish as Pru. But she wished it all the same.

Chapter Twenty-One

That volatile Friday began with a phone call from Maud. It wasn't clear whether Harriet had gone to the extension phone below stairs to make her own call, or whether she happened to be standing nearby and had picked up the second the phone rang. Whatever the case, Harriet could be clearly heard saying, "I don't understand. What constable? Where?"

Emily hurried out of the old parlor maid's quarters and snatched the receiver out of Harriet's hand, hoping that Harriet's grating voice hadn't disturbed Trevor and Constance in the master bedroom above.

Emily waited till Harriet had retreated a bit before saying, "It's Emily. Yes, Maud, go on."

"The message, love," said Maud, "is simply that our Hobbs, bright as a sixpence at this hour, would be jolly pleased to talk with you any time before things get underway."

"That's perfect. Thanks."

Emily hung up at once but had a hard time warding off Harriet's interference as Harriet continued asking about this constable's whereabouts and intentions. Soon enough, Pru came scurrying out of her room to see what all the fuss was about, and Silas emerged a moment later. Emily was then forced to hold a brief whispered conference well out of earshot in the oak-paneled hallway.

"As it happens," Emily said, "our stay here is hanging by a thread. Which means the Twinning portion and our whole itinerary is at stake if Trevor asks us to leave."

Cutting in, Harriet said, "Don't worry. It's all coming to a head."

Almost in tandem, Silas and Pru muttered, "Absolutely, has to stop . . . would ruin everything."

"Well," said Emily, directing the Curtises back to their respective rooms, "now that we all, finally, understand each other."

By the time breakfast was served in the old servants' morning room, things seemed to have taken a turn for the better. This was due in no small part to Silas and Pru's enthusiasm about exploring the village as soon as possible, making up for lost time, and getting on with their first stint on the posted schedule. The upbeat mood also seemed to rub off on Harriet just a bit, causing her to drop her veiled threats for the time being.

The order of the day called for Harriet to oversee the arrival of the flower show entries in the church vestry and organize their placement according to the defined categories. At the same time, Pru was scheduled to do a preview of her storytelling hour behind the church in the village hall, and Silas was to hold forth under one of the marquees in the far corner of the greensward. The marquee was also designated for the sale of tea and cakes, and Emily assumed Silas had been stationed there because the organizers thought he would be less lonely. No one had the heart to tell him that there may not be a great deal of interest on an early morn for a display of "memorabilia of the historical exchange of goods and services between the twin villages during the Colonial revolt." For the moment at least, Emily assumed her role as coordinator and guide.

Then, for some unknown reason, things got testy again. Silas eased out of his chair before he finished his egg-and-tomato omelet and returned immediately with his double-sided satchel. Harriet gave Silas an anxious look. The cook, a woman with gaunt no-nonsense features, offered to move the satchel to "keep things running ever so smooth between servings."

Silas replied, "No, no. Have to keep at the ready. Have everything in hand. Yes, yes, making sure, at all times."

Giving Silas a hateful glance, Harriet said, "Oh, really? Just you wait."

Silas closed his eyes and started counting to ten. "One for the money, two for the show . . . three to get ready and . . ."

Before Silas reached the count of four, Harriet pushed herself away from the table and stalked off.

Pru had nothing to offer except, "Uh-oh. There she goes again."

Emily had no idea what to make of this.

After the hasty breakfast, there was another hitch. Pru pulled Emily aside in the car park, glanced over her shoulder, and started in again. "You have to stick by me. Not like last night when you were gone, and that horrible beast was on the loose, and Harriet was back at it. You saw her just now. What if she actually does do something terrible?"

"I will keep my eye out."

"You mean it?"

"Good God, Pru, what does it take?"

Mulling it over, Pru looked up at the scudding dark clouds and nodded. "Yes, of course. You'll make sure. Act as lookout. And speaking of making sure, do you have your compass on you?"

To humor her, Emily snapped to attention, said, "Never fear," and patted one of her windbreaker pockets.

"Good," said Pru. Pointing down at her feet, she said, "I've got new walking shoes on plus an L.L. Bean sportsman watch with a luminous dial, and my topper is all set in the back seat. I followed your instructions."

"Look, Pru, let's forget about the hike in the moor and see if we can get through the next few hours. Agreed?"

Pru thought this over and said, "Okay, understood. I'm getting ahead of myself, aren't I? Harriet's threat isn't till noon. But what threat exactly? Can you tell me? Can you give me a clue?"

"Who knows? That's the whole point, isn't it? She's holding all the cards."

Emily slipped behind the wheel of the Vauxhall. Within seconds, Pru was right behind her, saying, "It's all hope and fear. That's what it is. And that's what makes for a good story."

Not bothering to answer this time, Emily switched on the ignition. Almost immediately, the other two took their customary positions and they were off.

Needless to say, the tension between Harriet and her siblings remained palpable. Emily met little traffic on the lane on the way to the approach to the village and, in short order, managed to find a parking space.

The silence between the Curtises continued during the saunter past the triangular-walled Green, the shops and petrol station closed for the holiday, and the clamber farther up the High Street to the gravestones and the ancient church. All the while, the three of them seemed to be girding themselves, flush with excitement and wary of what the morning might bring.

In the meantime, the scudding clouds had given way to a wash of slate gray, which was of some concern to Emily in light of Pru's fixation on taking a hike.

Back to her immediate concern, however, Emily surveyed the scene in all directions, looking for the local constable. The potential machinations of Doc and Cyril made Hobbs's presence all the more critical.

As more villagers began straggling in, Emily thought she caught a glimpse of Cyril's spiky red hair. Peering down the High Street in the direction of the Green, she could swear it was him darting between the tea garden and the all-purpose shop and post office. Then again, she'd turned so quickly it might have been the cascades of hanging baskets, their trailing clusters of flaming petals contrasting against the lavender, periwinkle, and whites.

Sloughing it off for the moment, catching up with the Curtises, she was immediately greeted by the Parish Council members. Gracious as ever, the jolly greeters gave everyone a cordial welcome.

A moment later, Harriet cast her gaze farther up the street and froze. The object of her attention was the uniformed figure of Hobbs ambling past the castle ruins and headed in their direction.

The next thing Emily knew, Harriet, Pru, and Silas were whisked away to their respective posts. Harriet kept glancing back and was soon out of sight.

Emily waited until Hobbs's ruddy face and beefy form was upon her.

"Well, well," said Hobbs, breaking out in a toothy grin, "if it isn't our Emily. I've had my eye out for you, lass, and here you are."

"I'll bet. With the other eye on your bangers and kippers."

Emily was teasing him, both out of force of habit and as a way of stalling, having no idea how to broach the subject, let alone what Cyril might be up to and Doc's whereabouts. She thought about beginning with Harriet's warnings, which, of late, had drawn the attention of Trevor and Constance. However, knowing Hobbs from past tours, he would put it down as an annoyance and nothing more. Anything to keep things on an even keel. She certainly couldn't go into the circumstances surrounding Chris Cooper's death and Doc's relentless pursuit. There was no way to put any of this succinctly and, even if she could, what would Hobbs make of it while greeting everyone in sight?

Not one to stand a lull, even for a moment, Hobbs said, "'Bangers and kippers?' It's my eyes only on my breakfast, is it? Or have you summoned me to admire my fine black uniform? Only temporary, mind, in honor of the occasion." Waving to a gaggle of middle-aged women carrying bins of bric-a-brac, Hobbs said, "So out with it, lovey. What is it you're wanting now you've got me all to yourself?"

Stepping forward in a bogus offer to help the ladies, Hobbs gave Emily a conspiratorial wink, knowing full well the women would claim they were hale and hearty enough to have a go without any assistance. Which they summarily did.

"Well, go on, go on," Hobbs said, back at Emily's side while eyeing a group of villagers armed for the white elephant sale.

"How about crime prevention?" Emily said. "And incriminating behavior?"

"With a possible spot of bother to do with Cyril, the wild rover, and a thick-set bloke of your own acquaintance. Maud gave me fair notice, you see."

Hobbs doffed his cap a few more times at a new set of passersby.

Worried that Hobbs's attention span was getting shorter and shorter in ratio to the number of villagers spilling in, Emily said, "Okay. First off, I'm sure I spotted Cyril in the past few minutes."

"Whilst I caught a glimpse of him scurrying round the earthworks. Quite typical, I'd say."

"Of what? What is he capable of?"

Pausing to retrieve the lid of a silver teapot that rattled on the pavement, Hobbs doffed his service cap once more, shook his head, and eyed the checkered black-and-white band that, doubtless, reminded him of his demotion. In return, the elderly lady tilted her straw hat as well, thanked him for his gallantry, and bade him a very good morning.

The service cap apparently did the trick as Hobbs went into Cyril's infractions. "Capable of what, you ask? Slapping his mum around. Making off with all manner of goods including horses and sheep for barter. Plus the odd scrapes with other lads, including breaking a few bones here and there. Will that do you?"

"And," Emily chimed in, "for a price, driving a wily Yank around, probably in a stolen car. I mean, who knows?"

"Or any number of silly buggers."

"So," Emily said, cutting it short, "what we've got here is a prankster and a smalltime hood at the service of a New York, streetwise guy called Doc."

"Ah. Is that the long and short of it?"

Pushing it despite herself, Emily said, "Tied in with the fallout from a possible recent felony back in my sister village in Connecticut, coming to a head on your watch in a few hours, involving one of my clients."

"Coming to a head you say?"

"By noon, if I'm not mistaken."

"And what is to happen, if I might inquire?"

Making her case as best she could, Emily noted the convergence of Doc, Cyril, and Harriet. She pointed out that Harriet was the one who had just gawked at Hobbs and froze as he made his way down, had recently made a number of threats, and was involved and in flight from a suspicious death.

"Something to do with being under the gun and an accessory," Emily said, pushing it, "and taking matters into her own hands. All of which is about to have serious consequences."

Taking in Hobbs's broad smile, Emily admitted, "Okay, I haven't a clue what those consequences might be. If I'm all wet, if I've been overloading the circuit the past few days, if by noon nothing happens, I'll go back to the drawing board. But if something does develop, I'll pass it on and am counting on you to intervene."

"And, by God's good graces, I shall tally all the incriminating details and soon be shed of this ever so temporary uniform and be back in harness." Still smiling, Hobbs turned his attention to the thickening tumble of slate-gray cloud cover.

"Tell me, lass, you haven't begun playing at Miss Marple and the like?"

"I am not playing. I've taken this deadly seriously and carefully monitored all the goings-on."

Offering a mock salute to another group of women and a few elderly men in cardigans and corduroys, Hobbs looked at Emily directly and said, "So, this is either a load of rubbish or, if we stretch it far and wide, a rather dodgy game. What Cyril and some sod from America might do, crossed with some lump of a woman making idle threats, makes my vote for a load of rubbish."

With more people streaming in from the Green and carrying on, all Emily could say was, "Fine. Just humor me, that's all I ask."

For his final answer, Hobbs widened his grin and held his hands up to the ever-darkening sky as if asking for divine intervention. "With heaven as my witness, I shall keep a watchful eye for anything untoward."

Emily had done all she could. If nothing else, the

situation was contained for now. The action was set to take place, or not, in a little more than three hours.

With a little luck, the preliminary activities of the mini-Twinning would consist of a trial run, then segue to a full-fledged, rural Devon fete. Soon, Tom, the slow-and-deliberate farmer's son, would have his horse and cart ready at the Green. Anyone who wanted a ride and a closer look at the wild Dartmoor ponies could hop on board.

The main events would start at noon. There would be games like "Whacking" a furry beanbag as it dropped down a long tube and reached the red spot, and "Timbola," where players reached into a wooden box in the hope of plucking a winning prize number. Under a nearby marquee, dressed like some B-movie gypsy, giggling Nell would do her Tarot readings and funny fortune telling. There would be a dog show, raffles to raise money for the Parish, three-legged races, sack races, and what-have-you.

Later on, the first performance of *Chippy Chippy Bang Bang* would take place with the usual local jokes, silly costume changes, and a goofy orchestra blowing on homemade instruments. As was the custom, a queen would be portrayed by some hairy farmer, attended by five local lads in wings and stingers dressed as bumblebee dancers. If all went according to plan, no mayhem would take place and all of Emily's anxieties and calculations would amount to zip.

Emily took a quick peek into the church hall and spotted a perky-looking Pru on stage, affecting a passable English accent, pretending she was a Devon pixie. A small group of village kids sat cross-legged on the floor directly below her in rapt attention.

Emily exited the hall, passed by the preparations under way under the marquees and circled around the far side of the church. There she spied Cyril again, threading his way in her direction past the ancient grave markers. Emily started to head toward him but was cut off by a few mothers carrying little children, joined by others toting various objects.

Then Cyril was gone and she couldn't say in what direction.

She glimpsed into the cool stoniness of the vestry. In full view were stiff wooden pews and buckets and baskets of all sorts of flowers including multiple shades of scented English roses. Beyond the mass of flowers, the ancient wooden pews and, to the side, the honesty box where a donation of fifty pence was welcome.

But there was no sign of Harriet.

Emily searched here and there and finally caught sight of her ungainly form making her way back to the High Street. Harriet had no sooner turned the corner when she was stopped in her tracks by a swarm of ladies carrying more floral offerings. Despite her protests, they ushered Harriet back across to the church grounds. As far as Emily could tell, one of the members of the Parish Council had intercepted and was politely scolding her and outlining her duties. She was to be at her post to receive and arrange all the entries. An interval would follow where she was to tend to the judging and final prizes.

After the council members left her to carry out her appointed tasks, there was a moment of calm until Pru popped out of nowhere wearing a storybook apron. She steered Emily over to the weathered tombstones by the church's front walkway.

"What is Harriet doing?" asked Pru. "I saw her trying to sneak out."

"All I know is she's been told to remain at her post. And what about you?"

"I was doing fine. I was a Devon pixie doing Ichabod Crane from Connecticut. You get the connection? Lydfield, in the Connecticut hills, linked with Lydfield-in-the-Moor. I did Ichabod by transforming myself into a gangly rubber band with a swiveling head like a weathervane, which the kids all giggled at. But out of the corner of my eye, I spotted Harriet scurrying around. I couldn't go on, couldn't concentrate. She is so-o-o obviously up to no good."

Grasping Pru's tiny shoulders, Emily said, "I can't do this."

"Can't do what?"

"Coddle you while trying to keep everyone in check."

Pru's eyes flitted back and forth. "Everyone? Harriet, you mean."

"Look, do me a favor, will you? Just go back to what you were doing. I'm sure the kids are waiting for you."

The mist drifted in and the temperature dropped a few more degrees. Pru buttoned her topper partway and glanced at her watch. Then she scrunched her little face and gazed up at the sky. "So much to deal with, so little time. I'm counting on you, Emily."

Without another word, Pru turned and scooted off.

Emily positioned herself between the long stretch of the church and the High Street some thirty yards behind. In this way, if she came across any difficulty, she could notify Hobbs who had stationed himself behind the church, close to the main marquee.

More villagers passed to her right and left, adding to the holiday mood, oblivious of the inclement weather. A few lumbering farmers who looked to be already tipsy, tugged on a hand cart loaded with drums of various sizes, stopping every now and then to beat out a rhythm to announce their presence.

More time passed. Two muscular men carrying a lopsided ring-toss booth moved past her, all the while arguing over a soccer match.

"Mate, it was a clean header that won the day," one said.

"Nah, it was a twitchy rebound from a wide kick against the crossbar," the other one countered.

Emily stepped forward to catch more of the argument as the two rival fans dropped the cumbersome booth on its side. She was drawn in by a world she knew, one with a level playing field and referees who'd slap you with a yellow card if you flagrantly broke the rules. A world with boundaries and a time limit. A world you could follow that made perfect sense.

"Bollocks," said the one with the close-cropped blond hair. "You lost the bloody wager, Rob. And you're clean forgetting how Dawes threaded it to Havers who settled the ball in full stride and sent it bang past the sweeper."

"Far back in the thirtieth minute, mind."

"And lovely all the same."

Apparently noting Emily's presence, playing to her as both audience and referee, the two carried on and became more animated.

"Brilliant," said the darker-haired one. "Whilst our lads kept it up, attacking all the while, your lot sat on its heels."

"Keeping your lot at bay, controlling throughout. And what about Havers's powerful header in the seventy-third minute from Morley's spot-on corner kick?"

"Who gives a toss? When it counted, who found the seams? A perfect touch, I'd say. Bloody perfect!"

This went on for several more minutes. More talk about offense and defense, each and every maneuver out in the open. Something Emily would give anything for at this point.

At an impasse, the bickering duo waved to Emily, hoisted their lopsided booth, and pressed on, circling around the church toward the burgeoning preparations.

Shortly after, an agitated Silas worked his way toward her against the flow of the oncoming crowd. Grimacing and peering over his bifocals, he said, "Ah, Emily. How to put it? Safeguarding . . . keeping things safe . . ."

At first, Emily paid no attention, assuming he was muttering about some papers he'd mislaid.

Flustered, Silas spoke louder. "Look at the weather. You must catch up . . . yes, you must, you must, before it all goes too far."

"Okay, Silas, what are you saying?"

He pointed somewhere into the distance up the High

Street and then frantically peered back at her. "Go now," Silas said, "while there's still time."

Emily looked up the High Street, in the direction Silas had been pointing.

Glancing back, Silas muttered, "Oh, my satchel, my things, must look after them. Must look after everything."

"Talk to me, Silas. For once, give it to me straight. What do you mean 'go'? Go where?"

"To the moor . . . by now, I suppose. Yes, yes, certainly by now. No good if something happens to Pru. No good, no good at all!"

Chapter Twenty-Two

By the time Emily reached Tom's horse and cart at the crest of the High Street, the mist had come down and the fog had rolled in. It was far damper and cooler than down below on the church grounds, so much so that Emily had to zip up her windbreaker and fasten the hood.

"I told her, miss," said Tom, his beanpole frame above her gripping the reins. "Of the dangers, spongy turf, prickly gorse and bracken, and such."

Snatching the compass out of her side pocket, Emily figured that Pru had at least a fifteen-minute head start. By now, she was certain to be disoriented, unknowingly headed down a sharp-sided ravine. Or in the direction of rushing water. Or meandering close to a mire or sucking peat bog or whatever in the world she might be getting herself into.

"But you see, miss," said Tom, "she was turning her head."

"Looking back like she was being followed?"

"Doing a runner, more like."

"Running from Cyril, or a stocky guy, or both?"

"No telling."

"Okay, I get it, Tom. I'll need you to stay put."

"That I will, my dray horse and me. Promised the little lady we'd be right handy, now didn't I?"

"That's good," said Emily, getting more and more concerned. "Now you're sure the map she had was of the beaten path? Up over the stile, past the stone walls and old farm buildings, and then the open moorland?"

"And a shepherd's hut between, I tell her. But no witch person or hut hereabouts. Not on the map Mr. Trevor drew. None at all. So which is it, a witch hunt or doing a runner?"

In too much of a rush to humor him, Emily poked around the back of the cart for some bright orange bags.

"Did she take one?" Emily asked.

"No, but I give fair warning. Those are signal bags if needs be, if the fog is too thick, I tell her. If you're lost, if you go too far."

"Okay," Emily said, snatching up two of the plastic bags in case. "You just sit tight."

Setting out, Emily hoped Pru had enough sense to hold still as soon as she realized no one was following her, not under these conditions. Whoever it may be had surely turned back. What's more, after hearing from both Trevor and Tom, she must have realized that her witch hunt was totally foolish. Then again, knowing Pru . . .

But Emily didn't know Pru, not really. Only what she seemed to have become lately, only more so. As pixilated as can be. And Emily certainly had no idea what Pru was like under pressure. The most sensible thing to do under the circumstances was wait until the fog lifted. And assume

Silas had alerted Emily to her flight and that Emily would guess Pru had enlisted Tom and his cart.

However, it was also possible that Pru had panicked, still believing in a kindred spirit she could call upon, and gone off the beaten path in search of the witchy woman's shelter. And was now floundering around, getting herself deeper in trouble. Despite her new walking shoes and adrenalin, frail Pru was not a hiker and completely unfamiliar with the terrain.

Emily took the narrowing track in stride, climbed over the stile through the break in the stone wall, and turned left. Though she'd never attempted this trek in a dense fog, she was fit and an experienced hiker, and knew more or less where she was.

She told herself that chances were good that Pru couldn't have gotten very far.

Able to make out the outline of the file of rock-pile fences, she pressed on, noticing the occasional tin roofs of the dilapidated farm buildings on her right. Her only immediate concern was tripping over the cattle grids, those gapped rusty bars dating back to the days of hauling and trundling.

Next, with that hurdle passed, she gauged the probable distance between herself and Pru before the mist and fog had closed in.

After a time, the ground rose and the silhouette of abandoned outbuildings fell away. Barely able to make out anything more than thirty feet ahead, Emily slackened her pace and tried to recall the lay of the land. In the near distance, there should be heather spreading out in all directions, sometimes as high as three feet, ordinarily edged in purple, but probably turning a grayish green at present. If memory served, the heather would merge with the moorland grasses. There would also be tangles of briars, head-high nettles, and lashes of brambles and thorns left and right of the beaten path, which would force Pru onto rocky hard going. Prickly gorse bushes and bracken would block her way like Tom had warned her, harboring green grass snakes with yellow markings behind their heads or an adder, with its zigzag stripe down its back and poisonous bite. An adder bite would do Pru in, leaving her writhing on the ground with no way to get her back in time.

So much for the "she couldn't have gotten very far" scenario but dismissing all thoughts of a snakebite, Emily pushed ahead.

She checked her compass. As far as she could tell, she was still in or around the path and hoped Pru hadn't strayed more than a hundred yards off course.

She called out. She called out again. There was no response, which told her that Pru hadn't at all done the sensible thing and stayed put and waited. With no other recourse, Emily picked up the pace and hurried on.

Emily wondered what she should have done instead of racing out here into the moors. She might have consulted with Hobbs, but that would have meant threading through the crowds and losing precious time. She could have told Silas to tell Hobbs she was leaving and for Hobbs to be on the alert. But on the alert for what? Besides, Silas had turned on his heels, much too distracted to take in anything Emily might have called out.

Just then, something caught her eye far up ahead. She couldn't tell if it was a figure, a weird twisted shape, or her imagination working overtime. Whatever it was, it was accompanied by a rustling sound. Then another. It could have been a woodcock or a fox. Or some meadow pipits or rabbits venturing out of their warrens.

Straining her eyes, all she could make out was a faint fluttering. Moving closer, she saw the grasses had been parted. A few yards closer and she came upon a stunted oak, twisted out of shape by seasons of untrammeled wind. As for the fluttering, a piece of Pru's apron was caught on the far edge of a gorse bush as high as Pru's waist.

Emily called out. Still no answer.

Checking her compass again, Emily's mind drifted to another set of worrisome alternatives. Finding herself engulfed in fog, Pru might have veered off the track, become startled by the specter of the tree, and run off farther to the right. That would head her in the worst possible direction. Eventually she'd hear the sound of the river below, which would put her close to a steep bank by the spongy peat beds. It would also put her in the vicinity of stretches of sphagnum moss. Once you stepped into the featherbed covering and began to struggle, it was over. You would sink over your head in no time flat and be gone.

A prospect equally as bad was skirting the bogs and mire, reaching the narrow riverbed, attempting to cross the rotting footbridge, and falling into the chilled, rushing water. Or, worse still, falling onto the slippery boulders below.

More over-the-top scenarios as fodder for Pru's campfire tales if she survived.

Emily called out again and waited. There was still no response.

She decided to drape one of the bright orange bags over the gorse bush and hang the other from a low-lying limb of the tree.

Switching to a more positive mode, Emily hoped that the moment Pru realized she was well off the track, she'd try to double back, spot the bright bags once the fog lifted, and use them as a marker. Failing that, if Pru had continued past the gnarled tree and bushes, she'd run smack into the thrusts of prehistoric granite. At that point, she'd at least surely have the good sense to stop in her tracks.

Opting for the latter, Emily adjusted her tack five degrees and headed for the stone circles.

A breeze kicked up and the mist and fog began playing tricks. Visibility opened up, enabling Emily to cover more ground and skirt around the gorse and bracken. Suddenly, as though changing its mind, the murk poured back in and it was back to silhouettes and brambles snagging her khaki slacks from all sides. When it began to drizzle as well, she tightened the hood of her windbreaker and trudged on.

She heard the bleat of sheep. Probably the ones with the light blue and crimson markings on their chests, stuck on a ledge somewhere. Or, due to their natural lameness, limping around bleating, as lost as scatter-brained Pru.

When the vista opened up again, Emily could make out rocky outcrops and a row of jutting granite shards, dappled in shades of purple and gray. If Pru had run into one of these, which were at a foot or more over her head, she would definitely have come to a halt.

But there was still no sign of her.

Emily glanced at her watch. It was almost twenty to eleven. Though she hadn't covered that much ground, she'd been tramping around for well over forty minutes. All the while, she'd kept Harriet's threats and the prospect of something impending by noon in the back of her mind. Which meant she had to catch up with Pru in the next fifteen minutes and, depending on the visibility, work her way quickly back.

Cutting through the stones, she immediately saw that she was surrounded by the symmetrical sites of prehistoric dwellings.

A chill ran through her. Drizzle continued to drip off her hood and find its way inside the windbreaker collar, trickling down her neck. Adding to everything else, given Pru's tiny frame, there was the danger of hypothermia. In all probability, it was only a few degrees above freezing.

A breeze blew a dent in the fog. The granite markers gave way, leaving only the scrubby undergrowth.

Then Emily finally heard it. It could have been a furry creature in dire straits. But as she drew nearer, it was more like a child's whimper fading off and on.

When the breeze kicked up again and the fog lifted, Emily could finally make out the scene in front of her. Inside a vast stone circle stood a shaggy Dartmoor pony, its eyes peering out through grayish-white forelocks, its long mane soaking wet, and its quarry, the tiny, flinching figure of Pru.

"Hold still!" Emily called out. "Don't move!" She wanted to add that the pony might kick or bite, but that would only add to Pru's panic.

Emily fully expected Pru to say something, to at least call out in gratitude. But she covered her face with her hands and didn't say a word.

Reaching the edge of the stone circle, Emily said, "Listen to me. Take one step back and then another, slow and easy."

But Pru remained rooted to the spot.

"Come on, Pru, you can't just stand there. You'll catch your death if you haven't already."

Pru pulled her hands away from her face but did little else.

"Look, there isn't time to wait him out. He might stand like that forever."

Still no response. Judging from the last episode with Tinker, the loopy Irish setter, the only solution was for Emily to step through the opening, stand in front of Pru, and back her out.

But Pru was so hesitant that even this simple maneuver seemed interminable. Emily had to back her away a few inches at a time. It was only when they had cleared the gap by a good four or five feet that Emily was able to shake Pru out of it and steer her away.

Shortly after, as if some switch had been turned on in her brain, Pru began to chatter inanely about the fog and the frightening shapes and the shaggy, dark creature. Letting her jabber away, Emily started doubling back.

"Do you think Tom might still be waiting with his

cart?" Pru asked, scrambling to keep up. "Oh, my, what an adventure."

Still doing her best to put up with her, Emily pointed out that Pru was shivering, needed to dry off as soon as possible, and her jabbering was only slowing them down.

Pru grew silent for a while then broke into another one of her flights of fancy.

"Oh, this is so-o-o good for story time. Pixies leading you astray in the soupy fog. Leaving you inside a stone circle to face your fate. But if you're strong of purpose, you won't be swallowed up by the fog or stomped on by the shaggy beast or ripped apart by the wisht hound. You'll be rescued by your trusty companion."

"Get it in your head," Emily said. "The fog can thicken again at any minute, you could come down with hypothermia, Silas is probably out of his mind with worry, people are waiting for you to perform and, last but not least, we've got the noontime ultimatum!"

Pru peeked at her watch and walked faster. "All right. But I did get rescued by a trusty companion. Now how about that?"

Emily and a now tractable Pru worked their way back. Pru managed to keep silent this time. Didn't even ask about the dangling bright orange bags that Emily snatched up as they passed by the gnarled oak.

It was only when they were back on the well-worn track that Emily brought up the fact that, barring any other mishaps like tripping over a cattle grid, there was only a slim chance of Pru drying off and being in any shape to perform.

"Oh, Emily," Pru said, "I'll be fine. The kids and parents will just have to wait and let me go on. Besides, while I was lost, I figured a way to work the headless horseman into my twin village story."

Emily wanted to say, "Is that all this meant to you?" but let it go.

Before long, with Pru laboring to appear none the worse for wear, they reached the stile. Emily helped Pru through the breach in the stone wall and led her traipsing down the path till they reached Tom's horse and cart.

Applauding wildly, Tom pulled off his makeshift umbrella, grabbed the two orange bags from Emily and tossed them in the back of the cart. He helped both of them up, flicked the reins, and they were off. Pru was seated on the plank bench next to Tom, trying to convince them that she was perfectly fine. Emily sat on the edge, hoping against hope that there would be no surprise waiting for them at the fete.

Down the lane they went, the bray picking his way until the mist slacked off at the crest of the High Street and the clip-clop on the damp cobblestones signaled they were back. As they passed the Castle Pub, Emily couldn't help thinking to herself, *So far so good*.

She was still leaning forward when she spotted Trevor, rushing up the street toward the pub. Not far behind, a large group had congregated at the foot of the slope that led to the castle ruins.

Realizing something was wrong, Emily told Tom to stop. She climbed down, asked Tom to take Pru to the marquees, and rushed over to Trevor whose face was flushed.

"What's going on?" asked Emily, blocking his way.

"As you see, I am sauntering up to the pub. Now if you'll kindly step aside."

The buzz of agitated voices down the street practically drowned out Emily's words. "Trevor, will you tell me what happened?"

"Can't a fellow take his customary walk without seeing . . .?"

"Seeing what?"

"Damned unpleasant business," Trevor mumbled under his breath. "Tearaways, hooligans, unpleasant business all round." Brushing past her, Trevor continued up toward the pub.

Spotting Hobbs down below, mobile in hand, Emily headed toward him. But Hobbs was soon swallowed up by the gathering throng. Within seconds, a paramedic was swallowed up as well.

Following Hobbs's lead, Emily reached the milling bystanders, some wary and holding back, some suggesting the incident, whatever it was, must have taken place beyond the ruins and over into the earthworks. Others simply jostled each other for a better view.

Threading her way through the bulk of the bystanders, Emily worked her way up the damp, grassy knoll, but the second she reached the top of the rise, she realized whatever had happened had nothing to do with the earthworks at all. She hurried back down the slope and managed to squeeze by the most ardent of the bunch who had guessed correctly. She ventured to the stone mound of the castle ruins and disregarded Hobbs's shouts to stand back.

The next thing Emily knew, uniformed men and women began to trickle in, bound and determined to break up the growing melee and cordon off the area with streams of blue-and-white-striped tape. The more boisterous members of the squad began ordering the onlookers to leave the premises; four or five others sought out witnesses.

Emily inched forward until she came up against the curtain wall that ringed the remains of the castle keep. Slipping in just before the stretch of scene-of-the-crime tape reached her, she edged her way along the dripping rampart until she finally could see what had happened.

Casting her gaze down the open, wet staircase, tracing the tumbling spiral past the conferring doctor and paramedic to the bottom of the dungeon, she caught a glimpse of the unmistakable twisted form. In that same instant, just before Hobbs yanked her away, she saw that the body was as stark and still as the granite floor itself. There was no doubt whatsoever that Harriet Curtis was dead.

Chapter Twenty-Three

"Listen to me now," said Hobbs, his beefy face getting more crimson by the second, "there's no blame here."

"Except that Pru scurried away on this very street and Harriet before her. Except that Harriet had also been looking over her shoulder the whole while."

"Right," said Hobbs, walking briskly past Emily farther up the High Street. "Next you'll be telling a one-man unit is required to be everywhere, guessing at sod all and not allowed so much as a hot cuppa in this bleedin' weather."

Emily let the drivel about a cup of tea pass, something he could have easily gotten at the refreshment marquee while he was supposed to be keeping watch.

Following on his heels, Emily asked, "How about at least getting a scene of crime officer to scour every inch of the grounds?"

"Well, if that's your idea of proper procedure, what can I say except more's the pity? Why can't you give over? You're soaked to the gills after keeping the little barmy one from slogging through the bogs. So high marks and the Victoria Cross and there's an end to it."

"Wonderful," Emily said, finally catching up to him.

"High marks and slough off the remotest chance someone did Harriet in."

"Oh, so now it's someone did for her, is it?" said Hobbs, walking even faster.

"Then explain to me why a clumsy woman would scramble across a soggy field to the top of soaking wet stone steps spiraling down with no guard rail? Why would she even go over there?"

Emily knew she was beside herself, grappling with circumstances beyond repair. But she kept it up until they both halted by the pub entrance under the still-gray canopy of the sky.

Harriet's body had been whisked away, all activities had been put on hiatus, and Hobbs had long since given up trying to get a statement from Trevor. For his part, Trevor was probably still inside, working on yet another round of Scotch. But Emily just wouldn't let it go.

Hovering over her, Hobbs said, "In Britain, you don't jump to conclusions and you work within the rule of law. You make inquiries, keep your ruddy eyes on the facts, and wait for the inquest. You let the bloomin' coroner form his opinion whether it's accidental, suicide, or no. Have you finally received my meaning?"

"You didn't answer my question."

"And you have given no bloody reason the woman didn't top herself or lose her footing. In Britain we need evidence to convince a ruddy Crown Prosecutor to bring a case. Here we've got sod all to fancy a case-number file, reports, photographs, and a flaming official inquiry."

"What about Doc talking about 'killing two birds with

one stone' with Cyril as his driver and the one probably chasing Pru?"

"Lovely! But why stop there? There's Cyril's uncle Basil who might have done after spending many a fortnight in the nick. And all who was at the fete who might have done and been known for a spot of bother or two. All unofficial, mind, but what the ruddy hell?"

In the silence that followed, Hobbs got control of himself and patted Emily on the shoulder. "It's the moor what's done it to you," he said. "All that fog and mist and scurrying about. Add what happened to the clumsy woman in your charge and it's no bloody wonder."

"For God's sake, that doesn't change a thing, Hobbs."

Maybe it was the quake in her voice and her disheveled appearance. Maybe it was the fact that, deep down, Hobbs hated to see Emily like this. In fact, had never seen Emily like this. At any rate, Hobbs softened his tone.

"Quite right. But in the meantime, you go right in and have Maud fix you a cuppa with a splash of brandy. Pay no mind to squire Trevor who wants nothing ever to do with what happened and the likes of Cyril."

"But that's the problem. He was completely rattled, rushing up here, calling it 'damn unpleasant business all around.'"

"Ah, well. Showing his true colors, Trevor was. Showing himself to be a bit of a prat."

"Oh, great. Terrific."

Neither Hobbs's softer tone nor his words helped. Nothing did. The sight of this second dreadful fall had shaken her to the core.

"So you have a bracing, hot cuppa," Hobbs went on. "Then, when you're a bit less knackered, you go and fetch the barmy one and her stepbrother. Still waiting under the marquee, I'll wager, still looking a fright. The lot of you will pop back to the manor, get yourselves into dry clothes, and gather your wits or, leastwise, calm yourselves down."

Emily just shook her head.

"All right, lass. Ring me on my mobile midday tomorrow, if you like. Can't say fairer than that."

This time Emily nodded. Pushing Hobbs any further was futile. She pocketed the card with his number and reached for the pub door.

"That's it, love. In you go."

Lingering a moment longer, Emily said, "But if I come across something?"

"Then Hobbs is your man. Dashing about with a warrant card, fancying my reinstatement. But for now, will you kindly push off?"

Another hesitant nod from Emily as she slipped inside. She looked past the bar till she spied Trevor slumped on the settle in the far corner of the snug. Maud commented on how poorly Emily looked and gave her a consoling pat on the shoulder. Emily moved in on the Squire of Penmead.

At first, Trevor didn't seem to realize Emily was even there. He drained his double Scotch and called for a refill.

Emily repeatedly called his name until he finally noticed her. Peering up, he tried to shoo her off with a wave of his hand.

"A leisurely stroll up the High Street 'twas what it was. Customary peals of laughter and thunderous drum beats but then, zounds! Ring the palace, call in the Grenadier Guards, Beefeaters, and Yeoman Warders, all and sundry."

"Trevor, listen to me."

"Can't you see I am trying to put the world to rights?"

"You saw something, I know you did. You said 'damn unpleasant business all around.' You can at least come forth and—"

"But wait. Not a spot of bother at all. Simply a case of nerves, our Emily assured me. All to do with judging the sumptuous flower show."

"It was something else. You know it was something else."

Propping himself up, Trevor waved his arms and raised his voice, as if addressing a jury in some amateur theatrical. "Quite. Dame Harriet, distressing others, including my own, sweet Constance. And causing sheer madness as our tour guide—running here, running there, running, running everywhere. I put it to you, how could our hitherto sensible Emily keep track, shepherding all three of her charges? And gaze solely upon troubled, troublesome Harriet? Not to forget our tearaway scurrying hither and yon?"

"Will you just make a statement?"

"So tiresome, really," said Trevor, waving her off again.

"Trevor," said Emily, raising her voice as a blowsy waitress replaced his empty shot glass with a one spilling over the top. "Don't you think you have a duty to—?"

"See to it, and I shall. I have rather liked you, Emily. Until this farrago, this utter sham."

Emily was unable to stop herself from asking the same question she'd asked Tom before she took off after Pru.

"Humor me. Before it happened? Did you see someone stocky lurking about? Or Cyril up to no good? Or both?"

Trevor closed his eyes and sipped his Scotch slowly, like a man trying to soothe a sore throat. Barely holding his own now, he murmured, "Must admit we'll miss the odd pound sterling. Have to thank Miranda Shaw on that score. That is, if Miranda is still about. It was she, after all, who initially put you on to us. Yes, indeed."

"What do you mean, 'if she's still about'?"

Slumping over, Trevor was unable to continue anything remotely resembling a conversation. There was no reply and none forthcoming.

The blowsy waitress returned and shook her head. Emily took the cue.

On the way out, Maud assured Emily that she was always at Emily's beck and call. Emily thanked her, said she might have to take her up on it, declined a hot toddy to see her on her way, and left.

Working against anguish, fatigue, and sore legs, she walked back down the High Street, averting the sight of the castle ruins. She found Pru and Silas sitting on a bench on the verge of the church grounds. By this juncture, the news had doubtless descended on one and all. Silas had his satchel at his side and was peering over his bifocals. He looked almost as far gone as Pru, who stared into the charcoal distance, possibly about to link Harriet's demise with some Devon folktale but seemingly too distraught to speak.

The threesome padded wordlessly past the Green toward the car, Pru's occasional shivering and moaning the only discernable sound. In the aftermath, there was no sign of Hobbs, Tom's horse and cart, or anyone else for that matter. Except for the pub, the village was now deserted.

Their silence held all the way back to Penmead through the passage of looming hedgerows onto the gravel drive. Emily let the two of them off without a word.

Moments later, she caught sight of Constance wearing an ankle-length raincoat and straw bonnet from days gone by and carrying a basket of freshly cut roses. Emily didn't wave. Constance drifted off, impervious to the presence of the forlorn pair walking past her. Emily stayed seated behind the wheel and stayed immobile for a long time.

Eventually, she thought of getting in touch with Will, but she'd assured him there was no danger and promised she would avoid any sign of trouble. Besides, he'd pick up immediately on the state she was in and there was no point in worrying him, as there was nothing he could do.

Other thoughts crossed her mind, most of them too hazy to amount to anything. There was the first time her father walked out, and she kept asking herself how she might have seen it coming and what she could have changed about herself. She remembered Chris insisting that it had nothing to do with her. From there, her thoughts drifted to something her mother said after the last red-hat lady had gone. "Got to hand it to you, Emily. No matter what, you carry on."

But none of this pertained. As Hobbs pointed out, the moor and the chase had taken its toll. No matter how she looked at it, the client who she'd suspected and unwittingly abandoned was dead. Although she couldn't truly mourn for Harriet, she was still shaken and greatly saddened all the same. However she tried to frame it, she'd let Harriet down.

Emily got out of the car with the vague notion of taking Hobbs's advice, resigning herself to her plight, and retiring to her room.

But the idea of letting Harriet down caused her to recall the moment she'd been dawdling, listening to those two carrying on about strategies and the ups and downs at a soccer match. Maybe it was a stretch, but Doc knew she'd been a soccer player and claimed to know all about the game. During that very same interval, caught up in the seesaw of the tale of the match, she'd lost track of both Pru and Harriet when she should have been keeping tabs.

Given the framework of soccer, she began to picture a calculated game plan. At the outset, utilizing Miranda's pseudo-leaking roof in the rain, whoever her opponents were exploited a weakness of overzealousness on Emily's part. Assumed the only obstacle was a young woman clearly out of her league who would have great difficulty keeping her eye on the ball. Especially if they used a combination ploy, applying constant pressure and distractions until striking when the moment was ripe.

At any rate, the day was far from over, and despite everything, despite her unsettling feelings, she was still on her feet.

She slid back behind the wheel of the Vauxhall and drove off. When she reached the turning, she proceeded north toward Bovey Tracey to make sure Miranda Shaw was, as Trevor put it, "still about."

All she knew was, she couldn't be relegated to the sidelines. She had to get back on the field and make up somehow for all her lapses. Try to get a bead on the way this crazy game was played.

At the moment she could think of no better place to start than at the beginning.

Chapter Twenty-Four

Emily's driving was fueled by an abiding sense she'd been sold short. Sloughed off as a rank amateur clearly over her head.

She had decided to track down Miranda Shaw and get an inkling as to why she had initiated this whole process by phoning Chris. In this way, she could somehow get onto the opening gambit. Then make the jump to the current maneuver. Out to "kill two birds with one stone" could mean that Miranda was next to cover up her part in the plot to eliminate Chris. Which may have prompted Martha Forbes, in cahoots with the GDC, to hire Doc to take the next flight overseas.

At this point, Emily quit pondering. She was speculating like crazy and getting way ahead of herself. Still and all, she didn't rule out any possibility. Nor did she dismiss the fact that Harriet, according to Mavis's list, made three aborted phone calls to Miranda early this past Wednesday from the Warwick Hotel. Up till now, Emily had been waiting for something to happen. It would be a step forward if she could be on the offensive, like any pro on top of her game.

She covered the remaining ten miles to the River Bovey in under a quarter of an hour, the dense charcoal of the sky giving way to glints of brightening as the sun did its best to poke through.

Approaching the main artery of the town, she came upon a hub of activity on this late Friday afternoon. Cars and tiny vans tooled around in all directions, stalking parking spaces unavailable to larger means of transport. Joining the fray, she managed to zip into a space vacated by another Vauxhall that had wedged between a brace of Mini Coopers. Her immediate destination was the tea shop on the tour itinerary Harriet had been aiming for, to use the phone or as a smokescreen for another getaway before Emily had zipped by the exit and stopped her. In Emily's case, the tea shop offered a quick way to make herself presentable. She would also down a scone and some fruit along with a cup of Earl Grey. In somewhat better shape, she would then locate Miranda's present whereabouts and hope for the best. Assuming, that is, Miranda had changed her mobile number and place of residence as she'd indicated during Emily's phone call regarding permission for Will to inspect her roof. Whether Miranda made these changes to her mobile, etc., as an offensive or defensive measure was another matter.

There was no problem getting a seat and ordering at this hour. No trouble popping into the ladies room to freshen up and brush her hair. Right on schedule, her order arrived and helped ease away the hunger and the lingering chill and dampness.

But at any rate, she was on the move, which was her stock in trade. Far from what was doubtless expected of her by the opposition, and far from bailing out.

The only snag was getting hold of Miranda's present address. With her fixation on makeovers, Miranda had apparently disposed of the last properties she'd renovated and gobbled up another in the vicinity. The question was where, provided, of course, that she was still okay. Given the best-case scenario, what country cottage in what part of town was she now tarting up? What results of "deferred maintenance" were being graced with central heating, fitted kitchens, brocaded curtains, and double-glazed windows? Not to mention the typical manicured privet hedges flanking a freshly laminated gate readied for a quick sale.

For Miranda, the trick was to live in one while she redecorated and workmen polished off the other. When that sort of thing grew tiresome, she'd flit back to the Connecticut hills, lodge at the B&B, and scout around for a new project, male or architectural or both. When that too proved trifling, she went flitting back once again, which, evidently, was the case at present, unless this time the act of flitting back had more ominous overtones.

Which, again, made her think of Doc's mission of killing two birds with one stone.

Emily pulled out her cellphone, hit the designated numbers, and called Fiona, the always-in-the-know estate agent on Fore Street.

She found out that, yes, Miranda was active, but given the fluctuations in the market, she was only renovating one cottage behind the Teign Valley Glassworks. No, Fiona was not at liberty to reveal Miranda's new mobile number, but Emily could probably get her precise address from the lads at the Pottery Road Garage where Miranda had her Jaguar serviced.

However, as it turned out, Miranda was not only very much alive and kicking, but someone else had been making inquiries about Miranda's well-being only a short while ago.

"Rather had me in a bit of a muddle," said Fiona. "The driver, a scruffy sod, apparently had been mucking about with my computer and pawing through my new listings. When I returned to my desk, neither him nor his guv—some dodgy bloke who'd been chatting me up—was anywhere to be found. Well, I tell you, I never."

Returning to her car, Emily was soon on her way along the A382, tooling along toward the southern end of the bypass near the House of Marble. She covered the remaining distance in minutes, pulled into the Pottery Road Garage, and took a moment to get her bearings.

Up by the petrol pumps, she spotted the rear end of a beat-up Morris Minor. At first, she couldn't be sure who was filling up his tank because her view was partially blocked by a lorry. As if obliging her, the lorry moved up to the far side of the pump island opposite and well past the little Morris, exposing Cyril's smirking face.

Something glittered in his right hand and disappeared under a shammy, the kind of sheepskin cloth used to polish silver and chrome. Like an amateur magician, he whipped the shammy away, making the object appear and disappear a second time. The clumsy sleight-of-hand trick afforded her a fleeting glimpse of the short, nickel-plated barrel of a pistol.

A familiar, raspy voice cut through the garage and engine noises to Emily's right, causing Cyril to cover up the gun and conceal it behind his back.

"Dammit, I thought I told you to ditch it or put it away!" Doc shouted.

Pointing directly at Doc, Cyril made an obscene gesture and deposited the gun in the trunk of the Morris, slammed the lid, snatched up a gas nozzle, and resumed his position at the pump.

As Doc appeared by his side, Cyril fended him off by pointing again, but this time in Emily's direction. Following Cyril's lead, Doc advanced toward her.

She could have backed out, driven around for a while until she was sure they were gone, and asked someone inside for Miranda's address. But taking into account Doc's control over Cyril, she was not about to be put off. Not out here in broad daylight at a busy garage.

She switched off the motor and stepped onto the pavement.

"What is this?" Doc said, moving right up to her. "Are you tailing me? Haven't you had enough?"

"Just wondering if you're through making your rounds. And if Cyril's prize possession is going to stay in the trunk."

"You're killing me, you know that? When are you freakin' gonna get off it?"

Calling out something unintelligible, Cyril slammed the petrol nozzle back into its cradle. He clapped his hands, either because he was itching to go or because he was egging Doc on. He cut over to the lorry, leaned against the tailgate, and folded his arms. When the surly looking driver suddenly emerged, Cyril banged his fist into his open palm, swaggered back to the Morris, got behind the wheel, and honked as the lorry's motor revved up.

"Wise up," Doc said, staring her right in the face, raising his voice over the mounting engine noise. "What you are is a tour guide who cuts out on her tour. A driver who is and is not for hire, and a sassy chick who's got no leverage. No authority, no nothin'. So why don't you do everybody a favor and hang it up?"

Emily let it go, not about to jump in again until she had something concrete to charge him with. She left him standing there and headed for the garage office.

Yelling as other revving motors joined the fray, Doc said, "So guess what, sister? You are damn well just asking for it!"

The feeble horn of the Morris beeped again. The lorry and a moving van rounded the far side of the petrol island and exited.

Doc strode over to Cyril as Emily reached the garage office. Caught between the petrol island and Emily, Doc hollered one last time. "Hey, forget about it. I am outta here."

The Morris took off, tires screeching, with Doc on board. While making a pointless loop around the pump island, Cyril made another nasty gesture. The look on Doc's face as it came into view was indecipherable. Completing the circle, the Morris whisked away, the whine of its motor strained to the limit, tailing off with a few taunting, farewell honks.

Before asking for directions to Miranda's present whereabouts, Emily took note of Cyril's concealed weapon and Doc's backhanded tip. She also took into account what she had learned the hard way. *Without leverage, without authority, anyone with anything to hide—like poor Harriet—can keep eluding you. As she'd done. As everyone had done. But, if they have no idea you're after something, if you're able to keep your feelings in check, this time you might actually catch someone off guard.*

This she told herself and vowed to keep it in mind.

"How very odd to receive your call," said Miranda, swaying a bit in her bare feet between the packing crates and freshly painted walls. "It must have been five days ago, surely, that you rang in the middle of the night. You were half asleep, I dare say."

"But still coherent, I hope," Emily said, warding off the odor of fresh paint.

"All the same, quite late for you, a bit early for me."

For a moment, Miranda seemed thrown. Then it came to her. "You were to pop round for tea. Report on what your handyman found, if memory serves. Absolving me of negligence. And here you are on my doorstep, days later, having given me no notice at all."

"Couldn't get hold of your new number. Just tracked down your address."

"Ah. Quite. Of course."

Still standing in the middle of the pristine white living room, Emily watched Miranda as she gazed quizzically at her unexpected guest, let out a sigh, and wandered off into the empty, equally spotless dining space adjacent to the kitchen area.

As soon as Emily rang the bell, she'd been greeted by that same quizzical glance. Wrapped in a flimsy white robe, which did little to hide her ample bosom and willowy figure, Miranda had halfheartedly attempted to pull back her honey-blonde hair and pile most of it on top. Wispy curls streamed down over her ears, adding to her usual blasé mode. But her lazy blue eyes darted here and there, which didn't go at all with her purring, mellow tone. Neither did the occasional twitch of her lips. Anyone who'd spent any time with Miranda would have to admit she was not quite herself.

Shuffling back into the living room, Miranda had another thought. "Then how did you manage to find me? And why aren't you at the fete with your clients? Doing your Twinning thingamabob?"

"I took a break. Felt guilty about not getting in touch. Made a call to Fiona."

The quizzical look returned.

"You know, Miranda. The estate agent."

"I see."

Emily filled the ensuing silence by asking if there was any possibility she could have a cup of tea. She mentioned she was on a tight schedule, having had such a hard time locating her, and could really use a little pick-me-up.

"Hmm."

Emily hoped that if Miranda was kept busy, she might be less wary. Given the awkward way things were going, it was worth a try.

"It seems, my dear," Miranda said, meandering back over to the glistening kitchen, "one never knows when one might be called upon to be a proper host. At all hours, as it were."

Emily took this remark to mean that either Miranda hadn't yet gotten over Doc and Cyril's untimely visit a few minutes before, or that the last thing she needed right now was Emily's company.

"But not to worry," said Miranda. "Kitchen's not only fitted but tidied up. I'll make us both a Tension Tamer. Ginseng and ginger root, chamomile flowers, and lemongrass. Do make yourself comfortable."

Her tone was colored now by more than a hint of growing annoyance.

With Miranda out of sight and the clinking sounds of cups and saucers in the background, Emily surveyed the area. In addition to the crates that lined the walls, she noted the two white-wicker chairs in the far corner facing a flimsy-looking three-tiered, white-wicker stand that blended perfectly with the walls and ceiling and Miranda's robe. Aside from the polished wooden floor, the only other thing that caught Emily's eye was a packet of photos lying on top of the wicker stand embossed with that unmistakable logo—the black hands of a grandfather clock and antique red lettering promising prompt and courteous service. A trademark of the Meadow Street Pharmacy at the edge of the Green in Lydfield, Connecticut. Judging from the ripped envelope and its haphazard position, it may have just been delivered by Doc and hastily tossed aside.

Emily stopped short of reaching out for the packet when

Miranda called, "Milk or lemon? One lump of raw turbinado sugar or a spoonful of honey?"

"Lemon and honey will do fine, thanks."

"And then we'll chat. Hear all about what actually brings you here. Nothing excessively tiresome, I hope."

"Oh, no. Not at all."

Emily sensed that anything directly implicating Miranda in any way would end tea time then and there. So she couldn't allude to the phone call Miranda had apparently made to Chris nor the recent ones she may have received from Harriet.

At the sound of Miranda's fake cooing, Emily sat down by the wicker coffee table as Miranda whisked into view, balancing the tea things on a white-wicker tray. Emily rose, intercepted Miranda and took over arranging the delicate pot and cups and saucers, leaning the tray against the stand to mask the photo packet.

Emily offered to pour. Miranda demurred, instructing Emily about the tea cozy and how "one had to wait till it was all properly hotted up."

Another awkward silence as they sat opposite each other. Emily asked about the new spa in Newton Abbot.

Playing along, Miranda went on about the Aquaroma-flow baths, smooth stones, and aromatic oil massage. Miranda then poured the steaming yellowish liquid into the fragile bone-china cups. "Now then, Emily. The reason for your popping in like this, my casual invitation aside. And your newfound—how shall I put it—cat-like stillness?"

"Sorry?"

"Rather as if you were about to pounce instead of the

usual forthright, New England manner I'm accustomed to."

Realizing she had to do something to get the focus off herself, Emily said, "I just wanted you to know there is no apparent negligence on your part."

"No apparent negligence. Odd turn of phrase."

"And, again, since I had no other way to reach you . . ."

"So you say."

To steer the conversation to the GDC's condo project, Emily alluded to the contrast between the development and Miranda's unsold, half-timbered, multiple chimneys, and slate-roofed McMansion. She hoped the subject of the real-estate market might get Miranda to loosen up a bit. But it only caused Miranda's eyes to go on another darting expedition.

While massaging her eyelids with her fingertips, Miranda said, "Is it local news on offer? Is that the gist of what's summoned you here?"

"In a way." Emily mentioned the GDC application and prospectus, and its probable acceptance by the Planning Commission by the middle of next week. But all Miranda could say to that was, "My dear, that's a foregone conclusion."

During the next pregnant pause, Emily would not have been at all surprised if Miranda chose to see Emily out before she had a chance to examine the photo packet.

With nothing else going for her, Emily said, "Miranda, do you still make that yogurt dish with dried fruit and nuts? The one you often whipped up while you stayed at the B&B? The tea is great but the truth is, I really am starving."

"After, I gather, you've been on one of your interminable

forays over hill and dale. Then drove here, ferreting out my address, tossing me a few bits and bobs, and now fancy my yogurt dish."

"If you don't mind."

Miranda rubbed the back of her neck and closed her eyes. "I sense your unfathomable behavior is due to a modicum of disease. Breaking the word down to its true meaning— dis-ease." Opening her eyes, Miranda added, "I shall bring you your dish. But you surely realize how perceptive I am and always have been."

Once more, Miranda wandered into the kitchen. Emily snatched up the packet from the wicker stand and took out a handful of glossy prints. The first featured the plastic smile, lacquered-down do, and vanilla summer suit of Brian Forbes in all his glory. The other snapshots zeroed in on Brian pawing different parts of Miranda's generously-endowed body on a dock somewhere on the Connecticut River. Some of the stills were less blatant, but it was more than obvious what was going on. Some blackmailing leverage vis-à-vis Brian and Miranda if they didn't beak it off, with the approval of the development in the balance. Without warning, Miranda came fluttering out of the kitchen into full view. "Oh, damn," Emily said, knocking over the tea tray.

"There, you see?" said Miranda, setting the white porcelain bowls on a crate while Emily dropped to her knees, holding up the tray to mask her attempt to shove the packet of photos back in place. "The body never lies, Emily Ryder. You are in a state, like a tightly coiled cat, surely."

Miranda began putting everything back where it

belonged. With the tea things sorted out and the bowls neatly rearranged, Miranda and Emily took up their respective positions. Skirting over the rising tension as best she could, Emily made cursory remarks comparing the weather and hiking in rural Devon with Connecticut's northwest hills. Forcing down the pre-prepared yogurt, fruit, and nuts as if she was actually famished, Emily looked for an easy exit.

Miranda began massaging the back of her neck and flexing her fingers. "There, do you see?" said Miranda. "Your dis-ease has quite altered the flow."

Miranda stood up, stretched her arms out wide and went into a half-limbering-up, half-dance routine, the same set of affected movements Miranda had performed on the front lawn of the B&B. Only this time, she was trying to cover up whatever had unnerved her—doubtless Doc and Cyril barging in on her, coupled with Emily, the cagey cat, suddenly dropping in as well.

Her voice and body straining a bit harder, Miranda kept on. "This technique is akin to the Chinese watercourse way. Just as water follows gravity and rises effortlessly."

She stretched high and in all directions and said, "It's curious how you mentioned my slate roof during your sleepy, early morning call. And here you are with never a mention what your handyman actually found. Nor how you came by the GDC prospectus highlighting the salient features."

She gave Emily ample time to respond, but Emily gave her nothing.

Straining even harder, Miranda gyrated to illustrate the difference between the rigid pine branch and the lithe and springy willow sloughing off heavy snow. The only problem was that, given the pressure of all that was apparently closing in on her, Miranda was so much better as the pine branch.

To break this up, Emily said, "Mind if I use my cellphone for a second? I have to check back with Silas and Pru, and the signal is bound to be less iffy here than the moorland terrain."

With another reluctant sigh, Miranda ceased her routine and motioned toward the kitchen area to afford Emily a little privacy. Before letting matters go, however, she said, "Speaking of realty, you haven't broached the subject of your mum and plans for the B&B either. Once again, 'curiouser and curiouser' as Alice, in the looking glass, would have it."

To Emily's mind, what was really odd was the fact Miranda hadn't shown the slightest concern over the fate of her fallen roofer, let alone noted that Emily was checking back with Silas and Pru and had omitted Harriet's name.

Miranda shuffled over to a picture window and peered out at nothing in particular. Emily walked back to the empty kitchen. She no sooner dialed and said hello when Trevor's drunken voice cut through all pleasantries.

"Right, spot on, splendid. May surprise you to know I have solved the whole troublesome business. Packed the two of them off, if you will. Rather, had my housekeeper do so. Trundled them off bag and baggage to Exeter. Wasn't too difficult to modify their flight plans—death in the family, that sort of thing. Getting rid of the lot of you, you see. Damn nuisance, of course, but nothing further need be said."

"Are you serious? Wait a minute, you can't just—"

"Made arrangements with Maud as well, only too happy to oblige. Put you up temporarily, spare quarters, no bother, no bother at all. Notified the British Tourist Authority as well. In a word, wiped the whole slate clean. No partial Twinning—erased, never happened, put out of everyone's mind."

She could hear Trevor's garbled directives addressed to Constance about retrieving Emily's things and some other leftover odds and ends. Another attempt on Emily's part to speak was met with the click of the receiver.

Emily returned to the living room and made her excuses. Miranda saw her out. Framing herself in the doorway, affecting a listless pose, Miranda said, "Oh, Emily, you *are* in a state. Ever so skittish. What is to become of you?"

Emily didn't bother to respond or say goodbye.

Walking by the newish, British-racing-green Jaguar perched on the gravel drive, Emily noticed a white leather suitcase and matching bags had been flung onto the plush back seat. Though it was clear by now that Miranda was not an intended victim, she definitely had a place in the scheme of things.

Emily, however, had no place. As if she hadn't been hit with enough, Trevor had seen to it that her two remaining clients had been shipped off, leaving her with no real justification for being here at all.

Chapter Twenty-Five

Constance slipped out of the portico of the manor house like a squeamish process server, her voice barely audible. Casting her gaze down and away, she held out a fancy blue shopping bag from Harrods.

"Oh, and here are some odds and ends, Emily. Left behind in all the rush, I gather. Trevor discovered them slipped behind the dustbin. You may, of course, keep the bag. Our pleasure."

Emily retrieved the shopping bag, tossed it in the trunk of the Vauxhall alongside her suitcase, turned back and, trying to hold her temper, said, "You needn't have bothered. I could have packed my own things and saved you the trouble."

Casting her gaze upward, still avoiding looking Emily in the eye, Constance said, "Actually, in view of the state Trevor is in, I . . . that is, we, thought it best if the two of you didn't, em . . ."

"Cross paths?"

After the next awkward pause, Constance went back to her rehearsed speech. "As for the accident at the castle ruins, rest assured I shall see to it, em . . ."

Ordinarily, when Constance couldn't avoid a situation

and was entirely on her own, she resorted to an "em" here and there in the hope that the other party would fill in the blanks. Coming to her rescue once more, Emily said, "See to it the spiral steps down to the dungeon are roped off?"

"Indeed."

"Off limits. Out of sight, out of mind."

The look on Constance's pale, equine features was so downtrodden that Emily wasn't about to take any of this out on her. After all, it wasn't Constance's idea to clean house so that Trevor could return to his self-appointed role as the blasé village squire without having to deal with loose ends and a pesky Emily Ryder to boot. Let alone the ghastly business surrounding Harriet's demise. He probably convinced himself that if he could swiftly return Lydfield-in-the-Moor to its quaint, historic coziness, he would have done his civic duty.

Making one last effort to smooth things over, Constance said, "In future we'll, perhaps, begin anew. Visit our quaint sister village again one day and, em . . ."

This time Emily left her hanging. There would be no sister village. Only flickering memories that, too, would quickly fade.

Facing the waning afternoon light, now tinted with dusty rose, Constance groped for some parting words. Then, as though recalling the end of her recitation, she said, "All the same, with nothing left for you here, perhaps you'd fancy motoring on to the Cornish coast as planned."

Emily stood by the side of her car, patiently waiting for Constance to finish her pointless goodbyes.

"Indeed," Constance went on, her voice quivering under

the strain. "You could meander around the, em . . . winding, cobbled streets in Fowey. Gaze at the lovely sailing vessels and . . . em . . . sort things out."

Breaking into a wan smile, Constance started to wave, couldn't carry it off, and slipped back through the portico out of sight.

Almost immediately, Tinker came tearing around the gravel drive, his mad eyes flaring, his drooling tongue flapping across his teeth. He looked here and there. When he found no small creature to torment or large, ungainly one to tease, he changed course and raced on.

The teasing madness of Tinker was the last straw. Emily got behind the wheel, hit the accelerator, and sped through the file of hedgerows, resolving that no one was going to send her packing like some misguided schoolgirl.

Nearing the access road, she braked, got out, and unlatched the trunk. She rummaged through the shopping bag to make sure Trevor had included her notepads with the rest of the "odds and ends slipped behind the dustbin." Once she saw that everything was intact, plus a great deal more, she pressed on.

As glimmers of dusty rose slipped through the break in the sky, she headed back to the High Street and her new, temporary digs. Fending off waves of fatigue, she decided there were four things left to do. Three were on her impending list. Procedures regarding Harriet's death could wait until tomorrow. For now, she needed to get hold of Hobbs and tell him about Cyril's gun. She'd call Babs and find out what had been happening at home this whole time, and then she'd call Will and keep in touch as promised.

What she would reveal to either one of them was another matter. So was her ability to remain cool and collected. It was all up for grabs.

Later that night, the fete resumed in earnest. The moratorium had ended as if Harriet's demise was an unfortunate item on the news cycle about someone no one knew and a matter of conjecture. What's more, there were so many diversions and amusements that whatever had been slated for the mini-Twinning portion of the bankers' holiday couldn't possible hold a candle. The flower show had been dealt with; there was no real need for Pru's storytelling antics or Silas's obscure offerings under the tea-and-crumpets marquee. Nor, as far as Emily could tell, was there any reason to notice her own determined presence as she squeezed through the swarms of people and looked high and low for Hobbs.

When she finally spotted his bulky form deep inside the village hall, he was too engrossed in the hijinks on stage to pay much attention to her. More interesting by far was Benjamin, the huge, hairy shepherd. In the role of the virgin queen—dressed in a grass skirt and sporting a pair of torpedo-shaped breasts—he was bawling over some bloke who had deserted him after promising "a right proper rave-on amongst the haystacks." Joining him in their own hokey grief was a chorus of farmers wearing outlandish gowns stitched together from shredded strips of sackcloth. The ditties that followed were so lame, they even included a rendition of the old clunker, "Run to the roundhouse, Nellie, they can't corner you there."

Realizing this was the only occasion for the otherwise diffident villagers to let down their hair, and unable to compete with all the howling laughter and applause, the best Emily could do was pass on her cryptic message.

"Cyril has a gun," she whispered in Hobbs's ear.

"Has what, love?"

"A gun. A pistol. A weapon."

Barely glancing at her, Hobbs said, "Ah, so it's more silly buggers, is it?"

"Listen to me."

"Lovely. And where and when did you arrive at this bit of news?"

"Bovey Tracey."

Glancing at her, Hobbs said, "Bovey Tracey? After I bloody told you to—?"

"Never mind. Look, I could only make out the glint of the barrel before he covered it with a shammy. I don't know where he is now. But that doesn't change the fact he stashed the gun in the trunk of his beat-up Morris Minor right after he taunted me with it."

Grimacing and shaking his head, Hobbs finally came back with, "You were well-knackered after one of yours scarpered in the moors and the other met her maker at the castle ruins. And here you are, peskier than I found you, with a new dodgy tale."

As Hobbs turned his attention back to the raucous goings on, Emily yanked on his arm and said, "Don't slough me off, Hobbs."

"Sod off, will you, lass?"

"No. You're a constable and I need you to act like one."

Doing another one of his pleas to heaven, Hobbs said, "Then, when you've long last gotten hold of yourself, put it down in writing—the details, mind, about the gun and sundry. And leave it with Maud. After my watch here at the fete, and pray, well past your bedtime, I'll see to it."

"You swear?"

"By queen and country and the bloomin' Scots Guard."

As a clincher, conscious of drawing attention to himself, Hobbs shouted over the encore of "Run to the Roundhouse," "Never let it be said Hobbs is ever off duty. We have a pact, mind, be it day or night."

After offering her a dismissive pat on the shoulder, Hobbs added, "You get some rest now, and that is a ruddy, flaming order."

The panto moved on to another raunchy skit featuring a pair of shy but lonely farm animals. Emily worked her way out of the hall and through the milling crowd. Putting it in the best possible light, she told herself that Hobbs needed a way to cover his own negligence, was unable to admit to anything after all he'd been through that landed him back on the beat, but might very well be open to a way to make amends, no matter how much he protested.

Ensconced in her cramped quarters above the pub, she wrote a note to Hobbs for Maud to pass on about her most recent encounter with Doc and Cyril, listing only the facts—who said and did what.

She returned to the bar and asked Maud for an envelope. Predictably, she had to ward off more ministrations over her plight as Maud provided her with a mug of tea laced with Irish whisky. This was soon followed by a little fishing expedition, prodding Emily for a clue as to the contents of her note.

"As you well know, pet," Maud went on, "I am a beacon for the Neighborhood Watch. Nothing dicey gets past these eyes and ears. So I might well have something to add to whatever you fancy may be amiss. Besides, the place is near empty given the fete and all, save for those two nutters playing whist in the back and making a pint last a fortnight."

"Truth is, Maud," said Emily, "I'm so out of it right now, I might let something slip that'll get you jumping to conclusions."

"Ah, but jumping to conclusions is not altogether amiss, from all the Sherlockian tales I've seen on the telly."

Moments later, realizing her prying and cheerful banter was getting her nowhere, Maud let out a dejected sigh. "But you will keep me posted, now won't you, love?"

Some halfhearted banter over paying for her accommodations at the pub was followed by Emily's thanks and a promise, bright and early, to run something by Maud apropos of the present situation. Cellphone in hand, Emily borrowed a flashlight, left the premises, and straggled up to the top of the lane. She needed to be well away from the jolliness of the festivities below and high enough to get a strong signal. It was time for the second and third items on her list.

"Come on, Ryder," said Babs, getting even more flabbergasted. "What do you mean you're switching gears and winding things up?"

Zipping up her windbreaker, Emily said, "Look, I'm standing outside, way up here in the dark."

"So?"

"So there's no telling how long this connection will last."

"Hey, you don't trust me with some UK number where I can reach you, call me whenever you feel like, and now you give me this? What happened with this Doc character, and what's the deal with Miranda?"

Actually, Emily felt bad about playing it so close to the vest but, at the same time, there was no way she could've handled Babs's interruptions prodding for updates.

Partly relenting, Emily told her that Doc and Miranda's business in the UK seemed to be over, and from what she could gather, each in their own way planned to head back to the States. In return, all Emily could get from Babs was news that the GDC's final vote of approval from the village Planning Commission was officially set for Wednesday. Plus banker Brian Forbes seemed a lot more chipper, while his realtor wife Martha had become a lot more testy.

Before Emily could ease her off the line, Babs began complaining that her take on the GDC project was still in limbo and started rattling on about her theory regarding the Lydfield goings-on, asking Emily to "try this on for size."

The way Babs saw it, all the drama had started because Harriet had skipped town without formally signing off on the right of way to the tract on the high meadow. Doc had to go after her because he was on the GDC payroll, and Martha Forbes was definitely in on the action.

Emily tried harder to cut Babs short as the shadows on the moor grew deeper and the connection began to fade. She wasn't about to broach the subject of Harriet's awful death and the fact that her two remaining clients had been subsequently whisked away. The last thing she needed was a lecture on the pitfalls and fallout of getting in way over your head.

Warming to her analysis despite Emily's protests, Babs ran on with her guessing game. She figured that with the Curtis property facing imminent foreclosure and Martha dying to know whether Emily's mom would throw in the towel, it didn't really matter what Harriet did or didn't do. And that's why Doc was called back.

"Okay," said Emily, "fine. Are we through?"

But Babs kept it up, insisting she was on a roll. At the Business Association meeting, Brian showed some projections and had started crowing over incoming revenue, a new strip mall, cinema-multiplex, pizza joints, gas stations, and a humongous cell tower that would service the whole area.

Emily caught a break when Babs suddenly announced

she had a call waiting. "Just a sec, Ryder, hang on, be right with you." The only value of Babs's slew of guesstimates so far was the prominence of all Babs didn't know.

Less than a minute later, Babs was back on line.

"Guess what, Ryder? I already checked all the car rental spots. Nothing. Just heard back from the Kent Livery Service and, bingo! Good ol' Brian Forbes is booked to pick someone up arriving on British Airways tomorrow at Kennedy Airport. Now I wonder who that could be, considering the fact that wifey Martha is holed up at a weekend realty confab in Danbury?"

"Oh?" Emily said, refusing to give Babs any ammunition that would take her off on yet another tangent.

But Babs still wouldn't let go. "Why aren't you excited? I mean, if the Twinning thing is over and all the action is at home, you should get your bod back here. Let's keep our eyes peeled, Ryder, and get with the program."

"I'll give it some thought."

"Terrific," said Babs, "you're on, kid, and I am back on track." With that, she finally clicked off for good.

Emily climbed higher up the hill, hoping for a steadier signal. When she'd told Babs she was winding things up, what she meant was that she would spend another day hoping to find some link between Cyril's weapon and Harriet's fall. Or, after being apprised of police procedure following Harriet's death, she'd leave everything on this end up to Hobbs, including getting a statement from Trevor.

At the top of the rise, she tried the B&B. No luck. The phone rang but Will didn't answer. He could have been out getting supplies or taking Oliver for a long walk. Lydfield Connecticut was a world away, probably bright and sunny on a quiet Friday afternoon.

In the silence, Emily's thoughts turned once again to Chris. How could people like Miranda Shaw write him off without a qualm? She must have known, must have heard about the final result of his fall from her roof. Harriet's suspicious death had also been given short shrift while host Trevor had gone so far as to rid himself of any trace of all three Curtises as fast as he could.

Adding these iffy factors to her collection, Emily waited a while longer and tried Will again. Still no luck.

Emily flashed her light on the narrowing path, moved up higher, and stopped at a spot close to the stile and the break in the stone wall. It was hard to believe that only ten hours ago, she'd managed to corral Pru and lead her back, only to come upon something infinitely much worse.

She hit the speed-dial number again. This time Will picked up and the connection was clear. It seems he'd spent the better part of the afternoon hauling bricks and stones, digging up the front walkway, replacing it with new pavers, and patching up the flagstone steps. As a result, he spoke in the lazy rhythm of a workman who could surely use a little downtime. A rhythm perfectly suited for Emily's last order of the day.

Yawning despite herself, Emily remained dead set on skirting around anything and everything the least bit worrisome. After a little small talk about her location high up at the rim of the moor to get a stronger signal, she knew she had to let on about the change of plans. She also had to skirt around what happened to Harriet to avoid any possible recriminations.

"I thought you should know that Pru Curtis, the dotty stepsister, got lost in the moor and I had to go traipsing after her. In the meantime, something happened to Harriet, the older sibling, which I can't go into right now. Anyway, the Twinning has been cut short and there's a good possibility the rest of the trip might have to be called off."

"But you're okay?" asked Will.

"Just bone tired after all the hiking."

"And the other two?"

"As well as can be expected."

"And this Doc fella?"

"Gone, I guess. Nowhere to be found." Emily hated being coy like this, but her run-in with Miranda was having an aftereffect. Sensing that everything was a game and she was still way out of practice.

"Well, now," said Will, as he took this all in, "I'd say you've had your fill."

"Chalk it all up, you mean."

"Look, I know how you must feel about cutting your tour short and all . . . and maybe you're still feeling down on yourself about what happened to Chris."

"But don't take everything so personally."

"Maybe. In a way."

She could hear him walking around, opening the refrigerator door, snapping the cap off a bottle, and taking a pull from a frosty Corona, doubtless still at a loss as to how to handle her.

Will hemmed and hawed and put his foot in it again when

he came up with the old saw about your best feature also being a shortcoming. Like his being easygoing to a fault.

"Will, if you don't mind, can we pick this up some other time?"

"You bet." There was another pause, as though Will was going over the way he should have put it. Then he came back on, sounding a little surer of himself.

"It's just when you expect yourself to be a certain way, always on top of things, and you don't come through, you take it hard. Or people expect you to be a certain way and take advantage of you. What I'm saying is, the time comes when you got to head on down a whole other road."

Emily pulled back for a second. It was only a nudge, not a flash. But it jibed with something Babs had just told her. "Okay, right. I hear you, Will."

"Do you? Well, now. And you'll maybe get Harriet squared away and get back here real soon?"

"Something like that. I'm working on it."

"All right then."

A little more yawning on Emily's part, some added small talk about the moor shadows, and then a soft goodbye.

After pocketing her cellphone, she heard something stirring close by. Flashing the light around, she caught a glimpse of the ragged face and wild gaze of a Dartmoor pony. It stopped moving and stood stock still, facing her just beyond the break in the stone wall.

Emily gazed right back at it, giving no quarter.

It wasn't the pony per se that held her; it was a combination of things. Fatigue, edginess, and something percolating in the back of her mind she couldn't put her finger on. A hitch here and there that called for a reshuffling of the whole picture.

Chapter Twenty-Six

After a fitful night's sleep, Emily found herself awake early Saturday morning, going over a few factors that had eluded her. Like the link between Cyril and Trevor.

During the moments surrounding the dreadful incident at the ruins, she recalled that Trevor had been rushing up the High Street muttering "damned tearaways and hooligans." He made for the pub and began drinking himself into a stupor. As a result of this and other prompts, she revised her agenda. Before departing from the UK, she first needed to touch on the Cyril–Trevor connection, and look into a few other matters as well.

Did Trevor have it in for Cyril, the "tearaway"? Did he catch Cyril (Doc's flunky), up to something in the vicinity of Harriet's undoing? What did this all mean?

Over a late breakfast, she learned from Maud that Trevor and Cyril went way back. Cyril, the tongue-tied orphan and delinquent, had shuttled from one degrading job after another during his teens. He wound up cleaning Trevor's chimneys, basement floors, kennels, and whatever other menial tasks Trevor could conjure up. To get rid of him, Trevor accused Cyril of stealing. In retaliation, Cyril stuck a knife in all four of Trevor's vintage Rolls Royce tires. Unable to speak in his own defense, Cyril was sent to the reformatory. When he got out, not long afterward, he lashed out, looking for all kinds of trouble and finding it, using silence to his advantage. Even his mates never knew what he was up to. He was cocky, strange, and unpredictable. Everyone's prime tearaway and the only one fitting that description.

Moreover, Emily had caught Cyril brandishing the nozzle of a pistol that Doc immediately ordered him to put away.

After duly noting these elements as part and parcel of yesterday's events, a drive to the Dunstone Constabulary established that Hobbs was right on one score. There would be an inquiry into Harriet's death followed by an inquest and a coroner's verdict whether the cause of death was accidental or self-inflicted, or occurred under suspicious circumstances.

Hobbs failed to tell her these procedures would take at least six weeks and Harriet's body would remain in a nearby mortuary till she was "done and dusted." Then, and only then, would her remains be shipped back home.

According to the constable on duty, Trevor had been apprised of this policy straight away, not long after Harriet's demise. Primed with enough aged single malt whiskey, Trevor had hopped back into his Rolls, fetched Pru and Silas, and had them identify the victim. He convinced the two of them there was no point in staying on and packed them off to Exeter, and back to whence they came. He had done this all in record time while Emily was tracking down Miranda in Bovey Tracey.

Taking this into account as well, Emily walked out of the constabulary into the diffused sunlight. She couldn't wait six weeks while the trail went cold and the mayhem continued or became lost and forgotten. Clearly the odds were against her and although she had no business delving into this at all, she seemed to be the only one really concerned. She'd have to come up with something really striking to prod the authorities.

But she was duty bound, no two ways about it. She owed at least that much to Harriet. And there was no way she could turn her back on what had befallen Chris.

Her last stop for the day was the fete, which was in full swing. She spotted Hobbs while making her way through the crowds to the whacking and thwacking Punch and Judy booth. Without any hesitation, she pulled him aside.

"Here's the deal, Hobbs. If I come up with something that would force Trevor to make a statement as a material witness and turn it over to you by no later than this coming Tuesday . . ."

"Crikey, lass," said Hobbs, completely taken aback. "Need I say I would be jolly well pleased to have a go at making squire Trevor do the right and honorable and confess? If, on the other hand, it's all bollocks, this rearranging sod all into a square peg, you will leave off, put your own house in order, and there's an end to it. Are you at long last hearing me?"

"Well, if you're going to put it that way . . ."

"The only way to put it. Now mark me."

"Okay, fine. You got it."

"Ah, and blessed be."

That settled, Emily went back to Maud, thanked her for everything, and promised she would keep her in the picture if anything developed. Then, trying to play both ends against the middle, she asked that if she needed further assistance while she was back clear over in Connecticut, could she contact her?

The smile spreading across Maud's broad face was all the reassurance Emily needed.

The rest of Emily's Saturday was a matter of logistics. She made the long drive back to Bath to drop off the Vauxhall and travelled via public and private transport to the Ascot House, an ex-coaching inn on the outskirts of Windsor. After a round of fish and chips and ginger beer, compliments of the genial hosts, she collapsed onto the four-poster bed.

In contrast, Sunday was a trial. An early wake-up call announced that her flight would be delayed three hours. After a taxi to nearby Heathrow, a security check-in line much longer than expected, a stressful spate of turbulence over the Atlantic, a bout over luggage at Kennedy Airport, and an overbooked shuttle flight, she arrived an hour and a half off schedule at the Bradley-Springfield-Hartford terminal.

On top of all that, there was another snag retrieving her luggage, a trek to locate her Camry in the long-term parking lot, and a meandering drive home through the hills and valleys in the dark and through the drizzling rain. She finally slipped into the cottage and flopped down in her own bed around 11 p.m. Eastern Daylight time.

The only bright spot was the ample time she'd had to

conjure up a totally new strategy—a game plan contingent on an irrepressible hunch that just wouldn't let go.

Chapter Twenty-Seven

The next morning, Emily took a cold shower and put on a light blouse and summer khakis. In contrast with the wilds of Dartmoor, it was a good fifteen degrees warmer in the Connecticut hills on this promising Monday. Promising, that is, if she could keep her mood positive before the jet lag and ordeals of the past few days took their toll.

Neither Will nor Oliver were around, so she left a note on the back door of the B&B, returned to the guest cottage, and called her mother.

Anxious as ever, too rushed to ask about Emily or even wonder where she was calling from, her mom carried on about how she managed to keep on the go—comparing menus, advertising, decorating schemes, room rates, and the like from the Berkshires of Massachusetts to the reaches of the Green Mountains of Vermont. She did ask if Emily had been keeping in touch with Will about any problems or news about the worrisome developer and Martha Forbes's latest sales pitch.

When Emily managed to slip in the fact that she just got back in town, as an afterthought her mother added, "How's Chris taking his lost cause? You know, preserving open space? Never mind, don't tell me, poor soul." The conversation was cut short as the proprietors of the Waybury Green Mountain Inn could be heard offering a peek at their accounting spreadsheets and cost-cutting measures if Mrs. Ryder could spare a moment.

Unnerved by her mother's query about Chris but continuing to try and keep her spirits up, Emily told her she would look into things at this end. And that all the ideas she'd been gathering up there would come in handy in time for the onslaught of the leaf-peepers. All the while, with all things considered, Emily wondered how in the world she could keep up this juggling act.

After a quick goodbye, Emily had a hasty cup of coffee and some granola and, once again, scanned the odds and ends in the shopping bag from Harrods she'd included in her luggage. Ever since Constance had foisted the stuff on her during her departure from Penmead, something had been nagging at her. She'd made a few stabs at putting the items in some kind of chronological order but nothing jelled, as yet. She was going to have to rely on her opening gambit to pan out so that everything else would fall into place. She was on a tight schedule and, considering the shape she was in, could only hold out for so much longer.

Her next chore was getting Babs to go along, no questions asked, while managing to keep Trooper Dave at arm's length.

Just before entering the Village Restaurant, Emily checked her watch. She had at least fifteen minutes before customers began filtering in from the bank, courthouse, and town hall on their lunch break. All she had to do was keep her eye out for Babs and come to some kind of understanding.

However, Dave Roberts spied her entering the restaurant, parked his cruiser right out front, barged in, and started badgering her. How come she was back so soon? Had she quit chauffeuring the Curtises around England and decided to take him up on his limo idea? The one about catering to retirees flocking to the new condos soon as the first units were up and ready? But what would she do in the meantime?

After deflecting his barrage of questions, she excused herself, walked through to the adjacent wood-paneled bar, slipped through the alcove, managed to intercept Babs just as she came around the corner, and asked for a little favor.

"Right," Babs squealed. "You just run along and take care of your father hang-up and leave me holding the bag. Stalling Trooper Dave while you're busy spinning your wheels. That's perfect. Whoop-de-doo."

It was Babs at her worst. Letting things thoughtlessly spill out of her mouth when she was totally flustered. Straining their friendship, which often only hung by a thread.

Emily had half a mind to tell Babs to forget it. She would go back inside the restaurant and have it out with Dave, even though that was the last thing she needed. She'd take precious time and energy to brush him off and delay the crucial first item on her agenda, which was backtracking to Chris's old place.

"Okay, okay," Babs said, going into one of her back-peddling routines. "Psychobabble, father thing, touchy subject. I get it. But I told you the bind I'm in. Stuck my neck out, so now I got to deliver on the condo upshot or be buried in the cutesy pages, or file for unemployment. And now you want me to stall good ol' Dave. What is that, a joke?"

With Babs's voice echoing all over the place, Emily stepped out onto the sidewalk with Babs scuffling behind.

"I know, I know," Babs said, followed by a typical Babs-ism. "A little louder and we'll dance to it."

"That's right. Look. I just don't want Dave out here pushing his stupid limo idea. What's the point?"

"And what, pray tell, is the point?" Babs asked, pulling Emily aside and lowering her voice. "If I get something out of it, okay? Thought I had it going but no real kicker, no scoop. The GDC wins, so what else is new."

"Yes or no, Babs?"

"Fine. You go off, do your thing and meet me back here on the Green in no later than twenty minutes and start leveling with me. Fill me in and quit pulling my chain. Yes or no, right back at you."

Emily nodded, having no idea what she'd toss Babs in the way of news. As Babs reentered the bar area, Emily left the scene, got back in her car, and was on her way.

Babs couldn't help wondering if Emily might be coming undone. She'd never seen Emily so bleary-eyed before. She had been acting a little odd before she left and had sounded uptight long distance over the phone. Babs was dying to know what had happened in between for her to wind up like this. Normally, Emily could hike, run, and play anybody into the ground. And now she apparently had quit her job, just like that. And certainly not because Babs had suggested she knock it off and get her butt back where it was all really going down. Emily had dropped her tour, flew back, and was running around playing hide-and-seek. But for what ungodly reason?

Shrugging it off, Babs whisked through the empty bar, strode up the aisle, and plunked herself down at the booth opposite Dave and the cross-hatched front restaurant windows.

Dave looked up from his menu. "I knew that was you hollering. What is this? And where's Emily?"

"Unlike you, she's minding her own business. Leaving me to put you straight."

"I don't believe it. What are we, back in grade school?"

"Maybe it's just you back in grade school, pal. Still making the moves on Emily with me as the go-between. What is it about no that you don't understand? Is it the *n* or the *o*?"

Before they could continue trading barbs, the waitress came by. Dave said he still hadn't decided, and Babs said she'd have whatever Emily usually ordered, which turned out to be an iced coffee and one of those fruit salads Babs hated.

Ignoring the passersby peering through the window, checking for vacant tables, Babs said, "Okay, Roberts, let's see if we can bypass the sexual harassment and the fact you're in uniform and supposed to be on duty."

"What is that supposed to mean? Dammit, what's going on here?"

"Exactly. How about what this GDC guy, Doc, is up to? Is he tied into your leaning on Emily to go in with you on some limo deal? To maybe service the new condo residents? Oh yeah, I heard all about it."

"Where did you get that?"

"Guess. Come to think of it, if it isn't the same old infractions on the Troop L blotter. Failing to yield the right of way, disturbing the peace, or malicious mischief at the high school—you can't handle it. So what does this tell us about the competence of Trooper Roberts and some more good ol' conflict of interest?"

"Don't mess with me, Babs. You want to dig up some dirt for that rag you write for, you got the wrong trooper."

"That does it," said Babs, faking a quick exit. "Calling my bluff? I'll just have to run this all by your superior, including Emily's take on your constant stalking."

"Hold it," said Dave, motioning her to remain seated as a few men in suits entered.

As more suits arguing trial lawyer chitchat joined the fray and sat down, Dave leaned forward. "What exactly are you up to?"

But before she could answer, one of the suits nodded to Roberts from across the room.

Dave turned his head and sat upright. "That's correct," he said, completely changing his tone. "For your information, Miss Maroon, any time assistance is required on a police matter, rest assured Trooper Dave Roberts is always on hand. Any local citizen can call 911, dispatcher relays me at L10, and I'll be promptly on the scene."

Jerking Roberts's sleeve, Babs said, "You can look at me now, officer. Your friendly judge has sat down and has his back to us. So here's the deal. Win-win. My best guess is that Chris Cooper's death, Emily's dwindling tour guide business, and her mom's B&B going down the tubes means it's all downhill for Emily. All you have to do is be on standby in case, while yours truly finalizes a one-on-one with this guy Doc. That is, to discuss why he hightailed it to jolly old England and happened to return at the same time as Miranda Shaw. Throwing in whatever else I know and can glom from Emily, by the time Planning and Zoning meets day after next, the public will have been informed about what really went on behind the scenes. Emily will be beholden to you, stalwart Dave, for playing watchdog and keeping Doc at bay, and stalwart Dave'll be in a much better position to compete with handyman Will."

"Since when?"

"Since when what?"

"Since when are you getting so chummy?"

"Like the saying goes, you hoist it up the flagpole and see who salutes it."

Babs neglected to reveal how she planned to shake any of this out of Doc, a man she'd never met. But no matter. The prospects and cheap thrills in the offing were her only compensation for a lousy love life.

Dave Roberts's face registered nothing. A chair squeaked. The portly judge looked back once more in his direction.

Roberts paid for his lunch before it arrived, squeezed out of the booth and said, "Excuse me, Miss Maroon, but I can't take any more time out from my duties. An important investigation is under way on that vandalism case. I'm not at liberty to fill you in on the progress we've made or the details at the present time."

Babs didn't know what to make of this one. She took it as a maybe. In any case, she couldn't help feeling something had to break. Otherwise, why was Miranda suddenly zipping back over to meet Brian Forbes at JFK? And why was Doc back on the scene as well, as Babs's call to the GDC main office had confirmed? The assistant had added that Doc was in touch now and then when the occasion called for it. Taken together, all bets were on that, by golly, today was the day.

Emily also thought there was more to the fact that Doc and Miranda had returned to the states at the same time, together with Brian Forbes in the mix. But that didn't change her immediate point of attack. Two people had lost their lives on her watch and this was her make-or-break chance for redemption.

Returning from her errand at Chris's place, Emily drove past the B&B to her right and slowed down. Everything had become too clear, too bright under the cloudless sky, as though the glare would erase anything that might appear troublesome. The sparkling brightness held true as she approached the Curtis property and noted the tiny red markers still in place, starting from the point where the side yard met the slope leading up to the tree line and the high meadow.

She pulled over for a moment and shifted her gaze away from the flags, directly beyond the elongated side of the house, over to the straggly garden next to the rose arbor. There she spotted Pru struggling with a weeding tool. The second Pru dropped the tool and moved out of sight behind the sprawling house, Emily drove on, passed the bank on her right and looked for a place to park.

She made a U-turn and took an empty space at the corner of the Green opposite the vacant bookstore. Turning off the ignition, her eyes strayed to the large sign covering the plate-glass window. There was no mistaking the new gold lettering etched in black. The venerable bookstore was now the local GDC headquarters and sales office, jumping the gun and readying itself for the inevitable buying spree.

Undaunted, Emily glanced at her knapsack nestled on the back seat, reached over, and patted it for good luck. When she turned back, she caught a glimpse of Silas's stooped form crossing the road. In that same instant, she caught a glimpse of Brian Forbes in his powder-blue suit a step or two ahead of Silas. She made a mental note and put it on the backburner for now.

For the next few minutes, nothing else of any import happened, unless you counted the sight of a Martha Forbes look-alike crossing at the intersection, making her way toward the post office. Admittedly, Martha wasn't the only rail-thin woman in town with a supercilious air about her, but it made Emily wonder what would happen if Brian, Martha, and Miranda Shaw should happen to meet.

But no matter in terms of her pressing, immediate plans.

A wave of jet lag came over her but before she had a chance to close her eyes, Babs showed up, slid onto the passenger seat, and folded her scrawny arms in a huff.

"Brilliant," said Babs. "This Doc character is driving up from the Bronx as scheduled."

"How do you know?"

"Never mind. But he wants to talk to you."

"What for?"

"Because I opened my big mouth, that's what for. Told him not only were you back, you were running around like crazy and totally out of it. That did it. He'll be right over around three thirty after his meeting in the Big Apple with good ol' Hacket, Martin Gordon's silent partner. Swell, terrific, just great. How do these things happen? How?"

At first, Emily couldn't handle it. Then she reminded herself all the players were on the move. That's how the game was played. No one was ever just standing still. It took some dickering and more stewing on Babs's part before Emily came up with something.

"Okay, Babs, I'll tell you what. Since Doc is planning to get here at three thirty, I'll make sure I won't be back to the B&B until four. You can tell him I was duty bound to help poor, bereft Pru tidy up Harriet's garden and that it was probably taking longer than expected."

"What do you mean, 'poor, bereft Pru'? Are you gonna console her about cutting short that Twinning thing? And what were you up to at Chris's old place? I mean, are you really okay, or is something going on with you that requires some real attending to? Why do I have this weird feeling you're either on top of this or unraveling right before my eyes?"

"Granted, I admit I'm suffering from jet lag. But I do have some personal matters to look into and I have a very tight window."

"What does that mean?"

"I can't explain. It's too complicated, and it's hard enough to try and keep all the balls in the air."

"Weird, Ryder. That's the only word for your behavior. Pretty damn weird."

"Call it what you will. I'll arrive late to the B&B and you'll act as my proxy. If anybody's good at winging it, it's you. Plus, think of what you might wheedle out of Doc. In exchange, all you have to do is lend me your pocket digital recorder."

"Wait a minute, hold the phone. I don't mind that you're wasted out of your gourd and running around half-cocked. What I do mind is a person who owes me one, if not a helluva lot more, still holding out and dictating my strategy."

Hesitating for a moment, Babs came right back with, "On second thought, you being out of the way until after four is a plus. But you're getting no pocket recorder till you fork something over for my first job, getting Trooper Dave off your back."

"And that's it," said Emily. "No more tit for tat, you hear?"

"But that's the basis of our whole relationship. So, let's

see now, I get a crack at this Doc character and a chance to finally blow the lid off this GDC scam . . . Okay, gotcha, you're on."

Emily followed Babs to her garage apartment by the rippling Housatonic. Babs pulled in and returned a few minutes later with the pocket recorder.

"Well?"

"Well what, Babs?"

"Divvying up for the proxy stunt with Dave. And don't tell me gardening with daffy Pru is any revelation."

Emily held back for the longest time and finally said, "Harriet had a terrible fall."

"Oh?"

"She didn't recover. She didn't make it."

For the first time in living memory, Babs was speechless. It took a while before she handed over the recorder and recovered her cocky style.

"Well there now. No wonder you tossed in the towel and don't seem to know which end is up."

Emily didn't counter Babs's little jab, Babs backed off, and that was the end of it.

As Emily drove back to the village, she reminded herself that despite all of Babs's put-downs, she was the only one who could call the game from the opening play to the final whistle. The only one haunted by a beloved guardian falling from a great height, tumbling and crashing to the cobblestones. The only one, as far as she could tell, who wanted to pursue the cause of Harriet's death and put things right.

Chapter Twenty-Eight

Pulling in past Will's pickup, Emily grabbed her knapsack and hurried inside the cottage. She placed the knapsack on the kitchen counter, pulled out Chris's answering machine, plugged it in, and was about to check on his calls last week when there was a knock on the door.

She flipped the latch and was greeted by Will's lean frame and expectant look. Oliver peered up from a few feet behind, wagging his tail.

"Glad you're finally in," said Will. "Guess we somehow missed each other."

He stood there as she searched for something to say and just gazed at her. Then, apparently sensing whatever response he was waiting for was not forthcoming, he reached into his denim shirt pocket, took out a whistle on a rawhide loop, and asked, "Hey, you got a minute?"

When Emily still failed to respond, he said, "I know you're kinda busy unpacking and settling back in and all. But lunch isn't on for another thirty minutes or so."

"Lunch?"

"So I was hoping you could give Oliver and me a hand with an experiment. Providing I can then really wing it with the recipe and the ingredients I scraped up."

Emily was still at a loss as to what to say. She realized there should be some kind of welcome home exchange after all this, but under the circumstances . . .

Then Will came right out with it. "This little practice session will only take a minute."

"Practice session? Right now?"

"As good a time as any. And, seeing how you look a little frazzled, which I can well understand, it might help get your mind off things."

"I'm sorry, Will, I—"

"I mean, just to ease off a bit while you get your bearings. What do you say?"

Emily had no idea where he was going with this, only that he was obviously stalling. There were those telltale shifts in rhythm and tone she had come to know that told her he definitely had something on his mind. In the rush of trying to avoid all the possible complications, she forgot to factor in Will. Whatever it was he was after, it couldn't have come at a worse time. Throwing her off track, a one and only opportunity possibly come and gone.

Undeterred, Will explained that Oliver had been incorrigible again, ignoring Will's commands and taking off after a small child strolling by the B&B with her older sister, scaring the kid to tears. As a result, an obedience trainer was called upon, who assured Will it was simply the nature of the breed and Oliver's young age. But with a little practice, Will or anyone else could gain control.

"Will, can't this wait?"

"Afraid not. If it isn't reinforced right after working with the obedience lady, if it isn't locked in, there's no telling."

"And if I don't or can't right this minute or—"

"Nothing to it, Emily. The whistle is the key. High-pitched sound can only be heard by Oliver and serves as a command to return to your side no matter what he's up to. Like that time with the turkeys up on the high meadow when I wasn't around. He'd have come tearing right back to me or you or whoever's blowing the whistle, and the problem would've been solved."

Unable to get her mind around this interruption, but unable to take the dejected look on Will's face coupled with a tinge of guilt over a missed reconciliation, Emily said, "Look, you'll have to excuse me. There is something I have to get back to and I can only spare a minute."

"A minute will do just fine."

She nodded halfheartedly as he told her to station herself about thirty paces up the trail and count for sixty seconds before blowing the whistle. She knew full well she was being standoffish as well as coy, but whatever Will really was after would doubtless take a couple of false starts before it was out in the open.

Will ordered Oliver to stay and walked into the kitchen while Emily waited up above, squinting under the dappled sunlight. It was all she could do to keep from calling this off. Apart from her mixed feelings about Will, she didn't know how much longer she could stay on her feet, sharp and fully functional. All she wanted to do was get back to the answering machine. Assuming her hunch rang true, she'd have to make a call to the UK and move into gear.

She blew the whistle. Oliver came rushing up after her and almost knocked her down in his enthusiasm to be released from his stay position, which did remind her of what may have happened to a small child he'd knocked over. But it didn't quite make sense under the present circumstances. The only good thing was that the little obedience lesson was quickly over.

After promising Will she'd be right back for a quick lunch, Emily worked on retrieving Chris's phone messages and adding the telling results to the items she'd placed in order in the Harrods bag Constance had foisted on her. Then she made a hasty call to Maud at the pub, explaining what she was after and making sure she realized there was a lot riding on Maud's return call.

Shortly afterwards, Emily sat in the spacious kitchen of the B&B watching Will prepare his version of a Florida Keys shrimp and avocado salad. All of this was confounded by trying to work around Will, who kept dragging his heels as to his true intentions, while she used the same disclaimer that she had something pressing to do with time running short. Antsy as can be, she continued to do her best to put up with Will's stalling, hoping he'd come right out with it by this time.

Instead, he went on, underscoring his past escapades as he fiddled with his recipe. Repeating yet again that he had run a charter fishing boat in the Keys and all the rest of it.

Any other time she would have gone along. But at the moment, getting more and more frustrated, Emily said,

"Okay, I'll bite. Why are you telling me this again? I don't get it."

He brushed aside the utensils and looked directly at her. "What I'm driving at is, I'm an older guy. I've been around. I know how to put up with things, to a point. But as soon as something or someone starts boxing me in—some tourist, some yacht owner's daughter who tells me about the wonderful life we're gonna have, or some proprietor stands over me and tells me how to do my work, I ease out of it and limit the damage."

"Oh, like my dad, you mean. Did Chris fill you in? Better to walk once the pressure builds. Is that the message?"

"No. I didn't mean it that way. I just meant—"

"The other way around. Keep from eating your heart out. Let it go through you, let it pass. But even when Chris gave me that option, he never let me turn a blind eye."

"Not what I'm saying either," said Will, as he shelled the jumbo shrimp. "Dammit, Emily, I still have that burlap sack in the tool shed full of incriminating evidence. Assuming my ol' buddy is right, and he's never wrong about people getting killed from power lines, storms, and loose wires and such. He's a damn expert."

"What burlap sack? What incriminating evidence? All you said was it was obviously no accident."

"Right. Upset you even more while you're clear across the ocean full of grief trying to do your job. Tell you all about strands of invisible copper wire up by the turret in that Brit lady's house. That would've really done the trick."

Really agitated now, Will let it all spill out. "So I keep

it to myself. I walk by the shed I don't know how many times. I go in, stare at the bag, open it up, go through it, the crowbar and copper wiring and all. Got to the point yesterday I called Troop L, asked about the chain of command. I lied and said it had something to do with the break-in at the high school, wanted to make sure what I found got to someone in charge. Dispatcher told me the commanding officer was a Lieutenant Neill. But I should deal with the resident trooper first, Officer Dave Roberts, who'd like nothing better than to run me out of town. So what do I do? What do I do about you, who might get real upset and is so all-fired independent and right now maybe up to something to boot? And then there's Oliver. I don't believe in tying up a carefree dog, that's not my nature. I'm just saying, something has got to give here."

The long silence that followed was palpable. So was the sense of the afternoon winding down.

Struck by Will's uncharacteristic outburst, taking in this new information but certainly not wanting to get sidetracked, Emily said, "Okay, so you're worried about Oliver and me, two of a kind."

Hearing his name called, Oliver scratched on the back screen door. Emily got up from the table but Will told her to pay Oliver no mind.

Will scraped the shells off the cutting board and tossed them in the bin under the sink. When Oliver scratched even harder, Will brushed by Emily, went to the door, swept his right hand down, and told Oliver to stay put. Oliver whined and reluctantly slumped down on the stoop.

"This isn't going right," said Will. "You're not hearing

me. You think I'm pulling some macho crap. But after what you saw in that downpour that's been eating at you ever since, and seeing the shape you're in, circles under your eyes . . . You just got in real late, been running back and forth, and I don't know what all you're about to do now."

"Such as?"

"Whatever it is, that is the whole damn point."

"So, as an older guy who has done it all except confront things, what is your mature advice?"

While toying with shards of coconut and a ripe mango, Will simmered down enough to begin alluding to the ivory-white flats of the Bahamas. He told her how a prize fish could be taken with a well-presented fly, provided you were positioned near shaded mangroves in the warmer channels. However, if you cast your line carelessly, your fish would flash away.

"Fish? We're talking about fish when you know darn well I've got to get cracking?"

"I'm saying, even if you think you hooked him, he can still surprise you, wrap around the mangroves, tangle the line, and bust free."

"Don't tell me. You've finally gotten around to it. You're talking about Doc."

"And how about you? When are you going to get around to it? What is it you're so hell-bent on doing?"

"Fine. You want it spelled out for you? I am simply going to drive a tiny, little ways down the hill, help a poor little thing with Harriet's garden which has gone to seed, and talk to her."

"Her?"

"Pru, as in Harriet, Silas, and Pru. Okay?"

"Now what do you want to do that for?"

"Because she's just lost her stepsister. Because I don't really want to go into it now, if you don't mind."

Like Babs, Will was completely thrown by the news about Harriet.

"It's too complicated, Will, and I don't have all the details."

Will started to speak, apparently thought better of it, and then came out with, "And I suppose you know that this Doc character called me not more than an hour ago and is driving up, on his way over here. He got the idea from Babs that you're still at it and is coming after you."

"Is that what he said?"

"In so many words. I thought you were trying to stay clear of him."

"That's right," said Emily, checking her watch while Will cut the large avocado in half and removed the pit.

Working some romaine lettuce into the mix, Will said, "If you've heard anything I've said, if you have any idea about the implications—I mean all of it, what happened to Chris and now this stepsister Harriet . . ."

"I'm going to talk to Pru, Will. Help her with the garden. I'm going to leave Doc and everything else aside, that's it."

Will scattered lettuce and coconut on two platters, absentmindedly added the other ingredients, and drizzled lemon and lime over the concoction. Setting the plates down on the table, handing Emily her ice tea, and plunking down his usual frosty Corona, Will sat opposite her. Neither of them spoke or began to eat until Will said, "So please, can we work this out?"

Emily started picking at the salad. The truth was, she was beginning to like the idea of Will close by on her side and, in some way, even Babs. It certainly couldn't hurt.

After sipping her iced tea, telling Will what a great salad he'd made, Emily rose up, pushed back her chair, and said, "Okay, I'll take it under advisement."

"Hold on," he said. "You're really only going to talk to Pru?"

"Garden and chat, Will. In broad daylight, out in the open, under the clear blue sky."

"Just you and—"

"This little bitty woman who I had in grade school. Who I've gotten to know better, who's afraid of big dogs and Dartmoor ponies and her own shadow."

"For how long? And when exactly?"

She checked her watch again. She needed to leave enough time to get back in touch with Maud, drive down the short distance to the Curtis house, set it up, and get some answers.

"I'll be there in about twenty minutes from now to no later than four-fifteen."

Will got up from the table, went outside, induced Oliver to flop back down, and stood there. Abruptly returning to the kitchen, he said, "A compromise, okay?"

Retrieving the silver whistle on the rawhide loop, Will admitted the training session wasn't just a ruse. After Babs called and told him she'd be by to waylay Doc while Emily

was beyond the high meadow over at the Curtis place, Will
had his suspicions. Worried that Doc wouldn't make it to
the B&B and just come after Emily.

"All right," said Will. "Now that we got it set that Oliver
will obey the whistle, this is what we'll do. Since I've got to
go to the bank anyway, I'll drive up around three-twenty,
way before the lobby closes, and when the bank is least
busy. I'll park my truck in front of the Curtises' side yard,
leave the tailgate down, walk the few yards and ask Chuck,
the security guard, to do me a little favor and keep an eye
out."

"Are you serious?" said Emily.

"Well, believe it or not, I've already given it a trial run."

"I don't believe this."

"No, listen to me. This way, Oliver will be at your
beck and call, sitting up at the rail of the open truck bed,
watching people and cars go by. Any sign of trouble, all you
got to do is blow the whistle. As soon as Chuck spots Oliver
bounding off, he'll alert me, and I'll come around to check
if you're okay."

Responding to the exasperated look Emily was giving
him, Will added, "All I'm talking about is covering a five-
minute gap in case Doc drives in early and happens to see
you out there. No pressure on my part, no keeping tabs on
you or crowding you, just a precaution. Seeing how I have
to go to the bank anyway, heard about him being on his
way, thought about him coming after you in England. And
now, especially after this news about Harriet."

"Will, this is so stupid."

"Fine, it's stupid. Take the whistle anyway. Meet me at

the bank, we'll intercept Babs and maybe all three of us will go after Doc with the burlap sack and have it out. I just want to end this thing."

When Emily still didn't answer, he said, "The long and short of it is, I don't trust any of it. No whistle blown, no problem. But if anything's wrong, if Oliver springs up, if Chuck or I spot him taking off . . ."

Feeling a bit lightheaded, Emily hesitated. At the same time, she wanted Will in reserve.

"Fine," she said. "Okay, you win." She snatched the whistle out of his hand and hurried out the kitchen door, startling Oliver. She headed straight for the cottage and waited impatiently inside for Maud to ring her back.

After making sure the items in the Harrods bag were in the exact order and checking back with Babs to make sure they were still on and she'd occupy Doc for a while, Emily was about to slip on her running jacket when the phone rang.

After Maud's comments about "possible dodgy evidence," Emily admitted that she had no idea how she was going to use this new information, let alone pry out the whole scenario. Especially in light of her fishing expedition with Miranda Shaw that turned into such a farce.

All the same, she eased Maud off the line. Yes, she would let her know soon as it was sorted.

For her part, if it came to anything, Maud promised to relay Emily's findings to Hobbs. "Let him deal with all and sundry at this end and, I shouldn't wonder, find his cheeky self back in the constabulary's good graces."

Emily hung up the receiver. With that item taken care

of, she patted the open mesh-pocket of her running jacket to make doubly sure she had everything, snatched up the Harrods shopping bag, and slipped out the door. The wired feeling that accompanied the pulsing on-again, off-again jet lag raised her adrenalin level higher, knowing once she started pressing for an advantage, she'd lock into the ebb and flow and damn well keep the ball in play.

Chapter Twenty-Nine

"It's so-o-o unfair," Pru called out from the opposite side of the rose arbor, reaching up with the long-handled shears and snipping at a vine. "Look at this. Where does it begin? Where does it end?"

Still looking for a way to get Pru's attention, Emily kept on working. She raised her spade, chopped off more woody tendrils of bittersweet, grabbed an armful of the invasive vine, and added it to the pile in the wheelbarrow

Dropping her shears, Pru moved along the trail of cocoa mulch she'd tossed under the scraggly line of laurel bushes, rhododendron, and lilac until she disappeared behind the rambling house. Like a child, she did an about-face and marched back, past the rose arbor, phlox, cosmos, and zinnias. She skirted by Emily, all the way to the swath between the red flags leading up the slope to the tree line and the high meadow.

Calling out again, Pru said, "We might have to start from up there in the trees, work all the way back down, and still never stop it. Still never keep the bittersweet from crawling everywhere and taking over."

It was yet another gross exaggeration. The swath consisted of overgrown grass and weeds. There was not a bittersweet vine in sight. But Pru being Pru had to make it into much more than it was, deflecting, avoiding anything too real for as long as possible. Even the terrible thing that happened to Harriet. Making Emily's objective here that much more difficult.

Another about-face, and Pru marched right back down the swath between the red flags, brushing by Emily again, up to the rose arbor, and pointed all around. "Clip and chop away and still never keep it from climbing up and choking the Don Juan roses and the honeysuckles. So unfair."

Emily couldn't help wondering how Pru was able to keep this up unless she'd really distanced herself from reality this time and was that far gone.

Another wave of fatigue came on. As it passed, Emily figured now was as good a time as any if there was any hope of getting Pru's attention. She pretended to tighten the laces of her running shoes, slipped her hand inside the open-mesh pocket of her jacket, and called back.

"Speaking of things being unfair, nothing is actually fair if you think about it."

Pru thought for a moment and said, "I suppose."

Taking that as a sign that Pru was back in the here and now, Emily said, "Like all that preparation you did. And coming up with a posh English accent to a T."

"Beg your pardon?"

"You know. That warm-up you did for the village kids at the Twinning."

"Oh? What about it?"

Emily stood up and moved closer. "How you had them

going with that posh accent. Just as good as Miranda Shaw's."

"Did I tell you that?"

"More or less."

"No, I didn't. I did not say that."

Turning her curly head, Pru engaged Emily directly this time. "But it is true how good I can be. If it hadn't been for Harriet slipping and falling like that, I could've gone back to those kids and really pulled it off."

"All that bad luck," said Emily, pressing a bit more, underscoring her words. "What happened to Harriet and right before that, you being chased and getting lost. Unbelievable."

"Yes. Not just getting lost but wandering aimlessly in the mist and fog and cold. That was really something."

Pru reached into her apron, pulled out some pruning clippers, shuffled by the near side of the arbor, and began deadheading sprays of Shasta daisies growing wild behind the zinnias. She looked over at Emily, shoved the clippers back into her apron pocket and said in that singsong voice of hers, "What do you mean, Emily? What are you getting at?"

Feeling her anger slipping in, Emily had to remind herself it would do no good to snap at Pru. She also reminded herself that chatter was worthless. Only strong indications of probable cause would do. She'd gleaned that much from Dave Roberts.

Easing off, Emily said, "I mean, it's still such a muddle. And the jet lag doesn't help."

"What's a muddle?"

Taking her time, Emily resumed her spade work. She moved past the arbor and chopped what was left of the bittersweet around the low-lying beds of creeping myrtle and said, "Well, you've got this posh English accent. Posh and sleepy like Miranda's. You know, perfect for *Sleepy Hollow*."

"Oh," said Pru, back to her singsong. "Now I get it— *sleepy*, like the Sleepy Hollow story. But did I really say that? And what do you mean about being chased?"

"You said you were being chased and ran off into the moor. Tom, the cart driver, told me."

Pru pivoted under the glinting afternoon sun as though unsure of where she was. Then she peered at the long side of the clapboard colonial as it led her gaze all the way out to North Street and the passing cars. She kept looking in that direction as if she might have heard something, perhaps out there on the main drag or close by behind a window. Then she pivoted again and peered behind her house where she'd tossed the cocoa mulch.

"Remember how things were, Emily?" said Pru, tracing an imaginary line from the far corner. "First the lilacs in bloom, followed by the rhododendrons and the laurels. Like a wave. The rambling roses cascading over the arbor next as the annuals joined in, marching like a colorful parade."

"What does that have to do with anything?"

Pru rubbed her eyes and said, "Whew, I'm just like you, I guess. Haven't gotten over the jet lag. Been back a few days and I'm still trying to get reacclimated. My body tells me it's after eight, time to start thinking about turning in, as if it was cool and dark. But it's only after three, isn't it? On a beautiful, clear afternoon. Right back here in the old home place where I belong. So-o-o different."

"Totally different."

"And it's getting hot and sweaty. How can you keep that running jacket on?"

"No problem, it's un-zipped. Besides, it has a wicking feature."

"Oh, what will they come up with next? Amazing how you can always find ways to . . . to . . . ."

But Pru didn't finish the thought. The way Pru was drifting in and out, she was liable to wander off back inside the house and that would be that.

In motion again, Emily piled up the bittersweet, grasped the handles of the wheelbarrow, made another trip to the rear of the arbor, and dumped the snake-like clumps. Then she decided she couldn't hold back, couldn't keep toying with Pru a moment longer.

She went to the spot behind the compost pile where she'd stashed the Harrods shopping bag. There, for the first time, she noticed a low wire fence running the entire length of the back area, marking off the old vegetable garden. Why she noticed the wire fence and what it might mean was beyond her, and she let it go.

With the file of wooden stakes, overarching annuals, and the bird feeder for cover, she pushed the wheelbarrow up to the back of the arbor, left it there, stepped inside, and started to rummage through the contents of the bag.

Taking the bait, Pru entered the arbor and joined her.

"What are you doing? And where did that bag come from? I thought we were going to conquer the bittersweet?"

"I know. But as I was saying, I can't stop wondering about things. I've been helping you and now, if you can keep your mind on it, perhaps you can help me."

Pru stared at the bag with the Harrods logo as though unsure of where she was again.

Pressing much harder this time, Emily said, "It's the logic of it all. Things just don't fit. And it's not as if I can pretend like you. I need to make some sense out of it and then check it out with Hobbs."

"Hobbs?"

"The constable, the one Harriet was so anxious to meet."

"Running away from, you mean. You saw her. Running off, like she ran off from here and left us in the lurch."

"You see?" said Emily, "that's one of the problems. Hobbs came down from the pub at noon. Before that, Harriet kept looking up the High Street. She was looking up the High Street when the flower ladies ushered her back to her post. She must have tried again but somehow wound up at the castle ruins. She wouldn't keep going up that way unless she was trying to get to Hobbs. Or at least get to a phone like those other times."

"What other times?"

"You know what other times. Like when she was so antsy in the car to get off the motorway, supposedly for a cream tea. And, speaking of running away, let's get back to you being chased by Doc or Cyril."

"Who?"

"Stick with it, Pru. Why didn't you have Tom drop you off at the pub so you could get hold of Hobbs or tell Maud or somebody, instead of running off? You see what I mean? It doesn't fit."

As a ploy, Emily glanced out past Pru. "Oh well, I guess I'll have to make a long-distance call to Hobbs, run the discrepancies by him along with these other things."

Tugging at Emily's sleeve, pulling her back deeper inside the shade of the arbor, Pru said, "What other things? What has gotten into you all of a sudden? And what does this silly bag have to do with it?"

Emily reached inside and pulled out the crinkled papers and computer printouts. "This bag, as it happens, contains what I've compiled. And the more you think about it, the more curious it gets."

"How come? And where did this come from?"

"Constance handed it to me as I was leaving. Since it was shoved behind a dustbin, you must've thought it would be thrown out. But that's not the way Trevor operates. He'll sweep up as far as any undesirable people are concerned. But he's not going to dirty his hands with leftover trash discarded in his spotless manor. That's strictly my responsibility. I have to see to it, sort it, and leave not a trace behind. And so, what have we got?"

Warming to the subject, Emily said, "These printouts are off the Internet using an old dot matrix printer—the kind they haven't made for years. The kind Silas has hooked up in his basement vault. These two pages are weather forecasts for the week in question for both here and Dartmoor—light fog and heavy rain for the time of

Chris's dreadful fall with a check mark next to it. Dense fog in the moors and precipitation in the lower elevations during the time of Harriet's fall also marked with a check. Nothing else highlighted or marked."

Pru's eyes locked on the Harrods bag, her body motionless.

Emily went on. "And what have we here? Trevor's hand-drawn map with a check next to the area where your strip of apron was found, and another check next to the stone circle dead ahead. No indication of any witch's hut, something that neither Trevor nor Tom the cart driver, nor anyone else for that matter, knew existed."

Still no response whatsoever from Pru.

"And another thing" said Emily, pushing her case, "even though you claimed you'd been corresponding, there are no e-mails or letters. Instead, we've got these crumpled printouts from websites like Devon Folktales with stories about the Dewerstone where the devil guided lost travelers. And you know what else? Those stories originated miles away from our sister village. And so did the one about the fickle maidens and all the rest of it."

With her eyes darting here and there, Pru finally spoke. "But when you add it to my adventure with the mist and the cold and the wild pony, you have quite a story to tell."

"When you add how scared you were out there, you mean. And how somebody put you up to it and it wasn't at all like they said it would be. But you went ahead anyway and followed the map. When I finally caught up with you, you kept looking at your watch on the way back, and all of a sudden, were relieved and cheerful. You even bypassed any mention of the crone storyteller like you knew it was all a crock in the first place."

Pru brushed past Emily, moving deeper into the arbor until she reached a back wall of rambling roses and honeysuckle, so thickly woven from top to bottom that her compact frame was completely in shadow.

"I don't follow?" said Pru, flinching as her back scraped against the roses.

"Yes, you do. Come on, Pru, stay with it. To get your apron snagged on the twisted oak, you had to unbutton your topper, rip off a piece, attach it, button up again and, when the fog lifted, move on."

"Who said, who said?" Pru cried out like a little girl.

"And well before that, as you rode up on the cart, you weren't looking back because you were afraid somebody was following. You were looking back so that Tom would tell me about it. And you were looking back because you were afraid good ol' dependable Emily might *not* be following."

Pru gingerly ran a forefinger along the rose thorns. She reached inside her apron, snapped her pruning clippers a few times, cut off a deep-red bud, held it to her nose, and smiled mischievously.

"How about this, Pru? You've been duped."

"Words, words, words."

"Don't you see? Don't you get it?"

"No."

"I'm telling you, you've been used. You've been had."

No mischievous smile this time. Nothing in the offing save for a faint shuffling sound nearby.

Then Pru went on the offensive. "So you say, Emily

Ryder. But it's all a jumble. Like these vines and roses and bittersweet. You couldn't tell a story if your life depended on it. Bits and pieces, that's all you've got. Bits and pieces and you can't put them together."

"Your voice is on the answering machine, dammit!"

"What did you say?"

"I said, your Miranda Shaw imitation is on Chris Cooper's answering machine, plus the exact time and date. Chris didn't tell me he talked to anybody. He only said he got a message impugning his workmanship. That's what sent him over there. And right after, high up in the driving rain, the voltage from the power line jolted his heart. Jolted him off the roof!"

Emily may have heard the shuffling sound again but was too close to the clincher to stop. She grabbed Pru's arm and yanked her up to the arbor opening.

"Look out there way past the side of the house. See the sidewalk and the cars going by? That's real, that's happening. And so is what you did."

Pru followed Emily's directive and gazed straight ahead, down the side yard out at North Street. But she didn't seem as though she was finally coming to her senses. She seemed as if the wheels were spinning rapidly in her brain.

Speaking as slowly as you would to a misguided four-year-old, Emily stood close by Pru's side and said, "I've got the answering machine with your voice on it. They've traced Silas's gun to the collector in Bath. It's the twin to the one that's missing from the glass case down in Silas's vault. The one I noticed while I was down there cleaning up for him the day before I left. The very twin he later hid in his satchel. The one Cyril found."

"Cyril? Found?" Pru said, back in her singsong tone.

"Stashed by the castle ruins."

Pru peeked out again. Emily followed her gaze until she spotted Will's pickup along with a glimpse of Oliver's blocky head. The truck eased to a stop by the sidewalk fronting the façade of the Curtis house exactly as Will told her. Will got out, may have waved to her—she couldn't tell—unhitched the tailgate, and was soon out of sight.

Emily had no sooner noted Oliver's muzzle protruding over the truck-bed railing when, out of nowhere, Silas slipped out from the shadows of the rear entrance, stepped in front of her, and blocked everything. Squinting over his bifocals, he said, "Not good, not good."

"Shut up, Silas," said Pru, flinging the rosebud at him. "You're supposed to be at the lawyer's."

"Turned around and came back. Emily and you alone in the garden. Coincidence? I don't think so."

"It has to be spun, that's all. So go away."

"Not if she's got you on an answering machine. Not good, Pru."

"Not good at all," said Emily. "So if you'll kindly get out of my way."

Silas shuffled back and forth before he reached into his back pocket and jerked out the nickel-plated .32 Smith and Wesson.

"What are you doing?" Pru said, glaring up at him.

"Emily knows. Knows what this regulator was used for."

"Forget it, Silas," said Emily. "It's over."

Silas shook his mop of woolly hair, his gun wavering as well. Trying to steady his hand, he said, "No, no, no. Not when you have a regulator. Kept it in perfect condition to fulfill its purpose. Yes, yes, to regulate, keep everyone in their place, where they belong."

"The twin to the one you retrieved from the dealer in Bath," said Emily. "Handy as can be the whole while, hanging up in the glass case down in your vault. We know, we know."

"Exactly. To regulate, restore, keep things going."

"I told you to shut up, Silas," said Pru.

"Which was why Harriet kept asking what you were up to," said Emily, "and what you had hidden in your satchel. Could it be that duplicate, the one Maud just confirmed?"

"Maud? Confirmed?" said Silas, shaking his head again.

"Over the phone, Silas, long distance. Poor Harriet tried to put an ocean between you, shake off being implicated somehow. Took money from the GDC and thought she could get lost in the flower show. Made calls to the hospital to see if maybe, somehow, Chris was still alive. Even tried to reach Miranda because it was her roof where it happened. Maybe she'd heard something. But when there was no way to shed herself of the two of you, no way to shake off the pressure of being complicit, what did she do?"

Silas's beady eyes seemed to lock for a second.

"She thought she could get hold of Hobbs, the roving constable. Right after judging the flower show. Reveal who the real culprit was. Isn't that the gist of it, Silas?"

Silas muttered and shook his head again as if it was all going much too fast for him.

Tired of humoring him, tired of humoring them both, Emily said loud and clear, "It's no use. You've had it. So step aside."

"Can't oblige," said Silas, brandishing his weapon. "Not like this. Oh no, oh no. Not until everything is regulated."

"Stop it," Pru said. "No more guns."

"That's right," said Emily. "We're going to notify the police. They'll take the gun. They'll take it all from here."

But the minute she said it, she glanced back and realized her cellphone was in the Harrods bag.

Pru glanced back at the arbor too, like she had some other way out right on the tip of her tongue. Silas didn't budge, watching Pru, waiting for a cue.

"Got it," Pru said, snatching up the Harrods bag, stepping out into the sunlight. "She's guilty of theft. And she's guilty of trespass. Yes! This is our territory. She's not in charge. She's on our soil. The gun is good, we can use it."

Silas backed off a short distance, nodding to himself.

Fully aware the .32 was still pointed at her, Emily drifted toward him, trying to distract his attention away from Pru. She kept going a few steps at a time until she was almost abreast of the flags and the upslope to her left. Were it not for the weapon, she had a clear path directly ahead, a dash to the sidewalk to her car, its hood jutting out in plain sight. Or a quick jog to Will at the bank. A clear path, including the open tailgate of Will's pickup and Chuck petting Oliver, his back to her, his service revolver holstered, a weapon that in living memory had never been drawn but was always at the ready.

But the escape route was obliterated the second Pru yanked out the dog whistle from the bag and said, "Look. Can you beat it? She was actually going to blow the whistle on us. Well, let me tell you, two can play at that game. We'll blow the whistle on her."

Silas spun around, placing Chuck and Oliver directly in his line of fire, his shaking hand signaling an urge to shoot at something. Coupled with Pru carrying on about "a citizen's right to bear arms as a matter of self-protection," the madness of it all was absolutely crystal. They'd both snapped. Perhaps just now, perhaps all along. Barking mad—the two of them.

In that same moment, Emily knew it would take nothing to provoke Silas, a man who couldn't abide confusion. Or Pru, up on an imaginary soapbox, the whistle close to her mouth, about to blow it like some agitated London bobby.

Reflexively, Emily cut to her left and sprinted up the slope between the red flags, counting on covering enough distance between herself and Silas, for Chuck to turn around if Oliver began to bolt, for Silas to lower his weapon, and for Pru, even for an instant, to see what was happening.

At first, Emily's run seemed to be paying off. She kept racing higher up the rise, to reach a safe distance, to reach the tree line.

But she heard the report of a gun, like a blown tire, along with the blare of a car horn. Twisting around, she caught a glimpse of the recoil as Silas's outstretched arms flew up and straightened like he was on a firing range.

The next thing she knew, Silas began to scramble up the slope after her, slow as can be, but bound and determined. The only words she could make out were "only a warning shot."

She scanned the area below for some sign of Chuck or Will or any passersby to no avail. She twisted back around and headed for cover toward a stand of maples. More beeps of a car horn as a second warning shot pinged off a tree trunk somewhere above.

At the same time, she could hear Pru's screams, perhaps at Silas, perhaps at a bounding eighty-five-pound retriever who may have heard the silent whistle or merely spotted what he took to be a perky child in an apron he could jump on and tussle with as it crumpled to his level.

Emily sprang forward, running harder, darting through the trees as the branches whacked her shoulders. She kept going until she hit the wide stretch of meadow. She ran on with no other thought than to cross the high grasses as fast as she could, all the way over to the downward rush of the trail in the distance that led to her cottage below and a phone. Or Babs. Or anyone. All the same, she figured there was no way in this world that discombobulated Silas could ever get this far.

For a moment, there was no more gunfire, no third warning shot winging by. She picked up the pace as the tracery of thick pines at the head of the trail drew closer. But just then, her right foot hit a snag, jerking her around, and sending her spinning onto her back. Stunned, she tried to right herself, but the pain shot up her leg from her ankle to her wrenched knee. The glinting rays of sunlight shifted behind a cloud and spilled out again, hurting her eyes, coupled with her hard breathing and exhaustion, all of it forcing her to lie still until the dizzy, whirling sensations subsided.

Chapter Thirty

A few minutes ahead of schedule, Will had cruised by Emily's Camry and pulled up to the curb by the verge of the Curtises' side yard. Driving fast and being ahead of schedule was unusual in his approach to things, but he did it quick enough in order to get there in time to glance over and see that Emily was okay. More than okay from the looks of things. She was standing close by a little lady who might very well have needed consoling. After finishing up with whatever help the woman needed with her scraggly garden, he assumed Emily would come walking up to Oliver and the pickup and, momentarily, they'd take it from there.

As practiced, Will put the tailgate down and, sure enough, Oliver took his station right up to the back of the cab. He stuck his head out to get the best view of folks going in and out of the bank, but mostly in anticipation for Chuck to come over, pet him, and reward him with some milk bones hidden in the pocket of his uniform.

One more "stay" command on Will's part and he covered the remaining few yards to the bank in no time. All he had to do was get by Chuck's small talk while asking for two little favors.

Like Will had figured, there was hardly any bank

business at this hour, with everyone still at work or having completed their transactions earlier in the day. Luckily, there was also no sign of any small children for Oliver to knock over.

Will took the stone steps in stride. Chuck appeared before Will reached the glass-paneled door, milk bones at the ready, pushing the same ol' subject.

"So, you say Oliver's so light colored 'cause he's English. Not like the dark amber or russet ones you always see, that American variety."

"That's right. Listen, Chuck—"

"And you say this yacht lady gave him to you because—"

"He'd gotten too big. And I still don't remember exactly who she got him from."

"Well, you see, in a funny way, he reminds me of me. Not that I'm frisky. But Oliver's so easygoing. He never gets riled."

"Sorry, got no time for this now, Chuck."

Another first. Cutting someone off. But Will had given himself only a few minutes to use Chuck as a lookout while cashing the check from Mrs. Ryder and scooting back to the pickup to meet up with Emily.

Will pointed out Emily's Camry across the Curtis driveway from his pickup and made certain Chuck knew that Doc was his main concern. If Chuck spotted a car with New York plates going by and making a U-turn, he was to notify Will immediately, whether Will was through cashing his check or not. Same thing goes if Chuck spotted Oliver taking off.

"But," Chuck said, "you left the tailgate down."

"That's right. For the next couple of minutes, I need you as a kind of safety net."

"Okay . . . I guess. Sort of on guard for real, you mean."

"You got it."

"And we can talk about English goldens some other time."

"You bet."

"Lucky, Brian Forbes just took off suddenly. Leaving me to my own devices, like they say."

"Lucky all around," Will said as he moved past Chuck into the bank.

Like clockwork, Will spotted the vacant window of the nosy-but-efficient teller. Even the mortgage consultant and customer service representatives sat snugly in their cubicles, pecking away at their computers, trying to look busy during the lull.

"Is Mrs. Ryder still scouting other B&Bs?" the teller asked Will in her usual crisp, cheery tone.

"Yes, ma'am."

"All around the Berkshires and the Green Mountains, I expect. Prime season thereabouts."

"Yup."

"Still, you have to wonder about her prospects, given the ups and downs of the tourist trade. Especially hereabouts."

"Uh-huh."

"And the threat of those condos. Not that I don't appreciate the revenue they might bring in. But it's got to add to her worries."

"For sure."

The good thing was that the teller was able to talk,

cancel the check after Will endorsed it, and dole out the fifties and twenties at the same time.

The bad thing was that, just when Will thought he was home free, the teller stopped counting at the sound of a car horn somewhere at the front of the building. The teller smiled and offered a guess that crotchety Mrs. Pritchett was at it again, probably having trouble removing her ignition key. Something about not being able to figure out how to shift into park, turn off the motor, and push the key all the way to disengage it. And not press the panic button.

A little miffed at Will's disinterest in how, no matter how many times Chuck explained it to her, this kept happening, the teller took her sweet time handing Will the rest of his pay. As Will pocketed the envelope, Chuck entered the lobby, shrugged, and spun around at the sound of a cane tapping at the door behind him. He gave Will a signal he'd be right with him while escorting the grumbling Pritchett woman to the customer service cubicle as she too took her own, sweet time.

Back outside the lobby door, Chuck said, "Oliver is fine. I checked on him and we had a high old time. No sign of any car with New York plates passing by either. But, naturally, I did have to hightail it back, what with Mrs. Pritchett's car horn blaring, making all that fuss, and me on duty to see to the smooth comings and goings. You see, it doesn't matter how many times I tell the lady—"

Will left him hanging and rushed over to his truck to check. But by the time he got there, both Oliver and Emily were nowhere in sight.

Midway down the Curtises' side yard, Will found the

dog whistle glinting in the grass and, almost immediately, noticed the little woman in the apron standing by a rose arbor, looking dazed.

As he approached her, whistle in hand, he couldn't help but be reminded of that spinster who rode the *Catfish Queen* riverboat. The one who had that same faraway look as he handed her another frosty glass of Southern Comfort and peach liqueur. It seemed she'd been searching the passing riverbanks for her old "angel of a love," pinning her hopes on the daydream he would reappear on this very crossing. Will had let her be and tended to his bartending like he let most things go.

But there was no way he was going to let this little Pru lady be, even if she turned out to be just as dotty.

"Excuse me, ma'am," Will called out. "Could you help me out here? I'm looking for Emily and my golden, and it makes no sense that Emily might've blown the whistle and dropped it. No sense at all."

With her blue-button eyes darting around, she broke out of her stupor and said, "Your dog? Well I've got news. He knocked me down, ran me over. There is a village ordinance covering that sort of thing. An ordinance protecting smaller citizens from unleashed hounds."

Moving away from the arbor, she set out for her sagging back porch. "I'm sure Trooper Dave Roberts would like to hear about this. And he'll do something too. For your information, he was a pupil of mine in grade school, not a stranger like you. And he has always been obliging."

Will tried to intercept her, recalling how Mrs. Ryder told him about the dingy interior, gloomy central staircase, and funeral room where the bodies were once laid for the undertaker. The last thing Will needed right now was to be sucked inside, hassling over stupid ordinances.

"Hold it, lady. You didn't answer me about Emily dropping the dog whistle, or her whereabouts, and Oliver, my retriever."

"That's right. I'd made up my mind to file a report."

"Fine," Will said, heading back to the arbor. "You go call Trooper Dave. You don't want to talk to me, I'll have to track Emily and Oliver best I can."

For some reason, she suddenly became very friendly, rushed back in front of Will and pulled him by a row of bushes. "Look," she said, "see the way the dog sniffed and messed up the cocoa mulch I just put down? It must be like some wonderful doggy dessert. He's way past the bank by now, I'll bet you anything. On to Main Street and beyond with Emily in hot pursuit."

Will took this in. It made sense about the cocoa mulch and Oliver sniffing and pursuing it far as it would go. But it made no sense that Emily would blow the whistle, drop it, let Oliver knock this lady over, and then take off after him.

Not knowing which way to turn, Will eyed the footpath leading behind the bank to the main street and then shifted back to Pru.

Still beaming, Pru returned to her post at the arbor, surveying the slope as it rose up to the tree line. Not at all like someone pinning her hopes on some old love. More like she was pinning her hopes on something else.

Chapter Thirty-One

Through the pain, woozy fatigue, and the stupidity of her predicament, Emily kept asking herself where she'd gone wrong. All she wanted was to jar something loose and force the authorities to step in. She had incriminating material. She had, at the very least, a sixty-minute window, she'd double-checked. She'd called Pru earlier to find out when she'd be free and clear to jointly tackle the weeds and such. She'd been informed that Silas would be at the lawyer's office blocks away on South Street. He'd be going over the details of Harriet's last will and testament, thereby leaving the two of them on their own. It was a perfect setup.

Another sharp jab of pain in her knee, followed by reeling thoughts about gaps in the story that still had to be filled. Otherwise Pru would be right. Just storytelling—bits and pieces depending on whose version you wanted to believe because Pru now had the Harrods bag. *Was it poor Pru the victim? Pru the co-conspirator? Pru the mastermind who, at this very moment, might be pulling something else?*

And, adding to the whir of her mind, a lingering image of Chris Cooper's fall.

Trying to snap out of it, she checked the open-mesh pocket of her jacket. She propped herself up on one elbow, the long shadows stretching over swathes of tall grasses right and left, a tracery of leaves quivering in the breeze. Save for an occasional scudding cloud, the heat and blinding afternoon sunlight held steady.

Through the muffled sound of traffic passing by in the distance, she thought she heard the faint echo of someone calling. It could have been Will, or someone else, or wishful thinking. After all, she'd never heard Will call out for anything.

She looked over to the brace of pines at the fringe of the trail, which still offered an exit and cover leading down to the B&B and cottage. If only she could get there. With luck, Silas (who, doubtless, had never experienced a smidge of physical exercise) was stuck by the flags along the upward slope, not only out of breath but in a muddle, talking himself into or out of this convoluted situation.

She sat up straight, brushed aside the ferns, and examined the thick vine and bracken that ensnared her right ankle. She scoured around until she came up with a gnarled, knobby branch with a forked end that had also succumbed to the undergrowth. Tugging it out, she peeled off the damp bark and snapped off a few twigs. Perhaps she could use it to brace herself and free her foot.

She tried to cantilever herself up, ignoring the pain coursing through her twisted knee and ankle, the bright sunlight streaming in and out exacerbating her wooziness. After three stabs at it, straining and swaying on one leg, she poked away at the vine and bracken. But it was useless. Not only was she hopelessly ensnared, everything was so tender that the slightest movement seemed to jolt her whole body.

She shielded her eyes and glanced back over to the way she had come, past the expanse of the meadow to the stand of maples masking the red-flagged slope down to the Curtis side yard. Still no sign of Silas. Only the muffled sound of traffic and perhaps a dog barking way off in the distance. No more cries or calling.

But then, she gradually made out the stooping form slipping through the break in the maples, advancing toward her. He was straggling, mopping his high forehead with a handkerchief, but drifting steadily closer all the same.

In effect, her dash had gained her no more than a few minutes' head start, an advantage that was now wiped out.

As though commenting on her mishap, the moment he spotted her, Silas shouted, "You see, it's all the rushing around!" Then muttered, "You, Harriet, Chris Cooper. The rushing . . . yes, yes, the rushing. But even so, I always give fair warning."

Stopping in his tracks, apparently scouring his memory all the while, he began to itemize. "Yes . . . I have it. Take the invasive creatures. The rabbits and deer in Harriet's garden. A shock of current and they got the message. They did, they did, of course they did."

Still poking away with the forked end of the branch, Emily began to decipher what he was saying. *He'd rigged that wire fence behind the annuals. His first trial run.*

Seconds later, Emily finally succeeded in freeing her ankle just enough so she could almost keep her balance.

Moving closer, his mind back on track, Silas kept

convincing himself how fair he had been. "Yes, yes. With Chris Cooper, a tad more was required. But I gave fair warning nonetheless. Every time, I did. I did, indeed."

Fair warning? Emily pondered. *Setting fire to Chris's greenhouse? Taking the skeleton keys and pick locks from his workroom to break in, using Chris's hot plate and magazines to set the smoky blaze? That was fair warning?*

Getting more and more anxious, she raised her voice. "Keep away from me, Silas."

But this time, Silas kept coming. "As for Emily Ryder, I fired warning shots. She must have heard, must have seen."

"Back off, Silas, I'm warning you."

"But what got into her?" Silas kept ruminating as he advanced. "She hikes, plays sports, guides travelers, and doesn't meddle. What did she see? What did she hear? What *was* it?"

Suddenly it came to her. Down in his vault. The multi-volt transformer . . . the short in the model-train tracks sparking like crazy, the tangle of frayed wires by the fuse box, the blown fuse—more practice. Then afterward, the buried burlap sack with the copper wiring after he'd done his worst . . . the damp, crumpled raincoat when he returned, lying by her feet beneath the gun case when she tidied up. All of it signaling to her. But she didn't get it, had no idea, and sloughed it off.

More shaky than ever, she hollered, "I mean it, damn you!"

But Silas trudged on. "Was it Harriet's badgering, wanting something done right away? Then Pru egging me on? Was Emily aware?"

Answering himself, Silas said, "No, no, impossible. Emily couldn't have known. Only I heard it, only I knew."

When he drew within less than twenty yards, Emily shouted, "Cut it out, Silas. It's over! Don't you get it?"

"Oh no. Oh-oh-oh no. Not if Emily is reasonable and all the fluster stops."

"Forget it! You are out of your mind!"

Silas stopped short. "You're not listening to me. When Chris Cooper pressed and looked for loopholes, that was not preservation. Causing the Planning Commission to vote no, the GDC to withdraw its offer, the bank to foreclose? Never. Something had to be done after my warning was ignored . . . done immediately."

Silas wiped the perspiration off his bifocals with his handkerchief and drew his gun out. "No time to calibrate, don't you see? Upped the voltage a goodly bit . . . so he'll fall off like those accidents before. Heart might be still beating . . . in a coma then, out of the picture for a good long while. Or out of the picture for good would be best. Stands to reason, all stands to reason."

As Silas hesitated and appeared to lose his train of thought once again, Emily leaned just a bit in order to catch what he was saying. But she couldn't make out a thing, lost her balance and barely managed to drop to her one good knee.

"Ah," Silas said, his voice rising again. "There was the rain. Not heavy at first, just enough to draw him over. Pru liked the rain, fit the bill. Then came the downpour . . . just in time. So providential, so perfect."

Barely up on her feet again, realizing that if it wasn't

for the wrenching pain and having to wobble on one leg, she could've taken advantage of Silas's sputtering lapses and been long gone.

Silas secured his glasses as the sunlight dimmed. "But then there was Harriet. Rushing off . . . threatening to betray us and turn us in. Gave her fair warning too. But she wouldn't listen. Too much in a rush. Was going to do something. Couldn't forego the flower show but immediately afterwards—hell-bent on ruining everything."

Looking directly at Emily, he said, "You can see it all now, can't you? Of course you can. Say it. Why won't you say it?"

Emily gave him nothing.

"All right then. You will obey when I count to ten, just like I did with Harriet. One for the money, two for the show, three to get ready, four to go . . . Of course, the precious old .32, the regulator, the twin was necessary. Had to retrieve it, had to have it handy to keep her in check, from getting to a phone or that constable. She saw the shammy cloth poking out of the satchel when the cook tried to put it aside, knew full well what was wrapped in it."

Recalling Harriet's initial protest that she was "under the gun," Emily was now completely taken with how it had all played out during Harriet's last run.

Silas went on, as if sensing Emily's rapt attention, as if turning to some phantom juror for validation. "Clearly, if she hadn't panicked, scrambled to the ruins . . . If she would've stopped screaming . . . I aimed above her head while the drums were beating. A warning shot, she must have known. But the drumming kept on, louder and louder.

And the second shot . . . by her ear, like herding sheep over a cliff, so clumsy, up to the ramparts she scampered, down the stone steps, wet and slippery . . . Providential once more. Providential, surely."

Scanning the sky, Silas said, "When you give fair warning and become an instrument, a vessel, there's an end to it. Order restored. Let it be, let it be."

The whole time, Emily had been tugging at her snare. This time, she yanked so hard that she broke free and turned sharply toward the trail.

"No, no!" Silas yelled. "Don't make me do it. Please! Please!"

Though the makeshift cane only enabled her to move awkwardly, she pushed on. Glancing back for a brief second, she saw Silas pressing his palms against his temples with his handkerchief, as though his brain had jammed.

Wincing, with the fringe of the trail dead ahead, she was determined to cover more ground and elude Silas before he came out of it. Somehow, she might even signal for help down below at the cottage if she made it that far. If not, hide as a last resort.

But the gunshot echoed all around the treetops. Shaken, with the pain shooting through her whole body, Emily froze.

"Put things back that don't belong to you," said Silas, coming after her. "That's all. All right? Say it's all right, Emily. It's the only way."

Twisting around, all Emily could do was secure her grip on the damp, knobby branch to keep from toppling over.

At the same time, Silas fumbled with the gun and the handkerchief, and pressed his palms against his temples.

He wiped his glasses and put them back on. "All they want is a right of way, you stupid girl. Blame the developers, blame them."

Silas's eyes drifted skyward. "Wait, wait. The old journal with the history of the greenwoods . . . offer it to the Historical Society in memory of Harriet. As long as Emily turns over the answering machine, as long as Emily promises to behave herself, why not?"

As Silas's gaze remained fixed on high, Emily sensed how close she was to the brink, only a couple of feet to the trail that was beckoning her. She shifted over another few steps.

But Silas came out of it and fired again. The echo merged with other sounds, possibly voices from all sides or just her desperate imagination.

She called out, got no response and realized that Silas was almost on top of her now, shaking his head so hard the sweat ran down his forehead and his glasses began to slip.

"You're making me do this," said Silas, wiping his glasses yet again. "Forcing my hand . . . no choice, no choice, unless . . ."

Bracing herself, Emily nodded as she turned back one last time and tightened her grip on the knobby branch.

Dropping his handkerchief, Silas's lips curled up in a half smile as he lowered his gun.

With a shudder, she lurched, screaming in pain, and flung the forked end of the branch in his face. He shielded his eyes, knocking off his glasses. In the swirling blur that followed, he fumbled for the gun, got control of it, and waved it around crazily just before a thick-set figure stepped in, smashed his wrist, and landed sharp, quick jabs to his stomach, sending him reeling and sinking to his knees.

Bent over, Silas moaned over and over. Then became silent. Motionless. Like a penitent.

The gun disappeared under Silas's handkerchief as Doc carefully picked it up. Emily thrashed about on the ground, yanking at the open-mesh pocket of her jacket, worried sick she might have broken something.

"Get away from me," Emily said, clutching the pocket recorder.

"Easy, easy. He's down, he's had it."

"Get away, I said. Don't you dare touch me!"

"Hey, cut it out. What is this?"

"You lose, that's what, Doc. You and the GDC lose!"

When she wouldn't stop yelling, he yelled right back at her. "Oh, for Pete sake—here! This time will you freakin' look at it?"

Mingling with the sharp throbbing pain in her knee were the cries of Babs calling for her at the foot of the trail. And Will's voice along with Oliver's deep-throated bark approaching from the opposite direction. But it was the business card shoved in front of her eyes that caught her immediate attention:

Bernie "Doc" Kletzky. Ex-Cop, Will Travel

Chapter Thirty-Two

It took a while, but after going over his whole experience in Lydfield-in-the-Moor it all began to make sense as Doc reconsidered Cyril's cockamamie story. At first, as far as Doc was concerned, Cyril was just a flunky driver. But later on, he was also a key witness. Under pressure from Doc badgering him about the .32, threatening to turn him in, for the first time Cyril actually strung some words together.

"But you can't grouse on me, mate. Only larking about the ruins whilst you was blinkered, now wasn't I? Heard a shot. Spotted this wanker from the tea-and-crumpets marquee hopping it toward the High Street, giving a toss to this lovely piece. Wrapped in a shammy, it was. By a drainage ditch with rainwater trickling by, like so much trash or a bloomin' rock. That bleedin' sod Trevor, pratting about up the High Street, saw it all too. Side by side, eyeball to eyeball we was when I gave him sod all and told him to push off. Had me eye on that lovely piece the whole time."

Back there in England, Doc didn't understand half the words Cyril spewed out, let alone who this "bleedin' sod" Trevor was. So, the second he caught Cyril fooling around at the garage in Bovey Tracey and showing off in front of Emily, he took the old .32 away from him and, soon after, handed it over to the Teignbridge Police Authority. It was only shortly after he clocked that whacko Silas up on the meadow, when he made a call to the gossipy pub manager Maud who, he'd been told, didn't let anything get past her. It was only then that he really started to put the story about Silas's antique gun finagling together.

"Ah," Maud had said, sounding breathless as though she'd just heard the news about Doc's actual part in all this, "seeing that it's yourself and not the bounder we took you for. That you're on the straight and narrow, so to speak. Mind, I'm only saying what I heard, not being one to tittle-tattle."

"Yeah, yeah," Doc said to her plain as can be. "Look, I'm close but there's something I'm missing. It's the old guns. One here back in Connecticut, one over there. I still don't get it."

"Ah, well you're right lucky you rang me because I have it from the horse's mouth as I told our Emily. If you'd been less of a prat whilst in my pub, you'd have gotten all this from her by now."

"Never mind about her, okay? So, as usual, you got it from some horse's mouth. Come on, will ya? Let's have it."

There was a pause as Maud was still having a hard time putting up with him dating back to their first run-in. "Constable Hobbs, for your information. Ever so diligent, mind you."

"Great, terrific. What did this diligent cop come up with?"

"Well now, the way it was told for my ears only, this antiques bloke in Bath had a consignment arrangement with a client of Emily's. A matched pair of dueling pistols, if you like. But this client, it turns out—"

"Silas."

"Right you are. This Silas was also shipping a—"

".32. You're saying this Silas character shipped an old .32 with the dueling pistols overseas, then glommed it back from this Brit antiques guy. Then used it to lean on Harriet to make sure she stayed in line. Am I right or am I right?"

"Gone right barmy, if you ask me."

"Yes or no?"

"Crikey, how you Yanks squeeze the life out of everything."

"Lady, I just want to get a handle on it."

"Well, if it's more you want, either get on Emily's good side or take it up with the proper authorities. Whilst you're about it, in future you'll need to make plain what you're playing at. And there, me lad, is an end to it."

As she hung up on him, he realized she was probably right. Shortly, he found himself racking his brains as to how he had fallen into this whole can of worms in the first place.

As near as he could figure, it started out by just doing Hacket, Martin Gordon's silent partner, a favor. Among his other properties, Hacket owned a high rise in Washington Heights back in the Big Apple. Hacket gave him free rent in return for security services, keeping an eye out for burglars and second-story men casing the neighborhood and stuff like that. But it turns out that that was the least of Hacket's worries.

"Look, Bernie," the wiry, little guy had said, pointing with his index finger in that annoying way of his.

"Doc. I told you, just make it Doc."

"Anyway, I've got this development project pending in a village up in northwest Connecticut."

"Like always," Doc said. "Little village, big score, right? One where you stand to make a lot of coin?"

With his close-set eyes twitching away, Hacket jumped right into the bind he was in. "At any rate, you wouldn't believe what I've sunk into prep work on this one. Architectural plans, surveys, you name it."

"Up front, you mean."

"Out in the open? Hell no, never. I invest and stay in the background. All that PR stuff and glad-handing the locals—all that politicking gets on my nerves."

At that point, Hacket switched to putting his hand in the pocket of his suit pants and jingling some loose change, a nervous habit Doc had the worst time putting up with.

"So," Hacket said, "it all comes down to whether or not this dowager, this Harriet Curtis, comes through with a quitclaim deed for a right of way. The only option is a skittish lady, a Mrs. Ryder, who owns a B&B on the other side of the site we're after, who, if you ask me, doesn't know whether she's coming or going."

"You're saying you need this right of way, is that it? On the double. And you thought it was in the bag."

"Of course that's what I'm saying," Hacket said, getting even more antsy. "There's no other access onto the site. But I just learned that the Curtis property is under threat of foreclosure plus a suit for tax evasion. Not only that, an environmentalist, a Chris Cooper, is at the head of the Planning Commission and may have found a loophole that would kill the whole deal. If that isn't enough, an adulterer is on the verge of scandal and divorce proceedings. But not just an adulterer, oh no. This Brian Forbes is a prominent member of the Commission, the chief backer of the project, head of the Business Association, and a prime candidate for conflict of interest. Could there be a bigger godawful mess?"

"Whoa, easy. How am I supposed to take this all in?"

But Hacket didn't slow it down. "This is what I get for trusting Martin to hawk the package. He said it was pre-sold. He had the Planning Commission in his pocket. He was putting the cart before the horse, that's what he was doing, and it's liable to go all to pieces. In a nutshell, I need you to take soundings before I invest another cent. I need assurances. I need you to nail this Harriet Curtis down and get a line on this Cooper guy."

"Hey, I don't know. This is not my thing. I don't do so good with dowagers and WASPs and uppity types from New England."

"Don't give me that. You're retired from the force and climbing the walls. Burglars and the rest of the lowlifes in Washington Heights have moved on. You have nothing better to do than hang out at your old precinct, swap stories, and work out at the gym."

"Now I wouldn't say that."

"Oh, really? What cases have you lined up since you got your PI license?"

"I got a lead on tracking down a paper trail on some insurance fraud. They'll let me know."

"Exactly. You've got zippo, zero, zilch. And you can forget any more free rent. Well? Are you in or out?"

It didn't take any more persuading before Doc said he was in.

But it had taken Doc a while longer before he was able to pick up the thread. Not only did he have to stay on Harriet's tail to nail her down about the quitclaim deed, Martha Forbes had hired him to put the kibosh on Miranda Shaw. Armed with some photos and letters Martha had found stashed in Brian's bureau drawer, with Hacket naturally turning a blind eye and keeping his fingers crossed, Martha used Doc to get Brian Forbes under the GDC's thumb and Miranda swept permanently under the carpet in the UK. Besides, as far as Doc could figure, there was no way Martha could move Miranda's McMansion anyway, a white elephant that was Miranda's excuse to keep coming back to keep her hooks in Brian. And the commissions on the condo sales looked really juicy if Martha could use some leverage and wangle an exclusive the minute the sales office opened its doors on the Lydfield Green. So, from the get-go, Doc's job was to keep tabs on Harriet as the owner or whatever of the Curtis property, plus this Chris Cooper guy, and get to Miranda somehow and keep her out of the way.

However, as Doc had predicted, he was a fish out of water. Part of it was the communication gap, and part of it bad luck. Some people in the village gave him grief because they didn't like his brash tone. The raincoat he borrowed from some guy on the GDC staff because of the weather didn't fit, wild turkeys attacked him, and Emily—though he tried to be friendly and even offered her his card—wouldn't give him the time of day. His guess was it was his streetwise tone again, plus Chris Cooper meant something to her. All of which got more convoluted when Hacket called when he was up on the site, wanting to know whether Cooper could be taken care of, wanted to know right away, and when Doc repeated it, Emily must've picked up on it.

Anyways, the more Doc thought about it, the more he was convinced he really had stepped into one of them WASP nests prejudiced against New Yorkers and regular, stand-up guys. After all, why did Martha Forbes say just the sight of him would shake Miranda up? Why did she keep saying, "You have that nasty look and manner from the city streets that will certainly give her pause and do the trick"?

But then again, the money she was offering for this shakedown while the iron was hot was hard to refuse, on top of the per diem from Hacket, keeping his rent-free pad in Washington Heights, expenses covered, and a bonus after the smoke cleared. What was not to like?

So it was kill two birds with one stone, everybody back in place, cut the static so Brian was free and clear to close the deal. But how was he supposed to know the shakedown had no legs? That when he caught up with Miranda in Bovey Tracey, she shook him off and was going to cut out anyway? That she and Brian had the hots for each other even ice storms wouldn't cool off, and there was no way to keep her from scooting back to her McMansion as her excuse to getting back together?

Which wasn't the half of it. There was that first accident off the McMansion roof and then Harriet, who had bought it overseas. One accident at what they call an opportune time, maybe. But Harriet Curtis after he tracked her down? No way. And that was when, after he delivered the photos to

Miranda Shaw in Bovey Tracey, he tried to warn Emily to wise up and quit sticking her neck out. Because, no matter how much she kept giving him a hard time, he liked her spunk and was getting worried about her. Plus, in so doing, he was starting to feel more like his old self—keeping the good guys out of harm's way, being much less of a gofer on the take.

To put it all in a nutshell, it was no wonder some people—especially Emily—didn't know how to take him.

And so, after wrestling with all this and getting it straight in his mind, he drove to the Sharon hospital the very next day to make sure Emily was okay. But he found her down on herself for not seeing it coming. He tried as best he could, but he couldn't talk her out of it. She kept saying how sorry she was for taking him at face value.

He went down to the hospital gift shop, got hold of some stationary, wrote her a note, and left it with the nurse in charge of her ward.

Listen, the thing of it is, you hung in there. Your half-baked moves aside, you deserve some points. I mean, it looks like you put a lot of stuff together. And maybe with a little coaching—I mean no way you can get worse at it, right? Fact is, I wasn't the sharpest pencil in the box. A real fish out of water myself, a bull in the china shop, words like that. On top of it all, oversleeping after losing five hours because of the time difference, letting Cyril sneak off on me. Not picking up on those two characters sitting by that church wall, all broken up when their act got cancelled but not a peep about their sister who just got carted off . . .

*Anyways, I hear from everybody you drive real good.
What I'm saying is, when you get back on your feet and
since your tour guide thing is down the tubes, you could
maybe give me a ring. I'm talking around your neck of
the woods and up the Hudson—who knows?*

*Besides, seeing how I don't ever want to be stuck again
with lowlifes like Cyril, you would be a definite upgrade.
And I can help you quit taking things personal and to
steer clear of psychos. But hey, give it some thought.
Whatever.*

Doc

In point of fact, the charges and incriminating evidence
against Silas continued to mount. There were the contents
of the burlap sack, the deadly assaults with the .32 on both
sides of the pond, and Emily's, Will's, Doc's, and Cyril's
sworn statements.

For his part, Silas claimed that his stepsister goaded
him, both before and after Chris Cooper and Harriet Curtis
were out of the picture.

"Not really my fault, you see," said Silas, giving his
statement. "Pressured into it. Victim of circumstance
and timing. Duty-bound, of course, a matter of heritage
and preservation. Oh, and didn't I say? It all started with
Harriet. 'Don't you see, something has to be done. What if
Chris Cooper ruins everything? What if? What if?' Then it

was Pru hounding me. 'Time is of the essence, Silas. Forget your stupid little warnings. Get cracking.' Rush, rush, everyone in such a rush. Yes indeed, constant pressure. And did I mention duty? And heritage? Mustn't forget that. No, no, not ever."

In turn, Pru resorted to a childlike façade when giving her account. "I really don't understand what all the fuss is about. I'm so tiny, like a Devon pixie, sprinkling a bit of pixie dust. Like Puck in *A Midsummer Night's Dream.* Like a will-o'-the-wisp. Like Tinkerbell. Goodness, I was only humoring Harriet who, as Silas must have told you, kept moaning, 'What if?' Silas too. Actually, Chris Cooper flying off a roof came to me in a dream. Sailing away, out of sight, out of mind. And what happened to Harriet was like hide-and-seek. That just came to me too, out of the blue. Played in the rain around a dingy old castle. Don't you see? Make believe is what I'm all about. A fountain of fantasies if that's what you want of me. So why not call the whole thing 'Let's pretend'? That's really all it was."

As a result, incorporating Emily's testimony and incriminating evidence, Pru Curtis was charged with counts of conspiracy and accessory before and after the fact. Silas was charged with multiple counts of assault, reckless endangerment, and murder. The issue of Silas's and Pru's sanity only compounded the case against them as the judicial systems here and abroad were brought into play, more charges brought to bear, and, as one counselor put it, "the time-honored wheels of justice began to turn."

As for Emily, between the time Doc and Will saw her safely to the emergency room and the time she was consigned as a physical therapy patient on crutches, more things began to unfold.

Piecing things together, she learned a great deal after getting back in touch with Hobbs. It seems that Cyril had officially implicated Trevor as an eyewitness. Hobbs then had no trouble identifying the bloke with the grey wooly hair who had been hanging around the tea-and-crumpets marquee. The very spot where Hobbs had milled around ingratiating himself while doing his best to avoid Silas's mutterings about the history of the sister village in Connecticut. Hobbs knew full well who "that sod Trevor" was Cyril was going on about. Always put off by Trevor's preening and supercilious ways and armed with Cyril's testimony, Hobbs was more than happy to break Trevor down at the Teignbridge station and take his statement vis-à-vis spotting Silas (one of the guests on Trevor's estate) running away from the ramparts and, together with Cyril, watching Silas as he hastily tossed his gun in a nearby ditch.

All the while, Trevor had pleaded with Hobbs not to let it be known he was in any way implicated with withholding evidence and obstructing justice. He begged for some assurance that Constance would never find out. Needless to say, Hobbs promised no such thing. In practically no time, the details were out to all and sundry regarding the smuggled gun and Silas and Pru's residence at Trevor Vane's manor house. Silas, the selfsame prime suspect, had last been seen in the company of Trevor Vane leaving the mortuary and driving off in Vane's vintage Rolls Royce. Trevor Vane, in effect, thus aided a prime suspect to abscond scot-free.

In short order, Constance resigned as chairperson from her various committees and withdrew from local society altogether. Even more conspicuously, while awaiting possible charges, Trevor hadn't frequented the pub. Rumor had it that the manor house was listed with an estate agent in Lustleigh, and the Vanes were no longer covertly taking in lodgers.

All told, Hobbs did get to "dash about with a warrant card, fancying his reinstatement in a proper uniform." He got in touch with Emily at the hospital and apologized for being "thick and, as it were, dragging me heels." He wished her a speedy recovery and promised to do his best to get them both reinstated after Trevor had issued his complaint to the British Tourist Authority and packed off her remaining clients.

She told him how much she appreciated his news of the past few days, brushed aside his apologies, thanked him for his well wishes, and took his offer of interceding on her behalf with the British Tourist Authority with a grain of salt. She did, however, accept his standing invitation for a hearty meal at the pub next time they chanced to meet.

While in the hospital, Emily was also duly apprised of the details of Silas and Pru's arraignment, the docketing of incriminating evidence, and Emily's future appearances as a material witness. She was also handed a clipping from the *Wall Street Journal* by a nurse she knew on her ward she couldn't help reading aloud:

"A spokesman for the Gordon Development Company

of Newark, New Jersey, stated that the company has withdrawn its application for site approval in Lydfield, a historic village in the northwest hills of Connecticut. The timing of this move is surprising in view of the recent assurances the GDC had given its investors that the venture was certifiably sound. Those assurances were predicated on the potential of this project to tap into the retiree market from the Manhattan metropolitan area, especially those buyers wishing to take advantage of the attractions offered by the Southern Berkshire corridor.

"CEO Martin Gordon was unavailable for comment. R. J. Hacket, Mr. Gordon's associate, cited health issues and the fluctuations in the housing market for his sudden departure from the firm. However, reliable sources note that the Lydfield Planning Commission's bylaws forbidding transactions with alleged felons and the refusal of Mrs. Ryder, owner of an adjacent B&B, to provide an alternate right of way to the site as the main factors necessitating the GDC withdrawal. In any event, the GDC storefront office on the Lydfield Green is now vacant."

On a more intimate note, Will visited Emily every day she was in the hospital.

To try and cheer her up, Will let it slip that Lieutenant Neill, Dave Roberts's superior at Troop L, had called Dave on the carpet for a number of things, including his preoccupation with petty vandalism at the high school and sloughing off the statements of two key informants—one of whom he was infatuated with—all of which had clouded his judgment. As a result, Officer Roberts's duties would be severely limited and his status was under review for disciplinary action.

Will then limited their conversations to small talk about the weather, how the restorations he was making at the B&B were going, and the way the leaves were showing a touch of crimson and amber that would soon brighten into something really special. He did this taking into account all the painkillers she was taking and her need for rest and peace and quiet to get over her ordeal.

When she felt up to it, the only thing left for Emily to do was write Doc a note. Once again, she wanted to let him know that for all the right and wrong reasons, she'd misjudged him and would always be grateful for his coming to her rescue at the last minute. But she didn't respond to his proposition. At this stage of the game, she had no idea how she was going to pick up the pieces, let alone become an ex-cop's sidekick.

But even after asking the duty nurse to post the letter, even after all that had transpired, there was no closure. Babs had sent text messages, indicating that she, herself, was at sixes and sevens. Moreover, with the leaf-peeping season almost upon her, there was no telling what Emily's mother's plans were or how in the world she'd take Chris's passing and murder when she returned from her scouting expedition of vintage B&Bs in two weeks. Lastly, Will had been extremely attentive and helpful but hadn't given Emily any indication they had any future together, and Emily was too prideful to ask.

Chapter Thirty-Three

A week after her torn ligaments were set in an above-the-knee cast, and a few days after the service for Chris Cooper atop Mohawk Mountain under a cloudless sky as she wished him peace and a safe journey, Emily was still in limbo. She still hadn't come to terms or, as the Brits would say, "truly sorted it."

And so, around midmorning, she hauled out a lawn chair and foot stool outside the cottage door and propped up her leg. At this point, the only thing for it was to bask in the sunlight and wait for Will to appear.

However, as luck would have it, in practically no time she found herself contending with Babs as she came scurrying down the drive and across the back lawn, ahead of schedule.

"Tell you what," said Babs, trying to catch her breath. "I'll tuck the kiddie trek which is about to transpire into a sidebar and lead with *In Harm's Way on the High Meadow*. I'll set it up, sketch in what I saw and heard, and guess what led up to it. All you have to do is nod for yes and shake your head for no. What do you say? I know all bets are off, and I'm in no position to ask, but this is the proverbial point of no return."

Emily countered with the same response. "Like I told

you, Babs, I'll give you a capsule version of what happened as long as you keep it to yourself."

"What is that, a joke?" asked Babs, plunking her camera down next to Emily's crutches. "Have a heart, will you? Give me something before the school bus pulls in here. You've had your hiatus nursing your wounds, wallowing in your scruples. I am in desperate straits. Starving for an angle, an insider slant, a now-at-last-it-can-be-told. Outflanking every dude in the business beating the bushes over this. Plus salvaging my non-existent investigative career before the screen goes blank and the credits roll."

Taking in the anxious look on Babs's sliver of a face, Emily said, "What do you want me to do?"

"Look, I'll settle for anything. My breaking story has stalled, the GDC has split, the cops won't give me back my recorder and—oh please, lady, I am screwed."

Running her fingers through her mop of tangled red hair, Babs went on with her rant. "And don't give me any more crap about being a material witness and leaking something to the press that might prejudice the jury. Can't you even tell me what you dug up at Cooper's old place? Call it begging, call it charity. Thank you, missy Emily. Thank you, thank you, thank you."

Pacing back and forth, Babs added, "Get this. I can't even talk to good ol' Miranda who's off again or hiding under a rock for all I know. Besides, there's nothing doing on that front except the same old, same old adultery and pending Brian–Martha divorce which everybody knows about by now. So, I ask you, after all I've put into this, where does this leave me?"

Still at a loss how to placate her while anticipating Will's return at any moment, Emily glanced over to the back stoop of the B&B.

"That's it, Ryder, ignore me. I'm on a deadline, dying here in front of your eyes, and you keep looking over there."

Emily shifted around, ignoring the itch coursing up and down her encased leg as best she could. "I'm not ignoring you." Not about to add that Will, at the moment, was dealing with her mother about his role and any possible future plans, Emily added, "I'm just wondering how the phone call is going."

"Oh, whoop-de-doo, a phone call. What phone call?"

"Never mind. Look, I'm sorry, Babs."

"She's sorry. The least you can do is toss me a bone. Think. There has got to be something up for grabs. Otherwise—are you getting this—I will have to make do with this cockamamie kiddie shoot with you still laid up, no kicker that'll send me winging off to the pantheon, kiss my gonzo news-hounding career goodbye, and end it all." She gave Emily a withering look, bit her lip, and snatched up her camera.

As if on cue, the school bus pulled into the drive, the kiddie entourage led once more by the same flustered first-grade teacher sporting a neatly pressed L.L. Bean outfit and tinted glasses. After the usual scolding and pleading, she herded her charges into single file and reminded them that under no circumstances would she allow any wandering off nor any other infractions.

"I really mean it," she added. "Otherwise no more field trips, you hear?"

Just as the class was about to advance up the trail, the towheaded twins Emily had previously encountered broke ranks. They ran up to Emily, demanding to know what happened to her and why she wasn't leading them. They also asked about the photos she was supposed to bring back, her visit to "the British kids like us," and all the adventures she promised to share for show-and-tell.

Ms. Flustered ushered the protesting duo back to their place in line. Turning toward Emily, she said, "I hope you know the class and I spent a whole unit on the wonders of a twin village across the sea. And there is nothing so disheartening as getting little children's hopes up and then dashing them."

Giving Emily no chance to remind her she'd made her apologies days ago, that she still had no idea what she'd be physically capable of, Babs chimed in, "You have to understand that Miss Ryder has not been herself of late. Been under a great emotional strain, which explains why she's let people down, even her oldest friend."

Unsure as ever, Ms. Flustered stood waiting for some other response. When she realized it was not forthcoming, she broke in with, "The truth is, these kids are a little spoiled. I am not a nature person, and they really took a liking to you, Miss Emily, during that brief time you met when you promised all you were going to bring back for them. I was really hoping you'd be taking over instead of me."

"I know," said Emily. "Look, we'll just have to play it by ear."

"No, it has to be now while they're still so eager about

natural habitats and all. Plus, the principal is pressuring me to come through."

Unable to take another person working on her, Emily said, "We'll see. Maybe I could fill the kids in after you return from your hike. Okay?"

With a half smile, sensing her pupils were getting out of hand again, Ms. Flustered said, "Oh, that would be so-o-o good. Coming, Miss Maroon?" She pivoted on her heels and joined her restless class. After succeeding in getting them back in line, she led the boisterous bunch up the trail.

"All right, pal," said Babs, still lingering. "You lost your job. You had nothing else going for you, glommed stuff from me, went through some heroics, and beat me out. You were there, in the trenches, on the front lines. I was just doing reconnaissance." Scrunching up her face, Babs tossed out her final zinger. "But you can at least tell me why. Good God, why would you stick your neck out like that? Bullets flying up there on the meadow. I have to know."

Emily fell silent, not sure she could get the words out. But after all the time playing it close to the vest, perhaps she did owe Babs something. Something candid, something straight. She started with "Because . . ."

"Go on, go on. Don't have all day, you know."

"Because I saw it happen and I couldn't stop it."

"Stop what? What are you talking about? Don't tell me it's still Cooper?"

Speaking half to Babs and half to herself, Emily said, "He looked out for me. He always looked out for me."

"So?"

"So, I was all he had."

Babs reached for a snappy comeback but came up empty. As her squinty eyes began to moisten, she countered with, "And Harriet Curtis? She got to you too? No, no, spare me the drivel. I can't take it." Babs shuffled away and stopped short. She peered up at the trail, paused a few seconds longer, and turned back.

"Hey, Ryder, how does this grab you? Speaking of Cooper, I could jazz up this feature. Throw in one of his old sayings, like the one from that old movie, 'A lost cause is the only one worth fighting for.' Yeah . . . right . . . perfect. Merge Cooper's lost cause and the kiddie shoot with the good ol' save-the-environment angle. 'At first it seemed there was no way Chris Cooper could win out over the forces that be. No way to save the open space we've cherished since colonial days . . .'"

In mock surrender, Babs threw up her hands and said, "Okay, I know, I know. A little drippy, needs work."

As Babs broke into a perky stride up the trail, Emily knew she was on to something. Her coveted "kicker." Babs would never let anything get her down for long.

"No sweat, Ryder!" Babs called back. "One door closes, another opens. Get yourself a paper for a change. You might be surprised!"

During the ensuing lull, with Babs off her list and Ms. Flustered and the kids on the backburner for the moment, Emily wondered if there was something else. Some detail that might have slipped her mind or been overlooked. But all she could come up with was a reminder to see to the harvesting of Chris's apples and peaches.

And so it all came down to this.

The lull held a little while longer until Oliver burst through the hinged flap in the kitchen door and darted here and there. In Oliver's wake, Will finally appeared.

Emily reached for her crutches. She pulled herself up gradually, not wanting to appear too anxious. Only to settle the issue and then let it go. Let it be.

"Well?" Emily asked, breaking the silence.

"Are we talking lunch?"

"Not really."

Acting just as nonchalant, Will said, "Or what's going on with your mom? Is that what you mean?"

Emily held on, allowing him the usual do-si-do around a touchy subject.

Will tossed Oliver a stick and then ambled over to her. "If it's about your mom, seems from what she was just telling me on the phone, things are still up in the air. About finalizing her plans."

"Uh-huh. But in the meantime?"

Oliver circled around, the stick in his mouth, wiggling his backside like crazy.

"In the meantime, she's still got the leaf-peepers in mind. That is, if there are any. No bookings yet. And if she goes ahead with making the whole place all light and airy, there's a chance . . ."

"Oh?"

"Of course, she still hasn't a clue about what actually happened . . . and about your leg and all. After what I just let on, she thinks the GDC must've hightailed it 'cause of Chris's efforts and the up-and-down economy. Plus, how she left Brian Forbes and Martha hanging."

Emily adjusted her grip on the crutches. "And so?"

As if knowing what she meant all along, Will said, "Now that depends." He stepped back, and snatched the stick out of Oliver's mouth. Oliver sat dutifully and waited. "Like they say, if you don't know how things stand, you got to keep on biding your time till . . ."

"Till?"

Gazing directly at her this time, Will said, "Till she finally gives you some kinda sign."

Gazing right back at him, Emily hesitated. She could have gone on with this coy banter, worked her way back to the lawn chair and asked, "Whatever do you mean?"

Instead, she let go of her crutches. Will dropped the stick and reached out for her. As they clung easily to each other like it was the most natural thing in the world, she forgot she was balancing on one leg. She forgot her losses, forgot everything. In the stillness, her rambles were suspended and the last of the Twinnings had come and gone.

Oliver waited a tad longer. Then, at the end of his patience, he scampered over to the trail and took off, bounding higher and higher, drawn by the sound of children playing, the woodsy nip in the air, a scattering of birds, and the scurrying of something wild.

About the Author

Shelly Frome is a member of Mystery Writers of America, a professor of dramatic arts emeritus at the University of Connecticut, a former professional actor, and a writer of crime novels and books on theater and film. He is also the film columnist for Southern Writers Magazine and writes monthly profiles for Gannett Media. His fiction  includes *Sun Dance for Andy Horn, Lilac Moon, Twilight of the Drifter,* and *Tinseltown Riff.* Among his works of nonfiction are *The Actors Studio* and texts on the art and craft of screenwriting and writing for the stage. *Murder Run* is his latest published foray into the world of crime and the amateur sleuth. *Moon Games* is slated for release in early 2018. And *The Secluded Village Murders* will release in the fall of 2018. He lives in Black Mountain, North Carolina.